MILLENNIUM:
Preparations Begin

Physics, Prophecy, and the Silence of Weapons

Book One of the MILLENNIUM Series

By: Greg Olsen

MILLENNIUM - PREPARATIONS BEGIN

First Edition: June, 2026

ISBN 979-8-9863707-1-2 ebook
ISBN 979-8-9863707-2-9 paperback
ISBN 979-8-9863707-3-6 hardcover

Dr. Rigel Emerson never imagined his equations would help prepare the world for Christ's coming in the Millennium.

When interdimensional beings appear with a mandate, the brilliant physicist is drawn into a divine Plan to secure absolute peace among mankind so the final battle between good and evil may begin.

His mission: Develop a system that renders every man-made weapon, including nuclear weapons, on Earth inoperable without harming a single soul.

"And He will judge between the nations... They will hammer their swords into plowshares and their spears into pruning hooks. Nation will not lift up sword against nation, and never again will they learn war."
Isaiah 2:4

Table of Contents

Prologue:

Dr. Rigel Emerson had always believed the universe obeyed unbreakable scientific laws. Then, with interdimensional guidance, he discovered the scientific theories to which he subscribed were only a subset of what was available.

One ordinary Tuesday, reality began to unfold. Beings of light and intention stepped through the rift and offered him a choice that would reshape the destiny of humankind. They carried a commission from the Throne: prepare the world for the Millennium.

When Christ returns to bind Satan for a thousand years, the earth must know perfect peace. No armies. No bombs. No instruments of death. In exchange for Humanity giving up their ability to war among themselves, they would be promised peace. Divine unions were to be sanctioned by God himself, and the resulting offspring would allow for the advancement of mankind. But before the Millennium, the weapons of man had to fall silent. Every firearm, every warhead, every blade must be destroyed without the spilling of a single drop of human blood in the process.

To the interdimensional emissaries, Rigel Emerson was the only physicist capable of rewriting the fundamental rules of physics and conflict. To Rigel, the mission sounded like madness wrapped in prophecy. Yet the weight of divine permission settled upon him. He was being asked to disarm the world with science, and nothing less than absolute success would be accepted.

Rigel must recognize the terrifying truth: The Millennium was coming and Dr. Rigel Emerson would work to assure humanity met it unarmed and finally at peace.

Chapter One

Rigel Emerson wasn't looking forward to his upcoming trip. He and his wife were trying to have a baby, and this trip was scheduled during her next ovulating cycle. She wasn't going to be too pleased, and he dreaded having to tell her of his need to attend. He also dreaded trips of this sort. He had no idea with whom he'd be meeting. All he knew was he had gotten his orders to be there.

He was an up-and-coming scientist in quantum mechanics specializing in propulsion systems. He had received his PhD from MIT and was one of the youngest to have graduated in that field. Science and math had always come easily to Rigel. He could look at equations others were unable to solve and figure them out with relative ease. He lacked a little on the social side. Rigel recognized this weakness and surmised it was one of the reasons he would prefer to avoid this trip.

His wife, Anna, had met him in college. She was initially attracted to his extraordinary good looks, but he shied away from her at first, as he did all women. Rigel had spent most of his life with his nose in books, so never really developed the social skills a normal person with his good looks would have acquired at this point in life. Instead, he was standoffish, mostly avoiding social situations. When Anna first approached Rigel in the hall of the Bosworth Building at MIT, she could tell that he was a little awkward around females, but her curiosity tempted her to pursue this attractive, yet awkward treasure. It wasn't easy at first. He had no interest in women, but once she warmed up to him and convinced him she wasn't a threat, he became more at ease. It also helped that he didn't have a whole lot of other friends.

Anna was very attractive and highly intelligent. She was constantly pursued by men, but as a result of her intelligence, normal guys just didn't measure up. She was looking for someone who could challenge her mentally while also driving her wild physically. In her mind, Rigel could easily fit that bill. Besides, she knew there was something very special about him; she just didn't know what it was.

Anna was pursuing a master's degree in engineering while Rigel was working on his doctorate in physics. Anna normally wouldn't be in the Bosworth Building, but that semester she had one physics course she needed to complete for her Masters requirements. That made her a visitor to Bosworth three times a week. She didn't believe in luck. She felt running into Rigel had more to do with fate. She believed in making her own opportunities and Rigel became her latest adventure. They began hanging out together shortly after that first encounter.

They both graduated from MIT with honors. While Anna's master's degree in engineering from MIT would easily open opportunities, Rigel's PhD had prospective employers pounding on the door. He had offers from all over the world. With a little help from his father, who was an extremely well-known physicist in his own right, Rigel made the decision to join DARPA. DARPA is the Defense Advanced Research Project Agency for the U.S. government and Rigel was immediately sent to Los Alamos National Laboratory in New Mexico. Although Anna received several offers upon graduation, she knew the job at Los Alamos was too good for Rigel to pass up. She could search for jobs there as well as anywhere. Besides, she figured they wouldn't be there too long before DARPA would transfer Rigel someplace else.

It had been two years now since they had moved to Los Alamos. Anna had received a few offers, but none in the immediate area. They could easily live on Rigel's salary, so finding a job wasn't urgent. They decided that maybe it was time to start a family and once the kids were grown, Anna could pursue her career once the kids were in school.

They had been trying to have a baby, but nothing yet. They weren't sure what the problem was, but both decided it was time to get some professional help. They had made an appointment at the fertility clinic just to find out what was going on, but now Rigel had to break the news that his recently announced trip was scheduled during the same week as their appointment. Appointments were hard to come by. They had scheduled this one several months in advance, so he hated to have to postpone it. The problem was he had no choice regarding this trip. He was told by his boss in no uncertain terms that he was required to attend.

Of all places, the meeting was being held in Washington, DC. He hated traveling to Washington. It was always hectic, and he was always expected to socialize with the people with whom he was meeting. He had gotten better at socializing since college, but he still found himself uncomfortable in most social situations. Worse off, he wouldn't have Anna there to keep all his male comrades entertained. She knew exactly how to capture men's attention and draw the attention away from Rigel's unease and awkwardness. Luckily, it would only be a few days.

When he finally broke the news to Anna, she was disappointed, but she understood. He didn't have a choice. She'd call the fertility doctor's office in the morning and reschedule their appointment.

Over dinner that night, Anna asked him what the meeting was about. Rigel kind of furled his brow before he informed her he really didn't know. They hadn't told him. They just instructed him to be in Washington, DC for a meeting scheduled at 1:00 PM on Tuesday, September 27th. He didn't even know where the meeting was to be held, only that he would receive further instructions once he got there. It sounded important, but you never really knew when the government was involved. It could be one of those meetings where you justified expenditures for upcoming budgets or were assigned a new project. Either way, Rigel figured he'd find out once he was at the meeting.

Chapter Two

When Rigel arrived at work the next morning, he found an envelope lying on his desk. He immediately opened it and found a plane ticket for his trip. Nothing else. He was hoping to receive a little insight as to what the trip was about but working for the government, he had learned to just follow orders. Questions were allowed only after the doors were closed. Reviewing the ticket, he saw he had been upgraded to Business Class. That's unheard of when flying on government business as everyone at his level always flew coach. He wasn't going to complain, however. He'd enjoy the extra leg room.

The day before the trip, his boss called him into his office. He informed Rigel that there had been a change of plans. Instead of flying commercially, a government plane would be flying him to D.C. When Rigel asked what he should do with his plane ticket, his boss told him to destroy it, that the reservation had already been cancelled. Rigel had flown on government planes before, so this would be nothing new to him. He figured there must be others going to Washington, D.C. as well, so it made more sense to charter the government flight.

His original plane ticket had him flying out on a commercial flight at 11:00 AM on Monday, September 26th to assure he'd arrive in plenty of time for their meeting on Tuesday. With this change in itinerary, he would be flying out at 6:30 AM on Tuesday from Sunport Airport in Albuquerque. It was about an hour's drive from where he lived, so he planned on leaving his house at around 5:00 AM.

The night before the flight, he felt Anna was a little down. "I'm sorry we had to postpone the appointment," he said to her.

"I understand completely," Anna replied, "I don't want you to worry about it one bit. Who knows, you may learn during this trip that you're being transferred, and we wouldn't want to start fertility treatments here only to have to move them to a new doctor somewhere else."

Anna was always so understanding when it came to things having to do with his work, but he still knew deep down she was disappointed. At least, with the new flight arrangements, he'd get another night with her. He held her tightly that night and felt her strength become his.

Rigel awoke on Tuesday still dreading the trip, but he knew he didn't have a choice. Anna had packed his bag the night before and was already up making him breakfast when he got out of the shower. He dressed, walked into the kitchen and without a word, held her in his arms for what had to be the longest hug of his life. He understood what he had in Anna and realized what a difference she had made in his life. He would have held her like that forever, but she somehow slipped out of his arms to turn the omelet she had made for him. "Darn it," she exclaimed, "it's a little overcooked on one side."

Rigel chuckled, "Not everything has to be perfection, my love." They were meant for each other.

The ride to Sunport Airport was uneventful. He listened to one of his favorite podcasts on the way. It was a podcast meant for the general public on quantum mechanics, and he got a kick out of how simplistic the podcaster always tried to make it. That always made him laugh.

When he neared the airport, he followed the signs to General Aviation which was on the opposite side of the runway from the Main Terminal. The Main Terminal was designed for commercial flight, while private planes used General Aviation. He parked his car and went inside. There to greet him was an Air Force Officer who introduced himself as Captain Graves. Rigel chuckled to himself; how ironic the person flying the plane would have the name of Graves. He hoped this wasn't an omen, but he quickly dismissed those thoughts. Captain Graves grabbed Rigel's bag, exited the building, and headed toward the plane. Rigel followed closely behind. As usual with private aircraft, there was no aircraft walkway. The planes were too small. Instead, you walked across the tarmac and boarded the plane through a retractable set of steps that led up to the door of the plane.

Upon entering the aircraft, he was greeted by a flight attendant who smiled and said, "Welcome aboard, Dr. Emerson" as she gestured towards the seats. There were eight individual seats on this plane, two seats facing directly across from another two seats and separated by the aisle, and four somewhat narrower seats further back in the plane all facing forward with two seats on each side of the aisle.

Rigel realized instantly that he must be the first to arrive as there were no other passengers yet on the plane, so he asked, "Where would you like me to sit?"

"Anywhere you'd like," the flight attendant replied.

Rigel shrugged and headed towards the narrower seats toward the back of the aircraft. He was raised to be polite and thought he would save the larger seats for other passengers. Just as he was about to sit, the Flight Attendant approached and said, "You'll be much more comfortable in one of the larger seats up front."

"I thought I'd leave those for other passengers," Rigel replied.

"You are our only passenger today, Dr. Emerson, so you can sit wherever you'd like," the Flight Attendant informed him before smiling and walking away.

"I'm the only passenger?" Rigel thought to himself. That's almost unheard of on government aircraft. Perhaps others who had been scheduled to fly on this plane had to cancel. It seemed strange, but Rigel thought he might as well take advantage of the situation. He moved to one of the larger seats up front. When he sat down, he realized these seats were much more luxurious and comfortable.

The Flight Attendant returned one more time before take-off and asked if she could get him anything.

"I wouldn't mind a cup of coffee, if you wouldn't mind," Rigel replied.

"Coming right up," the Flight Attendant replied as she wheeled around and quickly headed to the galley to retrieve it. When she returned, on her tray was a cup and saucer, an urn of coffee, what appeared to be two expensive cut-glass containers, one holding sugar, the other cream, and a danish roll on a small plate. "I know you only asked for coffee," the Flight Attendant said, "but the danishes are so fresh, I thought you might like to have one."

"Twist my arm," Rigel replied and gratefully accepted it.

Just before closing the door to the aircraft, Captain Graves and another Air Force Officer approached him. Captain Graves began, "I'm going to be your pilot for this flight and Captain Holmberg here will be the copilot."

"It's a pleasure to meet you, sir," Captain Holmberg said as he extended his hand for a handshake. Rigel returned his coffee cup to the saucer and shook the co-pilot's hand. It was a firm handshake, and Rigel immediately knew he was going to be in good hands. After exchanging pleasantries, the two pilots went to the cockpit and began preparations for the flight. The Flight Attendant closed and secured the door to the plane and got ready for departure.

Rigel soon heard the engines of the plane waking up and knew they would soon be on their way. He still couldn't get over how he was the only passenger on the plane. His thoughts were interrupted when Captain Graves' voice came over the loudspeaker and explained they had been cleared for takeoff. He added the estimated flight time was approximately 3 hours and 13 minutes, but reminded Rigel there would also be a time zone change. Rigel thought to himself that the flight time seemed much shorter than flying commercially, but then he realized private planes were allowed to fly higher than commercial flights and at much higher speeds.

Before long, he felt the plane begin to taxi. The Flight Attendant appeared one more time and repeated the normal preflight instructions including use of seat belts and exits on the plane. He smiled as she spoke and wondered how many really important people she had coached on this same subject. When finished, she returned to the galley at the front of the plane, pulled down the jump seat and buckled herself in. Before he knew it, they were in the air and on their way to Washington.

Chapter Three

When Captain Graves came over the loudspeaker next, it was to inform him they were starting their descent. He looked out the window of the plane and saw only miles of tree covered land. No large cities were in sight. As the plane descended, Rigel thought it was odd that he still didn't see any large cities. He felt the plane bank hard left, level, then bank hard left again before quickly descending.

It appeared as if the plane was going to land right in the midst of all the trees, but just as they approached ground level, Rigel could see a clearing under the plane. There still weren't any buildings. Where were they landing? He thought they'd probably fly into Andrews AFB or Bolling AFB, or at the very least, Reagan International or Dulles, but this surely wasn't any of those. He knew he wasn't being kidnapped, so he just sat back in his seat and enjoyed the perfect landing.

Looking out of the window of the aircraft, all he saw were trees at the edge of the clearing. There were no buildings anywhere. As the aircraft rolled to a stop, he saw a black Suburban. He unbuckled, waited for the Flight Attendant to open the door and rose to exit the plane. Just as he got to the door of the aircraft, Captains Graves and Holmberg both appeared, thanked him for flying with them and told him to enjoy his stay.

"Enjoy my stay? It looks like I'm out in the boonies, " he thought to himself.

As he exited the aircraft, the driver of the Suburban retrieved Rigel's bag from Captain Holmberg and proceeded towards him. "Welcome to DC, Dr. Emerson. I'm Rick and I'll be driving you to your engagement," Rick informed him.

"Nice to meet you, Rick. Where are we, by the way?" Rigel asked.

"We're on private property outside of Washington DC, sir. You'll learn more about it soon," Rick replied. Rick opened one of the rear side doors and Rigel jumped in as Rick stowed his luggage in the back.

It was a relatively short drive before the Suburban pulled up in front of a rather large house. There was a nice yard, but everywhere you looked beyond the area cleared for the yard were trees. It was rather secluded. Rick opened the door for him, and Rigel exited the Suburban as Rick moved to the rear of the vehicle to retrieve Rigel's bag. As Rigel walked towards the house, the front door opened and out walked his father.

Chapter Four

"What are you doing here?" Rigel asked before even thinking about properly greeting his father.

His father, Stan, responded, "I'm here for the meeting." That was quite a surprise for Rigel, but he rushed and hugged him.

Rigel had a very special relationship with his father. He couldn't even begin to imagine having a better role model. His father was not only incredibly intelligent, but he was also a top scientist in the physics field. On top of that, he was the best father ever. Even with all his father had going on, he couldn't remember even one time when his father didn't have time for him. Rigel didn't play sports growing up, but he was involved in all kinds of competitions, groups and camps, all science related, of course. His father had been there for him every step of the way. Rigel only hoped he could be as good of a father to his son or daughter as his father was to him.

"Did they feed you on the plane? Are you hungry?" his father asked.

"I could eat," Rigel replied. With his arm around Rigel's shoulder, Stan walked his son into the house.

The inside of the house was even more amazing than the outside. It was like a log cabin, but very large, and with a huge entryway that led to a massive family room. There was a fireplace big enough for a person to stand in against the outside wall. The fireplace was made entirely of stone and gave the place such a warm and comfortable feeling.

As the driver entered and dropped off his bag, Rigel turned to his father and whispered, "Should I tip him?"

"It's already been taken care of, son," his father responded.

Stan walked Rigel into the kitchen. It was enormous and looked like it could be used to feed hundreds. Everything needed to cook for a large group was in this kitchen. A lone cook was busy in the corner starting preparations for the evening meal.

"Jim, would you mind coming over for a moment? I'd like to introduce you to my son, Rigel," Stan called out. Jim immediately stopped what he was doing, walked to the sink to wash his hands, and then quickly walked over to meet them.

Jim extended his hand. "Hi, Rigel. It's a pleasure to meet you," Jim offered. Rigel took Jim's hand and accepted his vigorous shake.

"It's a pleasure to meet you, as well," Rigel replied.

"Jim, would you mind rustling up a sandwich for my son?" Stan asked.

"It would be my pleasure," Jim politely responded.

Stan led Rigel over to a large table where they sat and awaited the sandwich. When Jim arrived, he was carrying a rather large sandwich stacked high with ham on homemade bread. The presentation was incredible the way Jim had arranged leaves of lettuce, slices of tomato and onion, and a small glass bowl of mayo on the plate.

"Are we splitting this?" Rigel asked his father.

"No, son, that's entirely yours," his father replied, "I already ate."

Jim asked Rigel what he'd like to drink. "Just water, if I may," Rigel responded. Jim quickly returned with a well-chilled bottle of water and a glass filled with ice.

As Rigel looked around, he asked, "Where are the rest of the people for the meeting?"

"We'll talk about that later," his father responded, "right now, just enjoy your sandwich and then I'll show you around." The sandwich was so delicious, his father didn't need to tell him twice. Soon his plate was empty, and Rigel was ready to get started.

His father showed him around the house and pointed out some interesting memorabilia from the world of physics. It was obvious his father had been here before, but he never remembered his father talking about it. "How come you never mentioned this place?" Rigel asked his father.

"We call this The Lodge. As you will learn shortly, our meetings here are not to be discussed," his father responded. That was odd that his father had answered his question in that manner. He never remembered his father holding anything back or living in a world surrounded by secrecy. Maybe he was being too curious and making something out of nothing.

After their tour of the house, his father stated, "Maybe you should go unpack your things and when you're finished, we'll get started."

"Started?" Rigel asked curiously, "Where is everyone else?"

To which his father responded, "the right people will be here at the appropriate time."

That was Rigel's clue to go no further in his questioning. "What time do you want me down here and what's the proper attire?" Rigel asked two last questions.

"No special time, just whenever you're ready and wear something comfortable. We're informal here," his father responded.

Rigel did as he was told and went up to his room to unpack, but he was still curious about the other people. This was a long trip. "Who knows, maybe Dad just wanted some father and son time," he thought to himself.

Chapter Five

After Rigel had found his room and unpacked his things, he took a moment to look out the window. His bedroom was on the second floor. Just as he had observed when exiting the plane, for as far as he could see, there were only trees.

When he made it back downstairs, his father was sitting on a couch in the living room. "Where's the meeting going to be held?" Rigel asked.

"Right here. Have a seat," his father responded.

Still a little wary, Rigel took a seat in a chair to the right of his father. He noticed a solemn look on his father's face. "I understand you and Anna are wanting children, " his father started.

"Yes, we've been trying, but nothing has happened yet. We had an appointment scheduled at a fertility clinic this week, but I had to postpone it because of this meeting," Rigel replied.

With a very stern look, Stan began, "What I'm about to tell you cannot be told to anyone. It doesn't leave this house. Do you understand?" His father had never talked to him in that fashion before, so he knew this was important.

"Yes, I understand," Rigel replied.

His father opened a folder that had been lying on the coffee table in front of him. He removed some papers and handed them to Rigel. "What's this?" Rigel asked.

"Read through this carefully. These papers must be signed before we can go any further," Rigel's father replied.

It was a non-disclosure agreement. "What had he gotten himself into?", Rigel thought to himself. He read the entire document. It was mostly cookie cutter verbiage until it came to the very last paragraph. Right above the signature line was a statement that read:

"...unauthorized disclosure by the Receiving Party of certain proprietary and confidential information shared under this contract shall be considered a breach of National Security, result in immediate revocation of security clearances and may result in prosecution and subject to any and all punishments afforded to the authority of the United States of America."

"Wow! They mean business," Rigel muttered quietly and took a rather large gulp.

As he reached for the pen, his father reached out and grabbed his hand. "Are you really ready to do this?" his father asked.

"Well, number one, I don't know what 'this' is, but I'm sure you would not allow me to put myself or my family in danger, and number two, if it's that important and you want me to sign, I trust you implicitly and will sign it," Rigel responded.

Still holding onto Rigel's hand, Stan raised his voice and said, "Jen, would you come in here for a moment?"

The Flight Attendant from his flight immediately entered the room from somewhere behind the kitchen. Rigel suddenly realized he hadn't even asked her name during the flight. When she arrived, she said, "Hello once again, Dr. Emerson."

Stan released Rigel's hand, picked up the pen and handed it to Rigel. Rigel clicked the top of the pen to expose the point and signed the document. Stan immediately spun the document around to Jen where she signed, pulled out a stamp and notarized the document. The document was then placed in a manilla envelope and Jen took it with her as she left the room.

With that, Stan arose, walked toward the kitchen and explained to everyone that they were now free to leave. Jim, Jen, Rick and both Captains followed each other out the door. Once they had left the house, Stan walked over to the entryway, punched a code into the security box installed next to the front door, then bent his knees slightly and peered into a device which obviously was a retinal reader. Rigel heard a ding followed by some clicking as locks on each door of the house became engaged. A soft noise also began to fill the room. Rigel recognized it immediately as white noise. This would allow he and his father to have a discussion without the possibility of anyone else hearing.

Chapter Six

His father returned to the couch, looked Rigel directly in the eyes and said, "Let's get started." His father explained how he knew calling the last-minute meeting was inconvenient for Anna and Rigel as they had to postpone their appointment at the fertility clinic. He also explained their appointment was exactly the reason the meeting had to be called.

"I don't understand," Rigel exclaimed.

"It's complicated, Rigel, but I'm going to explain it to you as best I can," his father explained.

Stan began to inform Rigel that he wouldn't be able to have children naturally. "We were beginning to figure that out," interrupted Rigel, "that's why we made the appointment."

"No, it's more than that. You will never be able to have children of your own, Rigel," his father said.

"Why? What's going on with me that I don't know about?" Rigel shouted a little more emphatically than he meant to.

"You were born sterile, " his father replied.

"How do you know that? I've not even been tested," Rigel threw back trying not to lose his temper.

"What I'm about to tell you may seem unbelievable, but you have to trust me," his father began. "I'm sterile, too, " his father announced in a voice that was calm yet impactful.

"How can that be? You had me," Rigel interrupted. His father said nothing. He just looked back at him with the love he had been accustomed to receiving from his father.

Stunned by the concept, Rigel said, "Wait, you're not my father?"

"I will always be your father, Rigel, I'm just not your birth father," his father replied.

Rigel sat there in shock. He didn't know how to respond. All these years and now he finds out his father isn't really his father. How can that be? This man had been the best father any child could possibly imagine. He had been so blessed with Stan having raised him, how could he possibly not be his father?

"So, I'm adopted?" Rigel let it slip out without thinking.

"Yes, and no," his father responded. "Your mother is your biological mother, but I'm not your biological father. Your mother doesn't even know that."

"Wait, what? How could Mom not know it?" Rigel interrupted.

"Let me explain," his father replied.

Stan started by going way back to the time that he had been born. Stan explained that his father was also sterile. Rigel couldn't believe what he was hearing, but he kept quiet allowing his father to continue. His father began to tell Rigel how he wasn't sure how many generations it had gone back. It had to have included his grandfather, and no one knows before that. Each of the men in his family were sterile, but each had at least one child from the child's natural mother. The mother was not aware because they were impregnated during normal intercourse with their husband, but the semen came from another source.

"So, all this was lies to trick your wives," Rigel couldn't help from interrupting.

"It wasn't a trick, Rigel," his father replied, "it was necessary."

"Necessary for what? All right. All right. I'll shut up, but explain how any of this makes any sense," Rigel demanded.

Stan put his arms out to calm his son. He didn't touch him, but he made the motion of placing his hands on Rigel's shoulders and calmly settling him back into the couch. "We are only partially of this dimension, Rigel."

Chapter Seven

Rigel couldn't believe what he was hearing. Had his father gone crazy? This made absolutely no sense. He started to talk but held back and allowed his father to explain.

"You are half human and half something else, Rigel," his father just put it out there bluntly.

"What does that even mean?" Rigel asked unable to believe his ears.

His father took a deep breath and began, "I mean a part of you is not of this Earth. Part of you is inter-dimensional."

Rigel stopped him right there, "Now you're talking crazy. How could I be half 'inter-dimensional' as you call it. This needs to stop and it's going to stop right now. I'm not a fool, father, or should I even call you 'Father'?"

Touché'. That touched hard. Rigel had made his point, and Stan was hurt by the comment, but he knew he must continue.

"Rigel, have you ever wondered why you were so much smarter than the other kids while growing up?", his father asked.

"I knew I was a little different. Things came easily to me, but I guess I didn't pay attention that I was any smarter," Rigel responded, still smarting from the craziness his father was speaking.

"Well, you were and there was no disproving that," his father replied. "In fact, you were so smart that your mother and I had to keep you busy with other science activities so you wouldn't become bored. You graduated early with a PhD from MIT, for heaven sakes. No normal kid does that."

Rigel hit back, "So, if you're not my father, who is? I want to meet him."

"I'm afraid that's not possible, Rigel," his father replied, "we don't know who he is, where he is or how to contact him. We don't even understand how it works. All we know is that it's happening and we're part of it."

"Then explain it to me the best way you can," Rigel demanded.

"All right, here's what we know," his father began. "An inter-dimensional entity decided to prepare our Earth for their own use, should they ever need to do so. We don't know what these beings look like, where they come from, or if they're even people at all. All we know is they are much further advanced than we are. We don't even know if they are physical beings. They decided to create highly advanced hybrids on Earth to foster their preparation process. You and I are both one of their hybrids. I don't know how many generations it goes back, but at some point in time, they decided to use humans, to interbreed with and create a highly evolved race of people. At some point, they impregnated a human female, who had a child. That child was intentionally bred to be sterile. They didn't want, nor could they allow any dilution of the gene pool for their species. As the first male hybrid child grew, they must have informed him of their Plan and he must have agreed to continue the trend. We don't know how many of us there are or ever have been. We don't know how to determine if a person is a hybrid. The only trait we know about is high intelligence and sterility, but we know not all highly intelligent people are hybrids."

"If we, as hybrids, are sterile, then how does this work? How can we continue the Plan?" Rigel asked.

"Good question," his father replied. "Each hybrid must receive half of their DNA from their human mother and half from the inter-dimensional race. That means the inter-dimensional entity must impregnate the human female mother. We know they don't physically impregnate them, but a transfer occurs, and it occurs only upon the approval from the hybrid father."

"So, I don't have your DNA?" Rigel asked. "No, son, you don't," his father responded.

"So, couldn't they detect I wasn't related to you, or even human for that matter, by testing my DNA?" Rigel questioned.

"That's a logical assumption, but I'm afraid it's incorrect," his father replied. "If they tested your DNA, they would find it would look quite normal. In fact, it would appear from the DNA that you were a child of both your mother and me but that would only be what showed up on a DNA test. In actuality, you would be a child of your mother and an inter-dimensional male. The inter-dimensional race took care of everything and manipulated the DNA so it would appear you were my son but in reality, you don't actually carry my DNA. We don't really know what the inter-dimensional people are. Perhaps they are human or another form. Some have had visions of their inter-dimensional guide, but no one has ever actually seen them. Sometimes we get communications from them, but that's all the contact we're allowed. We're not allowed to ask questions."

This was all getting so weird for Rigel, but he continued listening. His father went on to say, "I don't know how it is for everyone, but I can tell you what happened to me. My father told me about all of this when I was a little younger than you. I was about to get married, and he must have thought he needed to tell me before we considered having children. In any event, I found out I was sterile, but I also learned there was a way of having a child, a child I could raise as my own. Even though you don't carry my genetic material, you will always be my son, and I've done everything I could do to see that you were properly raised. When your mom and I first considered having children, my father informed me about the inter-dimensional plan. They offered me an opportunity to have you. There would be nothing that would affect your mother. It would happen while your mother and I were together, but instead of my sterile seed, she received the fertile seed of the inter-dimensional entity."

"Does Mom know?" Rigel jumped in trying not to panic.

"No, and she will never know." his father replied. "There's absolutely nothing about being unfaithful. I was involved in the process. I impregnated her, but a different seed replaced mine."

Rigel couldn't believe what he was hearing. "Then you've lied to Mom all these years?" Rigel chimed in.

"Is it lying if I'm the one that planted the seed, I'm the one that impregnated her, I'm the one that loved her and cared for her all these years, I'm the one that raised you?" he responded. "No, Rigel, I haven't told your mother everything. I'm not allowed to tell her everything. The agreement I had allowed me only to tell you once you reached an age where it was necessary."

"Let me see if I've got this straight. You had sex with Mom and inserted someone else's seed to impregnate her?" Rigel shot back a little louder than he meant to.

"Not exactly," his father said, "they placed their seed inside of me. It replaced my own. To everyone else, I was the person who impregnated your mother. If a DNA test were performed, it would confirm you were my son, but we know that test would have been manipulated because in fact, you cannot contain any of my DNA."

Rigel stood up from his chair saying, "I think I need some time to process this. I need to go outside and be by myself for a while."

"I'm sorry, son, but that's not possible just yet. It's important that I tell you everything I know before you're allowed to leave," his father replied.

"So, now I'm a prisoner," Rigel vehemently shouted back at his father.

"No, son, you are a hybrid and it's time to find out what that means. You have some decisions ahead of you and you'll need all the information I'm going to provide in order to make those decisions."

Chapter Eight

Stan gave Rigel a few minutes to compose himself. While Rigel was processing all he had heard, Stan prepared them some coffee. It was going to be a long day.

When Stan returned with the coffee, Rigel still seemed quite upset. Stan started in, "I'm not trying to upset you, Rigel. I'm only trying to be honest with you and provide you the information you'll need to go forward."

Rigel took a deep breath and nodded his head for his father to continue.

"Let me explain what I know and then I'll answer any questions that I'm able to answer," his father began. "At some point in time, this inter-dimensional race decided they needed a Plan for the future. I'm not sure if they were concerned something was happening to their world or what the issue was that caused them to develop this Plan."

"What planet are they from and are they the ones that are causing all this UFO hysteria?" Rigel inquired.

"No, son. They are much more advanced than the UFO sightings people have reported. In fact, some of those sightings probably are real, but the inter-dimensional people call those cultures 'primitive' because they've not yet developed inter-conscious travel and must rely on vessels or vehicles. The inter-dimensional people can communicate with us. They do that through inter-consciousness. We don't see them or hear their voice; we just receive their thoughts. In fact, we don't know if these inter-dimensional people actually have physical bodies. They may live only in consciousness, kind of like a spirit, for all we know. We don't know where they are from or where they reside. Maybe someday they will tell us, but for right now we are on a need-to-know basis with them, meaning if we don't absolutely need to know something, they're not going to share it with us."

This all sounded like something out of a science fiction book to Rigel, but it was his father telling him and he hoped his father wouldn't make this stuff up. He could tell it pained his father to have to tell him, but the fact that he was doing so meant it must have some validity.

"So, what's the purpose of us hybrids, then?" Rigel asked.

"Our purpose is to advance humanity and intelligence here on Earth so Earth is prepared for their arrival should they ever need it," his father answered. "No one knows when the hybrid process started or how many generations of hybrids actually exist. They made it very clear that we are not to search out other hybrids unless told to do so. We do know that each hybrid is sterile, so in order to perpetuate the process, each male hybrid must sign onto the Plan to father a child with their seed. Each female hybrid understands they will never have children. I suppose there have been some male hybrids who have been unwilling to sign onto the Plan, and they've gone childless. That's always an option, but I saw the value in continuing the process and parenthood has become the most rewarding experience in my life. That's why I wanted to give that option to you, but that's something we'll talk about later. First, I need to explain the Plan and how it works."

"The Plan is to advance civilization here on Earth. This has been occurring for many, many years. There are hybrids in high position all around the world. The goal is to advance intelligence and technology, and be in a position to govern the world, should the inter-dimensional people require it."

"Wait, if the inter-dimensional people need it, what happens to all the humans?" Rigel asked urgently.

"We have been assured that all humans will be fine. In fact, they will be better off than they are today as there will be no war among nations on Earth. That's why they must be in control of every nation. Any uprising will be shut off before it even begins to start. They are promising peace, and I have every reason to believe they will be able to keep their promise."

"I don't understand how they intend to accomplish this," Rigel injected.

"Their Plan is being implemented over time. Each hybrid is specialized in a specific field or aspect of life. You, for example, are specialized in physics. There will be specialists in government, law, economics, education, medicine and all the various factions of this world. The hybrids are charged to make progress in each area. Just like you have made significant contributions to physics."

"What about Jim, Jen, Rick and the two pilots, are they hybrids? Rigel asked.

"Yes, they are or they wouldn't be allowed to participate," his father answered.

"Then if hybrids are supposed to be so gifted, why are they doing jobs like cooks, flight attendants or pilots?" Rigel continued his questioning.

"We must be careful not to judge a book by its cover, son," his father replied. "They undoubtedly have special talents, and we have no idea what their assignment may be. Right now they're serving in these functions, but who knows what their real assignment entails? I'm not allowed to ask about their assignments, nor are they allowed to ask about yours or mine. That's why they had to leave before we got started."

"What happens to those male hybrids that choose not to father a child?" Rigel asked.

"Nothing," his father responded, "they are appreciated for their accomplishments in their field. They are well taken care of and respected for their choice not to father a child."

"Why couldn't you tell Mom?" Rigel was always very protective of his mother and was concerned why she wasn't included in the plan.

"Your mother is not a hybrid. The inter-dimensionals will not allow hybrids to discuss the Plan with anyone other than another hybrid, and then only with permission. I struggled at first with the thought of not being able to tell your mother, but when you see the joy you have brought her, it makes it all worthwhile. She was not used. She made a choice to have a child, and she had one. Not knowing about the Plan will never affect her feelings for you or the love your mother and I share for each other. And, she will never suspect anything different because a DNA test would show you are my son. I don't think there's one single gift I could have ever given your mother that would have been greater than the gift of you. It's not unlike when you're working on a project at work with someone that has a lower level of security clearance. You can tell them everything up to the point of their clearance, but you can't go beyond that point. I have made sure I've told your mother as much as I could about my job, but I'm not allowed to tell her anything about the Plan. That's above her security clearance."

Rigel still didn't like it, but he was starting to catch on. There were several moments of silence as Rigel regurgitated everything he had heard up to this point. His father sat silently, respected Rigel's silence and allowed his son the time he needed to process.

Chapter Nine

It took a while, but Rigel was finally ready to move on. He had so many questions.

"I have some questions," Rigel said.

"I was hoping you would," his father replied. Stan knew that questions meant his son was at least considering the information and hadn't shut it out completely.

"What if I decide not to go along with this?", Rigel asked.

"You have that option," his father explained, "in which case you will have no memory of this conversation, we will talk about a new project that you will be working on, and you will go home at the end of our meeting not having a recollection of us ever having discussed the hybrid situation."

"So, they would erase my memory?", Rigel inquired.

"Only the memory of our hybrid conversation," his father assured him. "For the protection of the Plan, it's important that word of this arrangement doesn't leak to anyone."

"Is it possible to have more than one child?" Rigel continued with his questions.

"Yes, as a matter of fact, it is," his father replied. "Each child, however, would be sterile," Stan added.

"Could a hybrid be female?", Rigel inquired.

His father replied, "Yes, like Jen, for example. But even a female hybrid child is sterile and cannot have children."

"Why couldn't a female hybrid have a child?" Rigel asked.

"All hybrids are born sterile, doesn't matter if they are male or female," his father answered. "They have a way around being a sterile male, but there is no way around a sterile female. A sterile female can't have children regardless of what happens."

"Doesn't seem quite fair that a male hybrid can have a child, but a female hybrid can't" Rigel chimed in.

"Remember, Rigel, a male hybrid can't have a child either. They're sterile, but they can adopt the child they are given. A female hybrid may also adopt a child, but it would probably be a human child and not a hybrid. It doesn't matter if they're a male hybrid or a female hybrid, their purpose is to contribute to society and the advancement of humanity," his father responded.

"Why are the inter-dimensionals so concerned about preserving their gene pool, making everyone sterile and not allowing them to have children of their own?" Rigel said frustrated.

"I don't get to make the rules, Rigel," his father responded, "but the inter-dimensional people have determined that their gene pool should never be reduced below 50%. If a hybrid's child was not born sterile and had a child with a human, that would result in a child with only 25% of inter-dimensional genes. That would only dwindle further as each successive child had children. In order to make the Plan work, they must have decided that 50% is the limit they would be willing to accept and put sterility in place to protect that."

"How could I ever do this to Anna?" Rigel declared solemnly.

Stan got up and moved the few steps to Rigel's chair. "Stand up for a moment," Stan said.

When Rigel stood, Stan gave his son a hug and whispered in his ear, "I am fine with any decision you make. This has to be your decision, but the best thing that has ever happened in my life was you, and the best thing that ever happened in your mother's life was you. You have to decide for yourself if you want to give Anna and yourself this level of happiness. It comes with responsibilities. Sometimes it even comes with hard decisions, but I can promise you that having a child is the greatest gift you will ever receive."

In this heartfelt moment, something struck Rigel the wrong way. He pushed back from his father and with a bit of contempt he spewed, "But a child won't really be my child."

Stan wasn't expecting this response. He should have been prepared for it, but he wasn't. It took a moment before he could respond. He finally said, "Your son would be every bit a son to you as you have been to me." Hardened from all the tough experiences they had encountered, and all the world had taught them, they both suddenly had tears in their eyes.

When they both had recovered, Rigel asked, "So, there's no other way, is there?"

His father replied, "The decision on whether or not to proceed is up to you, as is the decision of whether or not to have a child. Either way, you are admirably serving the Plan. No one can change the fact that you are sterile. Unfortunately, if you and Anna truly want a child, you must either follow this route or adopt a human baby. Those are your only options."

Rigel thought about that for a moment. He wondered what Anna would prefer. Would she rather go through life with a baby she thought they created, or adopt a baby that for certain had no genetic material from either of them? The problem was he wasn't going to be able to talk to her about this. He would need to make the decision on his own, for the both of them.

Chapter Ten

Rigel and his father spent the rest of the afternoon discussing the Plan and how it was working. He learned there were thousands, if not hundreds of thousands of hybrids already operating in the United States and probably many more than that all over the world. He was concerned that the Plan was a way for them to take over the world, and in fact it was, but his father kept reassuring him all the people of the Earth will be better off if that happened. It was hard to imagine a world without war, but the inter-dimensional people had promised that. Could they deliver? I guess no one knew for sure. There was only hope, but hope was something, and it was better than the alternative to which it appeared our world was headed. In fact, he learned the inter-dimensionals had sped up the process because of the increasingly dangerous times we were experiencing. Saving the world was a huge task and not something we could do on our own. We had tried so many times and failed. The hope the inter-dimensionals provided may be our only chance.

"Father, am I wrong to think the inter-dimensionals' Plan may be the only hope we have for our planet?" Rigel asked.

"No, son, You aren't wrong and I tend to agree with you. I believe their intention was to provide a safety net for themselves, but now that they've seen what we've done to our world, their Plan has become a safety net for all of us," his father told him.

"So, this Plan isn't really a bad thing, is it?" Rigel asked.

"No, son, I believe it's a very good thing. I believe it's the only way to save our planet and save humanity. They have blessed us with high intelligence. They have provided us with well-paying jobs. They've taken care of all our needs. The inter-dimensionals have been very good to us, Rigel. There's no denying that. That's what convinced me to put my faith in them. Now you need to decide whether you want to be involved or want out," his father explained.

"What happens if I decide to get out?" Rigel asked.

"Then, as I said before, you will have no recollection of our conversation today and life will go on for you as it was before. You will continue your work in physics and probably make some new discoveries that will advance our knowledge. On the downside, you will find out that you are sterile and if you and Anna decide you want children, you will have to adopt. I wish there was some way to allow you to have children of your own, but there just isn't," his father responded.

"And if I stay in?" Rigel inquired.

"Then you will also continue your contributions to physics and may be called upon to get involved in other fields, as well. You will be given the option of having a child, albeit hybrid, but a child Anna will believe came from you. I know you, Rigel. You will be a wonderful father regardless of which route you take, and your mother and I will love that grandchild with all the love that we have," his father said smiling.

"You really love me, don't you, Dad?" Rigel couldn't help from saying.

"More than anything in the world, Son," his father replied. Both of their eyes became moist once again.

Shaking off the emotions and getting back to business, Stan said, "Don't make a decision right now. I want you to sleep on it. Really think it through. I want you to do what is best for you and Anna. For right now, we get to have a little father and son time. We have some trout waiting for us!"

"What? After the load you dumped on me, you want to go fishing?" Rigel shouted out.

"Can you think of a better way to spend the afternoon, son?" his father replied.

With that, Stan gathered up some gear stored in a bench under the window, turned off the security alarm and the two of them headed down to a small stream near the house. It was finally father and son time. No business. No pressure. No decisions. Just enjoying each other. Rigel wished it was that easy as he couldn't get the conversation they had shared out of his mind.

Chapter Eleven

Fishing was great and they caught several nice trout. They took them back to the house and gave them to Jim who was already in the kitchen preparing for dinner.

"I was hoping you'd catch your dinner," Jim chuckled. "I had a backup plan, just in case, but I trusted you'd come through for me. Go wash up and then come down for cocktails. I've prepared some nice appetizers to tide you over until dinner is ready."

"You're the best, Jim," Stan said as he put his arm around his son and they headed to the staircase.

"Do you always hold your meetings here at the Lodge?" Rigel asked as they walked up the stairs. "Our meetings have to be held in secure locations. We have those set up all around the world. I prefer this one because it's so secluded. I've been coming here for years. Before Jim, Bert did all our cooking. He was a heck of a guy. He retired about three years ago and Jim took his place. You're going to love his cooking. That guy is just magic," his father replied.

When he reached his room, his father said, "Meet you downstairs in ten." Rigel nodded and headed inside.

Once Rigel closed the door behind him, he suddenly felt a brain rush. Today was a lot to take in. He didn't know what to do, but he knew his father would respect and love him regardless of which decision he made. He still couldn't get over that his mother didn't know. How would she feel if she found out? How would Anna feel if he put her through this? So much to think about.

After he had cleaned up and changed his clothes, he heard his father's footsteps coming down the hallway. He opened the door and caught his father just in time. "I have a question for you," Rigel started.

"Is it about what we talked about earlier?" his father asked? Rigel nodded his head. His father then continued, "Then I'm afraid we'll have to wait until tomorrow to discuss it. I'm sorry to put you off, but we aren't allowed to discuss that unless everyone is out of the house and the house is totally secured. I hope you understand."

Rigel nodded his head. He didn't like it, but he understood. That meant he'd be stewing about it all night.

When they got downstairs, Jim directed them out to the porch where he had a tray of appetizers ready for them. "What can I get you to drink?" Jim asked.

"I'll have the usual," Stan responded.

"Just a beer for me, if you have one" Rigel answered.

Jim returned shortly with an Old Fashion for his father and a beer in a frosty mug for Rigel. "I could get used to this," Rigel thought to himself.

The time on the porch was spent enjoying appetizers and discussing life in general. There wasn't a lot of catching up to do because Rigel had always remained close and had frequent conversations with his parents. Somehow, they found anything and everything to talk about.

Through their chat, Rigel couldn't help but think how much he loved his father. He was absolutely certain he had been blessed with the best parents in the world. His father would always be his father regardless of the circumstances.

It wasn't long before Jim informed them it was time for dinner. Walking into the house, the aroma of the freshly cooked trout filled the room. Waiting for them at the table was the trout they had caught only hours before. There was also a lettuce salad, green beans and a mushroom risotto. Everything was delicious. Rigel had dreaded coming to this meeting, but it was turning out to be quite enjoyable with just him and his father.

When dinner was finished, Jim cleared their plates and returned with a slice of homemade apple pie for each of them. Sitting on top of the pie was a scoop of homemade vanilla ice cream. Now this was life. Jim returned a second time with coffee. The pie was just as delicious as it looked. Now he knew why his father so enjoyed coming here. He suddenly wondered how his father kept from putting on extra pounds.

After dinner, they returned to the porch. Jim offered after-dinner drinks, but they both opted for just coffee. Sitting out on the porch, they could hear the sounds of the squirrels chattering and running through the trees. It was so peaceful and quiet out there. It made for a perfect retreat and place to get away from all the chaos in Washington, DC. Here Rigel thought he was going to have to put up with all those people. Instead, he got to enjoy the company of his father.

As they were sitting there, Rigel pulled out his phone with the intention of texting Anna to let her know he had arrived safely. "That won't work out here," his father quickly chimed in. "The place is surrounded with jamming devices to make sure no radio signals get in or out."

"How am I going to communicate with Anna?" Rigel asked.

"Let me show you," Stan said as he led Rigel back into the house.

In the corner of the room was a desk with a computer and phone on it. Stan sat down and typed in his log-in credentials. The screen blinked for a moment and suddenly the face of a cell phone appeared. "Type your name in here," his father instructed him. When Rigel did so, the generic phone then switched to a phone with his name on the top. He noticed he was able to pull up his contacts from the computer screen. "Just pull up Anna and type in any messages you want to send her. It will appear on her phone exactly as if it was coming from your cell phone. If you mistakenly mention anything about today or what is happening with our meeting, the computer won't allow you to send it and, in fact, will delete it," his father informed him.

"Can I tell you I'm here with you?" Rigel asked.

"No. I would just let her know your meeting is going fine and you'll tell her about it when you get home," his father replied.

That wasn't exactly how he would have liked to communicate with Anna, but he understood. At least he'd get to talk to her. He sent his first message letting Anna know he had arrived safely, and the meeting was going fine. Anna immediately replied she was happy to hear that, there was nothing new going on there and that she loved him. He knew how lucky he was to have Anna in his life. Nothing meant more to him. He was going to need to do some deep thinking tonight to make sure he made the right decision. Rigel responded that he loved her, too, and that he would talk to her tomorrow. He immediately received a thumbs-up sticker. Anna knew Rigel hated thumbs-up stickers and she did it just to tease him, but it was quickly followed by a kiss sticker. He smiled and logged out of the program.

It was only about 9:00 PM, but they were both tired and he still had a lot to think about. They walked upstairs together, gave each other a hug and went to their separate bedrooms.

Once inside, Rigel got ready for bed. When he laid down, he found the bed luxurious and comfortable, actually more comfortable than his bed at home. He caught himself lifting the corner of the sheet to find out what brand the mattress was. "I have to get me one of these," Rigel thought to himself.

As he laid back in the bed, he began to go over everything he and his father had discussed earlier that day. He was anticipating a restless night because there was a lot to take in, but instead, he felt calm and relaxed. It was as if he knew he didn't need to worry. He'd make the right decision; he was sure of that.

Sleep came much easier than he expected. He slept soundly all night.

Chapter Twelve

Rigel awoke to a soft knock on the door. "Rigel, are you awake? Breakfast in 20 minutes," he heard his father say.

"I'm awake, Dad. Just lying here thinking," Rigel responded. He chuckled as he realized he had just lied to his father. He hadn't been awake and thinking. He had still been asleep. He thought how easy it is sometimes to just respond the way you think people want you to respond instead of responding accurately. He hoped he never did that with Anna. She deserved better than just a meaningless response when she asked him a question. Suddenly, the enormity of the decision he was soon going to have to make hit him. "How will I ever decide?" he thought to himself.

He jumped out of bed, brushed his teeth, shaved and then jumped into the shower. He knew he had to make it quick because his father had only given him twenty minutes. The shower was large and displayed more knobs than usual. He first turned on the water. A digital screen lit up immediately as the water began to flow indicating the temperature of the water was set at 100 degrees Fahrenheit. The screen then flashed, "Press to accept or adjust". He pressed the accept button. The water, already warm began to adjust to the selected temperature. There was a knob just above the water controls. When he turned it, water not only sprayed from the shower head, but now also began falling from a rain head just above his head. It was heaven. "I've got to get me one of these," Rigel thought to himself.

When he finally pulled himself out of the shower, he toweled off and then quickly dried his hair. He dressed and rushed down to the dining room knowing he was late. "Sorry, I got mesmerized by the shower," Rigel sheepishly confessed.

"Happens to me every time," his father chuckled.

Jim immediately appeared and poured Rigel a nice hot cup of coffee. There was already a glass of orange juice waiting for him along with a tray of assorted danish rolls. "How do you like your eggs?" Jim asked.

"Sunny side up, please," Rigel responded. With that, Jim disappeared to begin cooking.

It wasn't long before Jim returned with breakfast for Rigel and his father. Each plate held two sunny side up eggs, two sausage links, two perfectly cooked slices of bacon and a slice of toast. His father thanked Jim and they both got to work on their plates. Rigel didn't realize at first that he seemed to be gobbling up his food. When he caught himself, he slowed down to a normal tempo. There was something about being out in the country that made a person hungry.

After breakfast, Stan and Rigel took their coffee to the porch, allowing Jim time to clean up after breakfast. "All done," Jim stated as he appeared at the door, "Is there anything else I can get you before I leave?"

"You've already done enough, Jim. That breakfast was delicious," Stan said, "Go enjoy your day."

"Thank you, sir," Jim replied as he disappeared from the door.

Stan gave Jim a few minutes and then said, "Well, are we ready to get at it?"

"I guess I'm as ready as I'll ever be," Rigel responded. They stood up and went back into the house.

As they approached the couch, Stan placed his coffee cup on the coaster setting on the coffee table. Jim had already placed an urn of coffee on the table for them. Rigel followed suit and sat in the chair he had sat in the day before. Stan made a brief walk-through of the house, then went to the security alarm pad and set the alarm. Once set, he returned to the couch.

"How'd you sleep, son?" Stan asked.

"Like a baby," Rigel responded. Stan just smiled.

"I'm not going to ask you for your decision on a child just yet. That's going to wait until tomorrow, so you have more time to think about it. At this point, however, I do need to ask you whether or not you've made your decision to continue," Stan said.

Rigel had thought about that and had a couple of questions. "Am I putting Anna or myself in any danger if I decide either way?" Rigel asked.

"No danger at all," his father responded. "If you decide to join us, you will be protected. If you decide not to join us, you will continue your life as a scientist, but your memory of this meeting will be erased."

Rigel didn't like the idea of anyone playing with his mind, but he understood drastic steps probably needed to be taken to protect the Plan. "What will life be like if I opt in?" Rigel asked.

"You will continue to grow rapidly in your career and may be involved in other aspects of the Plan as well. Either way, your family will be aptly provided for, and you will never need to worry about a thing," his father responded.

"What if I opt in now, but somewhere down the line, decide to get out?" Rigel asked.

"Then at the time you exercise that option, your memory of everything involving the Plan will be erased. Your career will continue, but you won't see advancement at the levels you'd experience if you were still in the program," his father replied.

"Are there any downfalls in joining?" Rigel asked.

"I've been in the program for over 40 years, and I've never had a bad experience," his father replied and continued, "I understand your reluctance to accept, son, but it really isn't so bad. The way they have provided for offspring has made me a father, something I otherwise wouldn't have been able to enjoy. Any downfall has been compensated to me in ways I couldn't have even imagined but save that decision for tomorrow. Today I only want to know if you are open to learning more."

"I'm open and ready," Rigel declared.

His father smiled warmly and replied, "Then let's get started."

They spent the rest of the morning discussing details of the Plan including all the variety and levels of jobs involved. Stan reinforced to his son that he wouldn't be able to necessarily determine if someone was in the Plan or not, unless the inter-dimensionals decided to share that information, but as long as the Plan was proceeding, he should trust those around him. Stan cautiously reminded Rigel he was not to share anything about the Plan with anyone and not to assume anyone was part of the Plan unless he received confirmation from the inter-dimensionals.

"How will I know?" Rigel asked.

"It's kind of hard to explain, Rigel. You'll just feel it," his father replied.

The time passed quickly and before they knew it, it was time for lunch. Jim had made them some sandwiches on a tray he left in the refrigerator before he departed. Stan turned off the alarm so they could enjoy their lunch on the porch.

"Do you know how much I love you, Dad?" Rigel asked as he was enjoying his lunch.

"I do," his father responded, "just as much as I love you."

"It's going to be okay, isn't it, Dad," Rigel declared.

"Yes, son, it's going to be better than okay," his father replied.

After lunch, they returned to the house, Stan reset the security system, and they spent the rest of the day talking about details. Rigel felt himself becoming more comfortable with the Plan as the day went on. He knew he probably wasn't as comfortable as his father, but he was getting there. A world without war was a big goal, but worth working towards.

At 4:00 PM, Stan told his son they had enough for the day. They broached a lot of subjects, and the vision of the Plan was becoming clearer for Rigel.

"I'd like to take you on a hike," his father exclaimed. "Go put on some comfortable shoes." A hike sounded like just what he needed, so Rigel hurried upstairs to change. When he returned, his father had already shut off the alarm.

They headed back toward the small stream where they had caught the fish for the previous night's dinner. As they approached the bank, Rigel could see a path proceeded upstream. It wasn't a clear walking path, but more the path of an animal, like a deer, would use to navigate the area. There were leaves on the path, fallen from the canopy of trees above, but not much vegetation, so it was an easy walk. Since it was narrow, they had to proceed single file which made it difficult to carry on a conversation, but they both had things they needed to think about, and the hike provided them the solitude to do so.

After about an hour, they headed back to the Lodge. Jim was on the porch lighting a grill. "I hope steaks are alright for dinner," Jim said, "How do you like them cooked?"

"Steaks sound wonderful. Medium-rare for me," Stan replied.

"Same for me," Rigel piped in.

They went into the house to change their shoes and wash up before heading back out to the porch for drinks and appetizers. Jim had prepared a beautiful charcuterie tray for them and a nice bottle of wine was waiting for them on the table. "If you prefer something other than wine, I'd be happy to get it," Jim informed them.

Wine sounded perfect to both of them and would pair well with the steaks they would be eating. As the steaks sizzled on the grill, the aroma was enticing and made them both hungry. Being surrounded by nature would do that to you, but the aroma put it over the top.

"I can see why you like it here, Dad," Rigel said.

"It's one of my favorite places," his father replied, "I'm hoping someday I'll get to bring your mother here, not for meetings obviously, but just to enjoy the serenity."

"Mom's always on your mind, isn't she, Dad?" Rigel asked.

"Always," his father replied, "I love her more than anything."

Rigel savored those words for a moment. His father hadn't told his mother everything, but he still loved her more than life itself. Despite the secret, his parents had a relationship he could only hope to have as intensely with Anna. Tomorrow he was expected to give his father his decision about a child. He was still a little nervous and hadn't completely yet decided, but seeing how much his father loved him and his mother, he knew which way he was leaning. He still had some questions for his father about having a child, but he knew he'd have to save them for tomorrow. For now, people were in the house, and the security system was turned off.

His thoughts were interrupted with an aroma too delectable to imagine. Jim had removed the steaks from the grill and was carrying them into the kitchen.

"It's funny how your mouth waters when you smell something that good," he was thinking to himself, but somehow the words came out for all to hear.

His father chuckled. "How lucky I am to have such a wonderful son," Stan thought to himself.

Before long, Jim was bringing their plates to the table. Rigel and Stan moved over to the table and took their seats.

"Will you please join us for dinner, Jim?" Rigel heard his father ask.

"Oh, I couldn't," Jim responded.

"I insist. You're part of our family now, and I'd like you to join us," Stan said welcomingly.

Jim's face turned red. "Oh, I'll just eat in the kitchen," were the words that leaked out of Jim's mouth.

Stan's face grew solemn. He wasn't taking "no" for an answer and Jim sensed it. Jim turned even redder and said, "I'll get my plate." Rigel saw a smile spread across his father's face. He could be quite stern when he needed to be but was as soft as a pillow inside.

Jim returned with his plate and sat down at the table. Wine was poured, dinner was devoured, and all three men enjoyed their time immensely. Before they were done, Jim felt like part of the family. His father could do that to a person.

With dinner over, Jim began to clear the table. "Here, let me help," Rigel chimed in as he grabbed some of the dishes and followed Jim into the kitchen. Tears again began to well up in Stan's eyes. He had made the right choice to have a son. He hoped Rigel would come to the same conclusion.

"I hope you don't mind having apple pie two nights in a row," Jim said as he carried in the plates of pie and homemade ice cream. "I hate to see it go to waste," he continued.

"No objections here," Stan said and Rigel nodded in agreement. The pie and ice cream were so delicious, there was no way they were going to pass that up.

When Jim delivered the coffee, all three of them sat down to enjoy. "Thank you for asking me to dine with you and your son tonight, Stan. That meant a great deal to me," Jim said.

"The fact is, Jim, we should be serving you after that meal you prepared. It was amazing," Stan replied. Jim turned a little red, but his smile revealed his sentiment.

After pie, Stan said to Jim, "Care to join us outside on the porch?"

"Thanks for offering, but I need to get everything cleaned up. I'll take a rain check, if you don't mind," Jim replied.

"You got it," Stan smiled.

Rigel and Stan made their way to the porch carrying their coffee. It was almost dark. You could still see a glimpse of light over the tops of the trees to the right of the house, which meant the sun had already set and they were getting an encore of the beautiful day.

They each chose rockers this time. For some reason, rockers seemed appropriate. The difficult task had been accomplished. All that was left was for Rigel to make his final decision and that would come tomorrow. "It's so peaceful out here," Rigel observed.

"It makes you forget about all the chaos going on around us, doesn't it?" his father asked.

"It sure does," Rigel replied.

After about a half hour of enjoying the fresh air, Rigel turned to his father and said, "If you don't mind, I think I'm going to turn in a little early. I have some things to think about."

His father replied, "I don't mind at all. In fact, I was thinking about turning in myself. Don't force your decision, Rigel. Let it come naturally."

"I will," Rigel said. He smiled, walked back into the house and returned his coffee cup to the kitchen. Jim was already gone, so he rinsed the cup and placed it in the dish washer. Then he made his way up to his bedroom.

Chapter Thirteen

When he awoke the next morning, he was surprised at how easily he had gotten to sleep the night before. He thought he would have tossed and turned with such a momentous decision ahead of him, but that wasn't the case at all. He fell asleep immediately as soon as his head hit the pillow. Best of all, he woke up refreshed. The decision he had expected would weigh on him didn't seem tough at all. He knew how much Anna wanted a child and he would do anything to make her happy. He thought about the relationship he had with his father and wanted that same kind of relationship with his child. He jumped into the shower and couldn't wait to share his decision with his father.

While toweling off, questions suddenly began jumping into his head. He was still sure of his decision, but he wanted clarity to those questions before completely committing. He knew his father would give him honest answers and he felt the need to cover all his bases before moving forward. The scientist inside him was kicking in.

When he finished dressing, he went downstairs. His father was already waiting for him at the dining room table. "Jim has been called away for another assignment, so it looks like you'll have to do with my cooking, or we eat a continental breakfast, "his father said as Rigel approached the table.

"A continental breakfast sounds just fine," Rigel replied. "It's not that I don't enjoy your cooking but why go through all the bother."

His father smiled. "It's no trouble, Rigel, but there are plenty of danishes left and maybe even a piece or two of Jim's apple pie," his father replied.

"How about both?" Rigel said laughing.

He went to the kitchen with his father to see what they could scrounge up. There were plenty of danishes and they still appeared fresh. When Rigel opened the refrigerator, he saw two pieces of pie remaining. They had hit the jackpot. Stan made coffee, while Rigel loaded a slice of pie onto plates for them. When the coffee was finished, they carried everything into the dining room.

"How'd you sleep, son?" his father asked.

"Like a baby," Rigel responded and smiled. He continued, "I thought this was going to be a tough decision, but it really isn't when you weigh everything."

His father smiled and said, "We'll discuss the details once we're finished eating and I can secure the house." That was Rigel's cue to hold the remainder of their conversation.

After they finished breakfast, Rigel cleaned up while his father secured and set the security alarm on the house. When Rigel heard the white noise come on, he knew the job was complete.

Rigel questioned, "If I decide to opt in and have a child, my child will be sterile, won't they?"

"Yes, I'm afraid they will," his father responded, "and someday you will be having this discussion with them. I wish there was another way, but there simply isn't."

"If I opt out, I'll never have children, will I?" Rigel asked.

"No, son, I'm afraid you won't, but you could always adopt," his father replied.

"It sounds like that's what I'd be doing anyhow," Rigel responded a bit more snarkily than he had intended.

"I have never once in my life considered you my adopted son, Rigel," his father retorted, "you have always been my son and always will be my son."

"It's all a big lie, though. How do you live with that?" Rigel continued.

"Let me break it down for you in the easiest way I know," his father replied. "When I first had this discussion with my father, I was angry. Being born sterile felt like a part of my manhood had been stolen from me. My initial response was to rebel. I didn't want to continue this charade any longer. In fact, I had every intention of exposing the Plan to everyone. Something my father said to me made me change my mind. He told me that we don't always get to choose our way through life, but we can choose how we react to it. Sterility is the condition we were born with. There are many people in the world that are born sterile, but only the chosen are born with the ability to do something about it. We can either choose to father a child, or we can choose not to father a child. That's within our ability. To make that decision, we must open our minds to beyond just ourselves and see who would benefit either way. When I thought of your mother and how much she wanted a child of her own, the choice was clear to me. That may or may not be the best route for you and Anna, only you can decide that, but it was the best choice for your mother and I," Stan told his son.

Rigel thought about that for a moment and said, "The decision would be a lot easier if I could talk it over with Anna first."

His father replied, "I'm sure it would be, but I'm afraid that's not a possibility. When I made the decision for your mother and I, I knew your mother well enough to know what she would have wanted. I was comfortable that having a child was the right choice for both of us. If you feel you know what Anna would want and are sure she would make the same decision you have chosen, then you'll know deep down inside which path to choose."

"What if I turn down the child option now, but decide at a later time that I want to go the child route?" Rigel asked.

"I'm not sure there will be a second chance. Here's why. If you choose not to have a child, all recollection of our conversations will be erased when you leave here. In other words, you won't be aware the option of having a child ever existed. You would eventually find out you were sterile and not know why. You and Anna could pursue adoption, but the both of you would never know anything about the option you were once given," his father replied.

"What if I make the wrong choice?", Rigel asked with what seemed like the weight of the world on his shoulders.

"Life is full of choices, Rigel. Sometimes we know we made the wrong choice and have an opportunity to choose another path. At other times, the choice we made is the choice we must live with, even if another option may have been better for us. You chose to be a scientist. You could have just as easily chosen to be a medical doctor. Does that mean either one of those options would have been a bad choice? Certainly not. It just means you have chosen your path and are pursuing it. Whatever you choose today, Rigel, will end up well. If you choose to have a child, you'll get to enjoy being a father. If you choose not to have a child, you will still be taken care of. Ultimately the choice comes down to what is right for you and Anna," his father replied.

While pondering his father's words, an image of Anna appeared in his mind. She was beaming with joy while holding a baby in her arms.

"What would you do, father?" Rigel asked one last time.

His father responded, "I can't make the decision for you, son. It's up to you to make a choice."

Rigel let out a deep sigh and said, "I know what Anna and I want. I've had the best parents a person could ever possibly have. I want to be able to share what I've learned from you and Mom with my child. I know nothing would make Anna happier than having a child. I'm still not completely comfortable with the situation, but I think I'm ready to say that Anna and I want to have a child."

Instead of the smile Rigel was expecting from his father, he saw a frown. "What's wrong, don't you agree?" Rigel asked.

"I'm afraid it's more than just wanting a child, son. You have to be completely comfortable with the situation before we can continue," his father informed him.

Those words caught Rigel by surprise. "Like how? What can I do to get there?" Rigel frantically asked.

"You have to be committed to the Plan," his father replied.

Chapter Fourteen

What a turn of events this was turning out to being. When he awoke, he was sure of his response and was ready to agree with having a child. As he was talking to his father, all kinds of doubts and questions surfaced, and he found himself unsure again. Then after talking to his father, he was once again convinced to proceed only to find out a decision on a child wasn't enough. What else did they want?

"How can I become any more committed to the Plan than to agree to have a child?" Rigel complained.

In a calm soothing voice, his father responded, "You have to be committed to doing everything within your abilities to make sure the Plan succeeds, Rigel. That means you will have to work towards the Plan's ultimate goal. You will need to participate when asked to do something. You'll have to agree to someday have this discussion with your child."

"How do I do all of that?" Rigel asked.

"Let me explain it in detail," his father responded.

Over the next few hours, Stan and Rigel discussed every known aspect of the Plan. Stan reiterated to Rigel that there is still a lot that no one knows, but the inter-dimensionals had proven they can be trusted and he had learned to have faith in not only the Plan, but in the inter-dimensionals as well.

Where Rigel was uncomfortable at first, he started to come around as his father explained everything. Where he had been a little cold toward the Plan earlier that morning, he was starting to warm up. The more his father talked, the more he began to understand. There were still a lot of questions in his head, but he felt himself being more accepting of the premises.

He thought to himself, "This is kind of like religion. You don't necessarily get to see God in person, but you learn enough about him to put your faith and trust in Him."

It was only 10:30 AM, but Stan thought Rigel should have some lunch before leaving. They decided to hunt something up while they continued to talk. Rigel was scheduled to fly back at 11:00 AM, so they had a lot of discussion to complete before then.

When Stan opened the refrigerator to find something to eat, he discovered two plates of sandwiches wrapped in cellophane. It was Jim's last gift to them before leaving late last night. He probably knew they could get by without him for breakfast, but lunch was going to be needed to get his two guests through their day. Stan thought of Jim and smiled. "Always at his best," Stan smiled.

Also in the refrigerator was a container of iced tea. Rigel retrieved a couple of glasses and filled them with ice while Stan brought the sandwiches to the table.

As Rigel filled their glasses, he said, "I'm so lucky you were the one explaining all of this to me. There is no one I trust more in the world than you."

His father looked at him, smiled and said, "And there's no one in the world I'd rather have this conversation with." That made Rigel realize that someday he'd be having this conversation with his child. He realized what he had just done. By imagining this conversation with his child, he had already made a decision.

"I'm committing, father," Rigel said. The smile that appeared on his father's face was indescribable. He had never seen his father happier.

His father leaned over the edge of the table to hug him. "I love you, son," his father said.

"I love you too, dad," Rigel replied.

After finishing lunch, they spent a few minutes cleaning up and then returned to the couch. "Where do I sign?", Rigel asked.

"There are no forms or written contracts, Rigel. The contract is in your heart," his father replied. "You now know what you can and can't do and you know the steps you must take in the future."

Rigel interjected, "I thought after the NDA, there would be another signing ceremony."

His father chuckled, "That's just a formality, son. When a person enters into a contract, what's in their heart is more important than what's written down on paper. I know you are committed. You know you are committed. They know you are committed. That's all that matters."

"Where do I go from here?" Rigel asked?

"You go home to your beautiful wife and love her with all your heart and soul. When the time is right, you will feel the seed inside you, and she will conceive. Both of your lives will change for sure, but for the better," his father replied. Those were exactly the words Rigel wanted to hear.

Rigel had one more question, "What about my commitment and assignments?"

His father responded, "They will be in contact when they want you to do something."

"Now, I'm never supposed to discuss this with anyone, correct?" Rigel asked.

"Not unless you're told to do so by the inter-dimensionals. They may ask you to participate in projects or discussions with other hybrids and, of course, one day you will discuss this with your child or children, but other than that, you are not to discuss this with anyone," his father responded.

Rigel arose from his chair. His father arose as well. They approached each other and shared a hug that bore new meaning. His father had just shared something of such profound importance with him, something his father had waited all his life to do, so this occasion was momentous, and this hug declared that both understood.

"Now you better get packing. Your plane leaves in a few minutes," Stan whispered into his son's ear.

"What about you? Aren't you coming back with me?" Rigel asked.

His father replied, "I have a little more business to wrap up, but I'll be home soon. Give Anna a big hug for me."

"I sure will," Rigel replied as he rushed up the stairs to pack.

After quickly throwing his clothes into his suitcase, Rigel exited the room and headed for the staircase. On the way down, he saw his father and Rick standing in the foyer. He hadn't realized the white noise had stopped, but his father must have turned off the alarm and allowed Rick in while he was packing. "Hi, again!" Rick uttered. Rick grabbed his suitcase and headed off towards the SUV.

As Rigel went to hug his father, his father held out a gift. It was a small box wrapped in silver wrapping paper with a white bow on top. "What's this?" Rigel asked.

"Something for you to open when you're on the plane," his father responded. They hugged once again, but while doing so, his father said, "I love you, now get back home to Anna."

"Love you too, Dad," Rigel replied as he pulled away and headed for the SUV.

Rick already had the door to the SUV open, so Rigel jumped inside. It was just a short drive to the end of the runway where the plane that had brought him was waiting. When Rigel exited the vehicle, he saw Captains Graves and Holmberg waiting for him near the plane. As he approached them, Rigel jokingly said, "Is that all you two do is haul people around to meetings?"

The two officers looked at each other, smiled and Captain Graves said, "Not always." He left it at that, so Rigel didn't pursue the subject any further. Captain Holmberg took his bag from Rick and Rigel rushed over to shake Rick's hand before boarding the plane.

Once on board, he saw Jen. "Am I the only one on the plane again?" Rigel asked.

"You sure are," Jen replied with a smile. With that, Rigel selected one of the comfy chairs and sat down while still holding the gift his father had given him. Jen returned and asked if there was anything she could get him before taking off.

"No thanks, I'm good," Rigel replied.

Jen began her speech on flight safety and Rigel buckled his seat belt. As she spoke, Rigel looked in her eyes and wondered what her role was in the Plan. He realized he may never know but realized he probably didn't have a need to know. When she finished, Jen walked back to the front of the plane and buckled herself into the jump seat.

Rigel looked down at the present his father had given him. He opened it slowly. As the wrapping paper was removed, a box with a picture of a fly-fishing reel was revealed. He opened the box and sure enough, there sat a brand-new fly-fishing reel along with a card that said, "For our next meeting. Love you, Dad".

While he was tempted to start wondering what their next meeting together would entail, he couldn't stop thinking about how much he loved his father and how much his father loved him.

"What if this wasn't the right decision?", the thought popped into his head. "How could I possibly do this without telling Anna?", the racing thoughts continued. He felt his mind being bombarded with questions and he could feel his anxiety level rising. He felt himself drumming with the fingers of his right hand on the arm of the chair, a habit that he had developed when he was having difficulty solving a problem or became nervous about something. He started feeling heat spread across his body and found himself clawing at the neck of the sweater he was wearing. The sweater wasn't the least bit tight, yet it felt like it was choking him. What was happening? Was he having a full-blown panic attack?

Suddenly, as if out of nowhere, he felt a sense of calm come over him. The heat was gone, he no longer felt like he was choking, and his fingers were no longer drumming. Instead, he felt peace, as if there wasn't anything he needed to worry about. All the questions that had been plaguing him had stopped. The anxiety went away. In his mind he pictured Anna holding their newborn child. He was making the right decision.

Chapter Fifteen

The pilot came on the loudspeaker and advised they were starting their descent. The flight had gone much quicker than he expected. The calm was still there, and he couldn't wait to get home to see Anna. He still wished he could discuss it with her, but having security clearance at work helped him understand that some things cannot be discussed no matter how badly you wanted to do so.

The plane landed smoothly and taxied to General Aviation. Once the plane had come to a stop, Jen opened the cabin door and the two pilots appeared at the entrance to the cockpit.

Rigel gathered his backpack, placed the fly-fishing reel inside, and headed toward the door. Captain Graves remained at the door to say his goodbye while Captain Holmberg retrieved Rigel's bag from the luggage compartment area under the plane. Jen smiled as he walked towards her and said, "Thank you for flying with us, Dr. Emerson."

"Thank you all for being so kind," Rigel responded.

Rigel exited the plane, retrieved his bag from Captain Holmberg and headed toward his car in the parking lot. He still had an hour's drive ahead of him and he couldn't wait to see Anna.

Once in the car, he started the engine. The podcast he had been listening to on his way to the airport came over the radio. He didn't feel like listening to podcasts today. Instead, he switched the channel to his favorite music station. The song "Faithfully" by Journey came on. It was one of his favorites and he sang along with it, "I'm forever yours, faithfully." He couldn't remember the last time he had sung along with a song in the car, but it felt good. Life felt good.

The hour drive went quickly and before he knew it, he was home. He pressed the button to open the garage door and pulled into the garage. Anna's car was gone. That was a little disappointing as he couldn't wait to see her, but it would give him a little time to unpack and freshen up. He texted her, "I'm home!" Almost immediately he received a thumbs up sticker response. It was her way of teasing. He loved that about her. The next text he received from her said, "Love you. Be home soon." Rigel just smiled, retrieved his bag from the trunk and headed into the house.

After unpacking his suitcase, he placed it in the linen closet, smiling as he thought to himself how Anna had a place for everything. He knew she would be home soon, but he felt the need to pray. Unlike many scientists who believed in evolution, Rigel knew that God had created everything. He was certain of this. The universe was simply too complex for it all to have happened randomly. Rigel's faith in God had always been strong. It's how his parents had raised him. He imagined bringing his own children up with an equally strong faith. Anna was a strong believer as well. He couldn't have married her had she not been.

As he began praying, the words came easily to his mind. He didn't say them out loud, but from his heart, "Dear Lord, I thank you for this opportunity. I ask for your strength and guidance. Having children means the world to Anna and I want to be able to give her what she wants and needs. I believe you have provided me a way to do that. Be with me in this journey and guide my ways. Whatever these inter-dimensional beings are, I know you made them. Help them to be doing your will, as well. Finally, dear Lord, help me to be as good of a father to my children as my father has been to me. If it is your will, remove any doubts I may have and bless Anna and me as we begin this journey together. In Jesus' name I pray. Amen."

The calm and comfort Rigel had felt on the plane suddenly washed through his body once again. He would take it as God's sign that he was doing the right thing.

He no more than got his prayer out of his mouth when he heard the garage door opening. He rang to the garage and watched as Anna parked her car inside. She shut the car off, swung open the door, and without even shutting it, she ran towards Rigel. She jumped in his arms, wrapped her legs around his waist and kissed him as if she hadn't seen him in years.

She felt so good in his arms. They were perfect for each other. Their kiss lasted an especially long time before she finally let loose with her legs and slid down his body to her feet. "I missed you," she said.

"I see that. I missed you, too," he replied.

"Let's go make love. I still have one day left in my ovulation cycle," she said with the cutest little smile. There was no resisting her.

"Maybe we should shut your car door first," he replied chuckling.

"Good idea," she said, "maybe we should get the groceries out, too."

They retrieved the groceries, shut the door of the car and went inside. She hurriedly removed the refrigerated groceries from the bags and placed them in the refrigerator. "Everything else can wait," she exclaimed. She grabbed his hand as she ran by and led him to the bedroom.

She couldn't wait to rip off his clothes. Before he even knew it, he was naked, and it was his turn to start on her. He was taking his time removing her clothing when she looked at him curiously. "Are you into this or not?" she laughed as she ripped her clothes off. She once again jumped into his arms and wrapped her legs around his waist. They fell together onto the bed. He couldn't stop kissing her. She was the only woman he had ever loved, besides his mother, but this was a completely different kind of love. He wanted to crawl inside her body and be one with her.

As things were heating up, he felt something occur inside of him. It started with a tingling but quickly turned to a power. He was being filled with power. He had felt something like this before while having sex as hormones were being released in his body, but never to this intensity. This was different. This was intense. He felt the need to hold back so as not to hurt Anna, but he couldn't. He made love to her more passionately and intensely than he had ever done before. She was feeling it as well. When he finally exploded inside her, she came simultaneously making them both shudder with uncontrollable spasms throughout their bodies. Rigel knew instantly the seed had been planted; she had been impregnated.

As they collapsed together, neither spoke. Their hearts were beating too fast for anything else in their bodies to work. They laid in each other's arms and absorbed the moment.

After a few minutes, Anna finally said, "Well, I guess you DID miss me."

"I certainly did," he replied smiling.

"You have never made love to me like that before. I liked it," she continued.

"A man can do wonderful things when he's with the woman he loves," Rigel replied. They embraced once again and just held each other.

As he held her, Rigel realized what had just happened. He had impregnated her. There was no turning back now. There were no regrets, just anticipation of how their lives were about to change. Anna seemed happy, but she was about to become much happier.

Chapter Sixteen

After a few minutes of lying in his arms, Anna looked up and said, "I have some good news. The fertility clinic was able to move our appointment and get us in much earlier than I thought. Our appointment is in three weeks." A surprised look appeared on Rigel's face. He had forgotten about the fertility clinic and understood what had just happened. Hopefully by the time of the appointment, they would already know she was pregnant.

"Are you not happy about that?" Anna asked.

"Oh no, I'm very pleased," Rigel replied, "I just wasn't thinking we'd be able to get in so quickly. That's very good news." He pulled her close and hugged her tightly. He wasn't quite sure how he was going to get her to do a pregnancy test before the appointment, but he'd figure something out.

"Let's go to dinner," Rigel uttered.

"Go to dinner? I bought groceries so I could make dinner. I thought you'd be tired," Anna replied.

"I don't want you to have to lift another finger," Rigel responded.

Anna shrugged and said, "Works for me."

They both jumped out of bed and got ready. While she was still dressing, Rigel called Ricardo's, their favorite restaurant, to make a reservation. "Ricardo's" the person on the other end of the line answered, "this is Rachel."

"Hi, Rachel, this is Rigel Emerson," Rigel started.

Rachel jumped in, "Oh hello, Dr. Emerson, it's good to hear from you."

"Would you happen to have a reservation for two available at 7:00 PM tonight?" Rigel asked.

"I'm so sorry, Dr. Emerson, but we're all booked up tonight," Rachel started, but as she was talking Rigel heard a rustling and suddenly Ricardo himself was on the phone. "Rigel," Ricardo declared, "you come any time you want tonight, and I will make sure I have a table for you."

It was good to be well known.

"Thank you, Ricardo. We'll see you around 7:00 PM," Rigel replied.

"We always look forward to seeing you, Rigel," Ricardo exclaimed. As Rigel hung up the phone, he smiled as he realized his life was pretty good and about to get much better.

Rigel finished dressing and glanced at the clock. It was already 6:20 and they'd need to leave by 6:30. He hoped Anna would be ready as he thought to himself that perhaps he should have made the reservation a little later just in case. It suddenly dawned on him that Ricardo had told him, "any time", so he didn't need to worry about getting there at any particular time.

As he was sitting on the bed pulling up his socks, Anna walked out of the closet. She was wearing a beautiful silver strapless dress. Her long dark hair fell across her beautifully tanned shoulders. He couldn't get over how beautiful she was and how radiant she looked. He also couldn't get over how he had managed to win her love and affection. She could have any man she wanted, yet she chose him.

He caught himself staring. He had stopped in the middle of putting on his socks and just stared at her. "What?" she asked quickly, "is there something wrong?"

"Yes," Rigel proclaimed, "I don't deserve you."

She smiled and blushed as she quickly made her way over to him. "And I don't know what I ever did to deserve you," she replied. She pulled his head into her chest, and he just stayed there. He loved this woman more than anything in the world.

Chapter Seventeen

When they arrived at Ricardo's, the valet opened Anna's door and helped her out of the car. Rigel handed the valet his keys as he took Anna's arm to enter the restaurant. As they entered the door and approached the host's desk, Ricardo himself came around the corner to meet them. "I will seat them," Ricardo told the hostess with a smile. "Rigel, Anna, so good to see you both again. It's always so nice to have the two of you at our restaurant. Please follow me."

Before Rigel could even utter a word, Ricardo scooped up a couple of menus and darted into the dining room to seat them. Once at the table, Ricardo pulled the chair out for Anna and then helped scoot it in as she sat. He lifted the napkin folded in the shape of a rose bud that had been setting on her plate, shook it once to unfold it and then laid the napkin gently across Anna's lap. He immediately went around the table and performed the same maneuver for Rigel.

"Ricardo, you always take such good care of us," Rigel proclaimed.

"You are indeed two of my favorite guests," Ricardo responded, "and I have something very special for you tonight. My chef has prepared a lump crab seafood dip served with deep fried bowtie pasta. I think you will find it delicious." He no sooner got the words out of his mouth and a server delivered the special appetizer to their table.

Directly behind the server was a waiter carrying two wine glasses and a bottle of Rigel and Anna's favorite wine. Ricardo looked at them both and just smiled. "Your dinner is on me tonight," Ricardo informed them.

"No, you don't need to do that," Rigel began debating, but stopped abruptly as Ricardo raised one finger to his lips. "It would bring me great joy if you would allow me to do this," Ricardo replied. Rigel just shook his head with unbelief that they were being treated so kindly. Ricardo simply patted Rigel on the shoulder as he walked away from the table.

The thought suddenly popped into his head, "Does Ricardo know?" He realized he was celebrating tonight because he knew what happened earlier in the day, that Anna would soon be pregnant, but how could Ricardo know? Was Ricardo in on the Plan? There was no way of knowing and he knew he couldn't ask Ricardo directly. It could be coincidence, or it could be intentional, but either way, it didn't change the fact that he couldn't tell Anna.

Once the wine was poured, Anna and Rigel dove into the crab dip. They had never heard of deep-fried bowtie pasta, but it was delicious. Anna closed her eyes for a moment, and a smile appeared as she succinctly summed up her thoughts with the comment, "Oh my goodness." She had never before tasted something so delicious. Anna wasn't exactly a woman of few words, but when something like this took her breath away, she would almost become speechless. Rigel just smiled. He still couldn't believe this amazingly beautiful woman was his wife.

Suddenly Rigel felt panicked. If Anna was pregnant, should she be drinking wine and eating shellfish? He had heard those two items in particular were to be avoided during pregnancy. What was he going to do? If he suddenly made Anna stop drinking the wine or eating the crab dip, she would wonder why, and he definitely wasn't in a position to explain. Just as suddenly as the panic arrived, a sense of calm pushed the panic aside. It's too early in the pregnancy and, if the truth were known, she may not yet be pregnant. Sometimes it takes a little while for a fertilized egg to embed in the wall of the uterus which is a critical step in pregnancy. He decided she'd be fine for now, but it was something he needed to consider once the pregnancy had been confirmed.

"Are you alright?" Anna asked puzzled. She had seen the sudden change in his demeanor when the panic set in.

"I'm fine," Rigel replied, "I was just thinking about something."

"Well, I'm thinking about something, too! This amazing dip!" Anna chuckled.

Once the appetizer was finished, the waiter brought each of them a menu. There were so many scrumptious things to choose from, but they each had their favorites. Anna ordered Chicken Marsala and Rigel ordered the lasagna. Everything was so good in this restaurant it was tough to choose, but somehow, they always seemed to go back to their favorites.

The waiter poured Anna another glass of wine and topped off Rigel's before leaving the table. As they waited for their salads, Rigel caught Anna staring into his eyes. "I love you so much," Anna said.

The words "I love you more" came out without Rigel even thinking. This beautiful woman had changed his life completely and he realized he would be lost without her. They flirted with each other and made small talk until the salads arrived. The entrees followed shortly after that. As usual, everything was absolutely delicious.

With the main course finished, the waiter cleared the table and then brought out a dessert tray. On it were samples of tiramisu, Creme Brulé, cheesecake, a decadent chocolate cake and a truffle. Anna looked them over and declared, "I'm much too full." The look in Rigel's eyes, however, made her rethink her decision. She knew Rigel wanted her to enjoy every bit of this evening and he didn't have to twist her arm. "Oh, okay, I'll have the Creme Brule," Anna replied. Rigel chose the tiramisu, and the waiter quickly left the table.

When he returned, he had their desserts on a tray and promptly placed them in front of each of them. "May I interest either of you in a coffee?" the waiter asked. They both declined and started in on their desserts.

"How can Ricardo's chef make everything so delicious?" Anna proclaimed.

"The same way you do," Rigel responded with a smile.

Anna blushed and took the last bite of her Creme Brule. When Rigel was finished with his tiramisu, the waiter returned to gather their dishes. "Will there be anything else tonight, Dr. Emerson?" the waiter asked.

"Just the check," Rigel replied.

"There will be no check tonight, Dr. Emerson. Ricardo has taken care of everything," the waiter responded and then quickly left the table.

Anna finished her last sip of wine as Rigel removed his wallet from the pocket in his blazer. He removed a $100 bill and placed it on the table. He placed the saltshaker on top of it to protect it from blowing off. He arose, walked over to Anna, pulled out her chair and helped her from the table. As she turned, he snuck a quick kiss on her shoulder. He did this periodically, but somehow, he knew these kisses would come more frequently going forward.

As they exited the restaurant, they stopped at the hostess station and Rigel asked the hostess if she wouldn't mind summoning Ricardo. He appeared in a flash with a huge smile on his face. "How was everything, my friends?" Ricardo asked.

"As always, delicious. Thank you so much, Ricardo. You didn't have to do that," Rigel replied.

"It was truly my pleasure," Ricardo replied as he reached out for Anna's hand, lifted it to his lips and gently kissed the back of it. Ricardo was a gentleman beyond words. That's one of the reasons this was their favorite restaurant.

The valet retrieved their car and opened the door for Anna. She slid in and the valet shut the door once he assured she was safely inside. Rigel handed the valet a $20 bill and climbed into the driver's seat. As they headed for home, Anna once again said, "I love you." No matter how many times she said it, those three words brought immense feelings to Rigel. He considered himself the lucky one in this relationship. He couldn't have a better partner in life.

Chapter Eighteen

Two weeks later, Rigel was beside himself wanting to find out if Anna was pregnant. He brought up a pregnancy test at breakfast. Anna didn't seem enthused. "Why?" she stated, "It will probably come back like all the rest."

"You never know," Rigel replied.

"I don't have any left. If I think about it, I'll stop at the drug store today and get one," Anna responded.

Rigel was about bursting at the seams with excitement, but he couldn't let on just yet to Anna. He was almost certain she was pregnant but knew he couldn't push it as he couldn't let on that he was expecting a positive result. It was killing him. "Patience" he thought to himself. On his way to work that morning, he stopped by the drug store just in case Anna forgot to pick one up. He'd figure out a way to bring it up if she didn't do so first.

Rigel arrived at work and began burying himself in his computer. He still hadn't caught up from being away and was diligently trying to do so. Suddenly his phone rang. When he glanced at the screen, he saw it was Anna. He immediately hoped nothing was wrong as she rarely ever called him at work. He picked up the phone, hit the button and put the phone to his ear. "We're pregnant." Anna was still a little in disbelief but was extremely excited to tell him.

"I'll be right home," Rigel replied.

"No, there's no need to come home. I just couldn't wait to tell you," Anna responded.

"I'm coming home anyhow," Rigel laughed as he closed the call.

He immediately shut down his computer, gathered his things and walked out to his administrative assistant's desk. "Sorry, something has come up and I have to leave. Would you mind clearing my schedule for this morning? I believe there's a meeting we'll need to reschedule," Rigel told Judy, his administrative assistant.

"Absolutely. Is everything okay?" Judy asked.

"Everything is perfect," Rigel yelled as he ran out the door.

Chapter Nineteen

As soon as Rigel pulled into the driveway, Anna came rushing out the door to greet him. He barely made it out of the car before she flung her arms around his neck, jumped into his arms, wrapped her legs around his waist and gave him the kiss of a lifetime. He had never seen her so excited. "Are you supposed to be jumping around like that?", he asked teasingly.

"I'm not sure, but this is the most exciting thing that's ever happened to me," she answered.

"Better than marrying me?", he asked.

"That comes in a close second," Anna taunted.

As she slid down and her feet touched the ground, Rigel found himself entranced with how happy Anna was. He was now sure he had made the right decision. The best part was he was no longer second-guessing himself. Seeing her this happy was all the confirmation he needed.

"Shouldn't you get it verified by the doctor?", Rigel asked.

"One step ahead of you," Anna replied. "I made an appointment and see her on Monday. In the meantime, let's just keep this between us, just in case." Anna was always the level-headed one. Had she have not said that, his next move would have been to call his parents with the news. "Prudence is the better part of valor," he thought to himself.

As they made their way inside the house, he could tell Anna was already gearing up. She grabbed his hand and led him into one of the spare bedrooms. "I was thinking this could be the nursery," she told Rigel.

"I think this would make a perfect nursery," Rigel said. "It's quiet and warm and you'll find it very comfortable when you're up all night with a crying baby," he teased. Anna loved the way he teased her but was always quick with a response.

"Shared duties. You got me into this and now you're going to have to pony up to some responsibility, Cowboy," Anna replied.

For a quick moment, those words struck Rigel awkwardly. This wasn't really his baby. As quickly as the thought appeared, it vanished. This was as much his baby as he was for his father.

"Something wrong?" Anna asked as she detected Rigel's mind had wandered.

"I was just wondering if I had shut down my computer at work before I left," Rigel replied trying to cover for the odd look on his face that must have given Anna concern. He didn't like lying to Anna, but from the conversations with his father and his familiarity with compartmentalizing top-secret information, he knew sometimes you needed to keep your true thoughts to yourself.

Rigel decided to take the remainder of the day off. He called his administrative assistant to inform her. "Everything okay?", his administrative assistant asked.

"Everything is perfect," Rigel replied, "I just have some things I need to catch up on at home since I've been away."

When he returned to Anna, he informed her she may want to change her clothes. They were going for a walk. She ran towards him, planted a kiss on his lips and ran to change. They spent the rest of the day at the park. Rigel especially liked the lake at the park. It was just large enough to be classified as a lake, rather than a pond, but still quaint and small enough to be able to see people enjoying themselves in every direction. He realized he better enjoy this time alone with Anna as much as possible because soon their alone time would be limited. They had new priorities arriving.

They spent the evening just enjoying each other's company. Sometimes just spending time with someone makes your life feel complete.

Chapter Twenty

On Monday, Rigel went with Anna to her gynecologist appointment. Rigel waited in the lobby while the doctor conducted her exam. Blood was drawn and submitted to the laboratory. Once the exam was completed and Anna was fully dressed, the doctor asked the medical assistant to take Anna to get her husband and meet her in her office.

Anna followed the medical assistant out to the lobby. She saw Rigel look up immediately when he heard the door open. She couldn't help but see him as a sad little puppy begging for good news. He stood as she approached and they hugged. He whispered, "Well?", in her ear.

"I don't know anything yet, but the doctor wants to talk to both of us," Anna replied.

Panic immediately penetrated Rigel's mind and body. Was there something wrong? Was she not pregnant? Anna sensed it immediately.

"Don't get your underwear in a wad. She just wants to talk to us," Anna teased.

Rigel and Anna followed the medical assistant into the doctor's office. When they reached the door, the doctor waved them in and asked them to have a seat. The medical assistant exited and shut the door behind her to give them some privacy.

"Dr. Anston, this is my husband, Rigel," Anna said.

"It's very nice to meet you, Rigel. Let's get right to it. All indications are that you are pregnant, but we'll need to get the results of the blood test in order to know for sure," the doctor began. "Anna's in excellent health, so I'm not expecting any problems. I like to talk to both the wife and husband if they are going to be first time parents. Sometimes when I talk to only the expectant mother, some things get lost in the message, so I've found it beneficial to go over pregnancy do's and don'ts with both. As I had mentioned, we'll need to wait for the results of the blood test to know for sure and we should have those back by tomorrow or the day after. In the meantime, I'd like you to start changing your diet and exercise routine as if we had already confirmed you were pregnant. I'm going to go over some details, and I will provide you with written information of things you should avoid eating beginning immediately. While I want you to stay in shape and continue exercising, there are some exercises I recommend you avoid."

Anna's doctor was laying it all out for her. "She wouldn't be doing this if she wasn't pretty sure Anna was pregnant," Rigel thought to himself. For a moment, he found himself daydreaming of their beautiful baby instead of listening. Anna picked up on it immediately and gave him a little tap on his arm. He got the message and returned to listening to everything the doctor had to say.

When Dr. Anston was finished, she handed Anna some papers which covered most everything the doctor had just covered. The doctor asked if they had any questions. At this point, both Rigel and Anna were so elated, their minds were too occupied to come up with questions, so they shook their heads indicating they had none. Dr. Anston rose from her chair, extended her hand to Anna for a handshake and then repeated that gesture with Rigel. They both picked up on the smile the doctor was wearing. They took that as one more hopeful sign the blood test results would come back positive.

With that, the doctor opened the door and pointed them down the hall to the lobby. "We'll be sure to call you as soon as we have the results," Dr. Anston said.

"We can't wait," Anna replied exuberantly.

Chapter Twenty-One

They made their way to their car in the parking lot, but upon reaching it, Rigel didn't open the door. Instead, he enveloped her in a hug. Good news or bad news is always better with a hug. They remained in their embrace for a long time before Rigel released, put his hands on her shoulders, looked her squarely in the eyes, and said, "I love you, Mommy!"

Anna smiled, but being the more prudent of the two, said, "We don't know for sure just yet."

Rigel let out a chuckle. "Who are you trying to kid? Did you see her smile?", Rigel smiled.

"I did and I loved it," Anna giggled.

They were both unusually quiet on their way home. Their minds were deep in thought. Their lives would soon change, and it was a change they both looked forward to. Rigel's mind was visualizing playing catch with his son on the front lawn or dancing with his daughter at her first Father/Daughter Dance. Anna's mind was focused on holding her child. It didn't matter if it was boy of a girl. It only mattered that the baby was theirs, created by love, protected by love, and cherished in love.

"What would you like to do first?", Rigel asked as they pulled into the driveway.

"Send you off to work," Anna replied. Rigel wasn't expecting that. "I've got a lot of things to do around the house to kind my mind busy until the blood test results come back and I don't need you getting in my way. Besides, somebody in this household better be earning some money," Anna said playfully.

Rigel got it. He knew he could be impatient and a bit of a pain when it came to things like waiting for results. He realized he'd probably be better off at work.

As he got out of the car, he hurried over to open her door to help her out. "What, I haven't had this kind of treatment in our entire marriage, but now that I might be pregnant, you're treating me special?" Anna teased.

Rigel didn't even reply. He just kissed her. "I love you," he said.

Chapter Twenty-Two

Sleeping that night was impossible. Rigel just kept tossing and turning in bed. Although Anna seemed like she was sleeping peacefully, he didn't want to take any chances of waking her, so he got up and made his way to the couch. He hardly slept at all that night. When he saw the sun peeking through the drapes, he got up and started getting ready for work. After showering and dressing, he was ready to go. Anna was still sleeping, so he tiptoed out of the bedroom and made his way to the kitchen. He made himself a cup of coffee in the Keurig as he jotted a note for Anna to read when she woke up. His note said, "I never realized how incomplete my life was until I met you. I love you so much."

When he arrived at work, Judy, his administrative assistant, informed him of an important virtual call he would need to attend at 9:00 AM.

"Do you know what it's about?", Rigel asked.

"No, sir. I was just asked to inform you as soon as you got in," she replied.

He still had an hour and a half before the call, so he began catching up on all the loose ends that had been dangling from him being out of the office so much in the recent days. Time flew and it was 9:00 AM before he knew it.

He shut the door to his office, opened the virtual call app and waited to be connected. Turns out it was a call from his department head, and all of his cohorts were on the call. The department head discussed a new project that would be coming their way. He informed them he wasn't yet at liberty to reveal it just yet, but wanted them to be prepared as some of them may need to drop current projects to begin working on this new one.

He was still in the middle of this virtual call when he saw his phone light up. "We're PREGNANT", the message said and Anna had emphasized it with his favorite...a big thumbs up.

His boss picked up on the big grin on his face and said, "Rigel, you seem to be excited about this project."

"I am, sir, but the smile comes from some good news I just received from home. Anna and I are going to have a baby," Rigel boasted. Everyone on the call clapped and threw out words of congratulations. Once everything calmed back down, his boss finished providing what additional information he could and then ended the call.

As soon as the call ended, Rigel called Anna on her cell phone. "Hi Momma," he said when she answered. He could tell she was on cloud nine.

"Hi, yourself, Poppa," she teased.

"How are we going to celebrate?", Rigel asked.

"By being responsible parents and getting started on that nursery," Anna replied. "I love you," she said.

"Not nearly as much as I love you," Rigel responded. He realized they could argue that point until the cows came home. The fact was their love for each other was equal and intense. Now they were about to add someone to their fold.

"I have to run to another meeting, so see you tonight?", Rigel asked.

"What? Are we still dating?", Anna chuckled, "of course you'll see me tonight!"

After hanging up, the thought of the Plan popped into his mind. Anna was as happy as he'd ever seen her and he was happier than he had ever been in his entire life, so he knew he had made the right choice. He realized he was already referring to this baby as their baby. Even if it wasn't his seed, this baby was his and Anna's. "That must be what my father was trying to tell me," Rigel thought to himself.

Chapter Twenty-Three

Anna's pregnancy proceeded normally. She really didn't suffer from morning sickness, but she still adhered to the doctor's strict rules on things she could or could not eat, as well as avoiding things she was not supposed to do.

Rigel and Anna each had their own opinion about learning the gender of their forthcoming bundle of joy. There was something in Anna that made her not want to know until the baby was born, although she enjoyed watching all the clever techniques people were using at Gender Reveal Parties to learn the sex of their child. Rigel, on the other hand, was eager to learn the baby's gender. He wanted to know if he would one day have that special talk with a son, or maybe even a more difficult discussion with a daughter. He knew it would be awkward either way, so he decided to leave the decision up to Anna.

Anna, usually always driven by logic and comfortable in her decisions, continued to struggle with this one. While a Gender Reveal Party could be fun, what if something happened during the pregnancy? While such an event would be devastating, wouldn't it be all that much worse if birth had already been celebrated at a Gender Reveal Party or shower? Anna remembered a cousin of hers who had been pregnant, had a baby shower, and then lost the baby. The loss of the child was difficult enough but having to look at and make a decision about all the gifts they had been given at the baby shower, made things even worse. She saw a Gender Reveal Party bearing the same risk. Rigel knew this was a sensitive subject for Anna, so he kept his opinions to himself and allowed Anna to make the final determination.

Most parents do a Gender Reveal Party around four to five months into the pregnancy, shortly after the routine anatomy ultrasound. Anna was already four months into her pregnancy and knew the ultrasound would be coming up shortly, so she knew she had to decide soon. Who would she even approach to plan one? It was customary for a close friend or relative of the couple to take on this job so the pregnant couple could be as surprised as everyone else at the party, but who would she pick? Her Maid of Honor at her wedding was her best friend, Kaitlyn, from college, but Kaitlyn lived in Boston, and it would be unfair to ask her to travel to take on this additional responsibility. She hesitated to ask a relative as she would want whoever was available to attend to enjoy the surprise without having to taking on the responsibilities of making the party happen. So, she continued to procrastinate in deciding.

That night, Anna turned to God and asked for His guidance in prayer. She didn't feel an immediate response, but knew God handled things when the time was appropriate. She slept peacefully that night knowing the decision was in God's hand.

The next morning, she cooked breakfast for Rigel, who devoured it as usual. Once finished, he gently hugged her, kissed her like a man thoroughly in love with his wife, whispered, "I love you!", in her ear, and then scurried out to the car to beat the morning traffic. He was so predictable, so routine, and so perfect. She thought about how lucky she was to have Rigel as a husband and a partner. She envisioned him holding their baby for the very first time. She anticipated the tears running down his cheeks.

Just as she started to become tearful herself, her cell phone rang. When she picked up the phone, she saw Kaitlyn's picture announcing the call. "I was just thinking about you," Anna said as she answered the call.

"I've been thinking about you, too. How are you feeling?", Kaitlyn asked.

"Fine," Anna responded, "I don't know why all these mothers complain. This has been a piece of cake."

Kaitlyn replied, "That's only because you're doing the right things and have kept yourself in shape. Not everyone has your perfect body, Anna."

"My body is far from perfect," Anna interjected.

"Care to trade?", Kaitlyn cut in. "To think the men I could have had if I had your body." Both ladies giggled at that one.

Kaitlyn cut right to the chase, "So when do I plan your Gender Reveal Party?"

"Who says we're having one?" Anna replied.

"Me!", Kaitlyn immediately interjected. "You're not going to cheat me out of this. You still owe me big time for all the interference I ran for you in college."

"What interference?", Anna asked.

"From all the men knocking down your door trying to ask you out," Kaitlyn replied.

"Quit exaggerating," Anna said."

"Do I need to name them? There was Ken, then Robin, then Charles, oh, who could forget Charles, then Adam, then Taylor," Kaitlyn continued.

"Okay, okay, but that was only until I found Rigel," Anna interjected.

"Yes, thanks for Rigel. It wasn't until you met him that I could finally concentrate on my own social life. Not that it made much difference. I'm still single," Kaitlyn responded.

"You'll find someone," Anna inserted, "you're too good of a person not to."

"Well, thank you for that, but when is your ultrasound so I can begin planning?" Kaitlyn asked.

"It's going to be at my next appointment on the fifth," Anna responded.

"So, pick any weekend after that and we'll have your party then," Kaitlyn stated.

It didn't look like Kaitlyn was going to let up on this. Just then, her discussion with God the night before popped into her head. "Thanks for guiding me, God," Anna thought to herself.

Anna finally agreed and told Kaitlyn she would talk it over with Rigel and give her some dates that would work. She loved Kaitlyn. Anna had already planned on making her the Godmother, but who would she pick for a Godfather? She knew that decision would come when the time was right.

Chapter Twenty-Four

Anna felt Kaitlyn's call was the answer from God she was awaiting regarding the Gender Reveal Party, but as a highly educated engineer, she knew coincidence does not prove a theory. She wanted Rigel's buy in. If she received validation from him, she was pretty sure it was God working the plan.

After dinner one evening, she decided to bring up the subject.

"What are your thoughts on a Gender Reveal Party?", Anna asked.

"I'm fine with whatever you want," Rigel replied trying to be cooperative.

Anna knew this about Rigel. He was always focused on what pleased her, but this time she wanted his honest opinion.

"That's not what I asked. I know you're just trying to be polite, but I really need to know how you feel about it," Anna responded.

Rigel thought for a moment and said, "There are pros and cons either way. On one hand, it would be nice to know so we can plan the nursery accordingly. The con is, we won't be nearly as surprised when the baby is born."

"And, as much as I hate saying it, there is always the risk that something will happen to the baby between the Reveal Party and the baby's birth," Anna added.

"Nope! Nothing bad is going to happen. I'm sure of it," Rigel quickly responded.

"How can you be so sure? Things like that happen all the time to couples and it can be devastating," Anna asked.

"Because I have it from a good source that this pregnancy is going to go perfectly and we will soon be enjoying our newest addition to our family," Rigel replied.

"Oh, you do, eh? And who might this source be?", Anna inquired.

"Let's just say someone not of this world told me," Rigel replied.

Thinking Rigel was referring to God, Anna accepted his response with a quick kiss on the cheek, then quickly turned and ran from the room.

"Hey, where are you going?", Rigel shouted, "I thought that response deserved more than just a peck on the cheek."

"Oh, you'll get better than that later," Anna shouted back. "Right now, I have to call Kaitlyn."

Rigel just smiled to himself at how cute Anna could be. He hadn't even actually answered her question; he'd just eased her angst about deciding. It wasn't often Anna let him off the hook so easily. He knew there was nothing to worry about, or at least hoped there was nothing to worry about, regarding this birth, but he wasn't able to explain to Anna why he felt so. He had gotten past the stage of feeling guilty about keeping the Plan a secret from Anna. Just like top secrets, she was on a need-to-know basis, and this child would bring her the purpose in life she had been looking for.

Chapter Twenty-Five

When Anna returned to the room, she was all smiles. She couldn't wait to share the excitement with Rigel. Kaitlyn was overjoyed with their decision to allow her to host the party. On the call, Kaitlyn's mind was racing a mile a minute as she rambled from one idea to another. Anna had to calm her down several times, but that was Kaitlyn for you. She was so full of ideas and the best friend a person could ever have. She would make a perfect Godmother for her child.

They had decided on the weekend of the 21st. That Saturday would be convenient for everyone. There was talk of food, beverages and an invite list. Since it was still too early to get an accurate weather forecast, Kaitlyn was going to plan most of the festivities to be done outside but capable of being brought inside in the event or rain or storms.

Rigel was on board with all of it. He smiled to think how happy this was making Anna. Suddenly, Anna stopped talking, turned a little white and said, "Oh no! That means we need to get the nursery ready so people can see it!"

"Whoa, whoa, whoa, Cowgirl," Rigel teased. "Aren't you getting a little ahead of yourself? How are you going to decorate the nursery without knowing the gender?"

"I could do it neutral," Anna replied starting to calm down a little.

"Wouldn't it be better to know the gender and actually decorate the room specific for that gender?" Rigel asked.

Anna thought for a moment before replying, "Yes, you're right. If it's a boy, I'm going to want sports things and if it's a girl, I'm going to want girly things, so why not just wait until we know?" He loved how excited Anna got about things and how logical she became when he had to talk her down.

"I guess that means I have nothing to do until the 21st," Anna said a little sadly.

"You can take care of this ugly mug," Rigel teased, "because once this baby comes, I'm going to be chopped liver."

Chapter Twenty-Six

The 5th arrived before they knew it. Anna awoke that morning a little surprised. Usually, on a weekday, she would hear Rigel's alarm go off and as he made his way to the shower, she would head down to the kitchen to start the coffee. Today, when she awakened, Rigel wasn't in bed and there were no lights on in the bathroom. "That's strange," she thought to herself but let it slide by as she got out of bed and put on her robe.

As she headed toward the kitchen, she smelled coffee brewing. She also picked up a hint of bacon. She wondered why Rigel would be cooking breakfast instead of getting ready for work.

"Are you ready for some breakfast?", Rigel asked as soon as Anna entered the kitchen.

"Why aren't you in the shower? You're going to be late for work," she responded.

"Well, number one, that's not what I asked, and number two, I'm not going to work today. I'm going with you to your appointment," Rigel replied.

"I thought you'd probably just meet me there," Anna interjected.

"This is an important appointment and I'm devoting my entire day to you," Rigel said emphatically. This was rather unusual for Rigel as work was extremely important to him. Anna recognized and appreciated how he was demonstrating how important she was in his life. She ran to him, placed her hands on his cheeks and pulled his face to her. She kissed him lovingly, deeply, and validated that she had received his message loud and clear.

After a full breakfast of eggs, bacon, toast and coffee, all of which Rigel cooked on his own, it was time to start getting ready for Anna's ultrasound appointment.

"It takes you longer, so you go ahead and get ready while I clean up after breakfast," Rigel said. Anna appreciated the thoughtfulness but realized she would be recleaning the kitchen later that day. Rigel was good at many things, but his cleaning skills were not his forte.

Chapter Twenty-Seven

Once they were both ready, they headed to the appointment. In the car, Rigel said, "Are you nervous?"

Anna replied, "Not really nervous, just excited." She was only being half-truthful. While she didn't really care about gender, she was nervous they would find something of concern on the ultrasound. It's every parent's fear. She realized many parents had their excitement abruptly interrupted when the doctor took a little longer performing the ultrasound and then ordered additional tests. Anna prayed this wouldn't be the case today.

When they arrived at the parking lot of the medical center, Rigel found an open parking space right up front. That hardly ever happened. Perhaps it was a good omen. After exiting the car, they walked hand-in-hand into the building. The walked to the elevator, pressed the button and the doors magically opened. "Wow, that's a first," Anna said, "usually you have to wait for the elevator." Once they entered, Anna pressed the button for the 6th floor and the elevator doors closed. They were the only ones in the elevator, so Rigel decided to take the opportunity to show Anna how much he cared. He pulled her to him and kissed her, sending all the warmth and love he possibly could through his lips to hers. She felt it.

They must have been lost in that kiss a little longer than they intended because the elevator dinged announcing they had reached the 6th floor and the doors open. This surprised them both and they suddenly realized the elderly lady standing in front of them waiting to get on the elevator had caught them in the act. "I'm so sorry," Anna apologized.

"Don't apologize at all," said the elderly lady. "It's refreshing to see two young people so much in love."

When they got to their floor and exited the elevator, Rigel was still a little embarrassed. The elderly lady grabbed his arm as he walked past her and whispered to Rigel, "Don't ever let her go. She's a keeper!"

"That she is," Rigel replied, "and I'm never ever letting her go."

Even though they had whispered, Anna heard the exchange. She just squeezed Rigel's arm a little harder letting him know she approved.

They entered the doctor's office and Anna went up to the window to check in. Rigel found two empty seats along the wall and sat down. He pulled out his cell phone and placed it on silent. He didn't want to be disturbed. Anna found where he was sitting, walked over and sat down. She immediately reached for Rigel's hand. Although he and Anna had never shied away from holding hands in public, the immediacy and intensity of Anna's gesture made him realize perhaps she was a little more nervous than she had originally let on.

They only sat for a few minutes before Anna's name was called. As she stood, she turned to Rigel and said, "Ready?"

"As ready as I'll ever be," Rigel replied.

They followed the nurse back into a row of examining rooms. The nurse showed them into a room, took Anna's blood pressure, asked if she was having any problems, and then told them the doctor would be in shortly. As the nurse left the room, Anna looked at Rigel and smiled. "Here goes," she said.

Dr. Anston entered almost immediately. She was young but professional and eluded confidence. "Well, let's take a look at this baby," she said as she helped Anna onto the table. After adjusting clothing, the doctor pulled the ultrasound machine closer, applied what seemed like an exorbitant amount of lube on the probe and then warned, "This may be a little cold."

She placed the probe on Anna's abdomen and began moving it in various directions, within seconds, she found the fetus. Although Rigel and Anna couldn't really tell what they were looking at on the monitor, they could hear the sound of the baby's heartbeat coming from the machine. Nothing in the world sounded so sweet.

The doctor began pointing out the baby's head, torso, legs, arms, hands and feet. "Now, just to confirm, you want me to keep the gender secret, correct?", the doctor asked.

"Yes, please," Anna responded. "I've brought a stamped envelope and would like you to send the gender results to our friend who will be planning the gender reveal party."

"How fun," Dr. Anston replied, "I'll be happy to do that for you."

The doctor finished in no time and said, "Everything looks just fine." Both Anna and Rigel let out a sigh of relief. Perhaps they both had been a little nervous about this appointment.

"I'll have a nurse come in to help you get cleaned up and I'll be back in shortly to discuss our next steps," the doctor said while exiting the room.

Rigel and Anna looked at each other while the color drained from both of their faces.

"What's that supposed to mean?", Anna whispered obviously shaken.

Trying to be brave enough for both of them, Rigel replied, "I'm sure it's nothing. She probably just wants to discuss the schedule for future appointments." At least that's what Rigel was hoping the doctor would be discussing.

When the nurse finished, she exited the room and Dr. Anston returned. Anna couldn't hold it in any longer, "Is there something wrong?"

"No, no, everything looks just fine. Why do you ask?", the doctor replied.

"It's just that when you left you said you would be back in to discuss the next steps," Anna responded.

"Oh, I'm so sorry to have worried you. No, I simply meant we wanted to discuss the next few months as we get ready for the delivery of your baby," the doctor replied.

A load of worry was lifted from them both. The rest of the appointment was spent talking over exactly what the doctor had said, how she would be feeling the next few months, what changes to her body she could expect, and how to prepare for her going into labor. While all of this was important, both Rigel and Anna realized they hadn't listened as well as they should. In fact, they each were busy saying silent prayers thanking God for this wonderful gift and for the good health which He had bestowed on Anna and the baby. Since they were both a little embarrassed about not listening as closely as they needed, they didn't ask any questions, but the doctor seemed to know.

"Most couples are a little overwhelmed at this point, so before you go, the nurse will provide you with some handouts of everything we discussed," the doctor said. This wasn't the first time she had dealt with parents of a firstborn and knew they would probably only absorb a portion of what they had heard. You only learn these tricks from experience.

The doctor asked if they had any questions. They couldn't think of any, so the doctor said, "Keep up the great work and we'll see you in a month." With that, she exited the room. The nurse returned shortly with the handouts and escorted them to the lobby.

When they got into the elevator and the doors closed, Rigel whispered to Anna, "I told you there was nothing to be worried about."

"Ha, you were more nervous than I was," Anna quickly retorted. Rigel couldn't really refute that, so he left it alone.

On the drive home, Anna asked, "Would you like me to fix you some lunch before you head to work?"

"I'm not going into work today," Rigel replied, "I'm spending the day with you."

Anna looked at Rigel who pretended to be intensely focused on driving. That was one of the things she loved most about Rigel. He could be so thoughtful but sought no credit. He was thoughtful for the right reasons. She realized how lucky she was to have him in her life.

As she continued to stare at him, Rigel said, "What are you staring at?"

"Just the most wonderful man in the world," Anna replied.

Chapter Twenty-Eight

The day of the Gender Reveal Party was here. Kaitlyn had flown in the night before and was staying with Anna and Rigel. She would only be there for the weekend, but when they picked her up at the airport, she had two large suitcases.

"Are you planning on moving in?", Rigel said to Kaitlyn when he saw them.

Kaitlyn loved how Rigel felt comfortable enough to tease her. She loved even more that he was the perfect husband for her best friend. "Most of that is decorations for your party, so just load them up, monkey boy," she teased right back."

When they got home, Rigel carried Kaitlyn's luggage to the guest room. Anna went into the kitchen to put out some snacks. She knew Kaitlyn would probably be hungry. She also knew Kaitlyn would deny it if asked, so setting out snacks was the perfect solution. That way Kaitlyn could nibble without feeling like she was imposing.

"Look at you," Kaitlyn said to Anna. "I never thought it would be possible, but somehow you're even more beautiful than you were in college. Pregnancy suits you."

Anna blushed, "I've been very fortunate to have an easy pregnancy, but I have to give most of the credit to Rigel. He just always seems to know what I need before I even let on that I need it."

"What do you mean?", Kaitlyn asked.

"Like the nursery. Without even asking him, he took it on himself to prime the entire room. Now, once we know the gender, we can paint the room for the baby. What husband does that on their own?", Anna responded.

"Not many, I would guess," Kaitlyn replied.

"And he has taken over many of the chores I used to do because he doesn't want me to get too tired. I used to cook dinner and then clean up the dishes before joining him in the family room to watch tv. I still cook, because he's working, but he now insists on cleaning up the kitchen after dinner while I relax," Anna shared. "I got the perfect husband, didn't I?"

"You sure did and I couldn't be happier for you," Kaitlyn said as she rushed to Anna and hugged her. They must have hugged thousands of times over the years, but this one seemed more emotional for both of them. It was deeper, lasted longer and brought tears to both their eyes.

"Look at us," Kaitlyn interjected, "I think you're sharing your hormones with me." They both laughed.

When Rigel entered the kitchen, he saw tears in both of their eyes and said, "Okay, what did I do wrong?" He was half joking; at least he hoped he was.

Both Anna and Kaitlyn ran over to give Rigel a hug. "You did nothing wrong. Those were tears of joy."

Even Rigel got a little teary eyed on that one.

Chapter Twenty-Nine

The next morning Rigel awoke when he heard footsteps in the kitchen. He initially thought it was Anna, but when he turned his head, he saw she was still sound asleep. He realized it must be Kaitlyn making the noise. He looked at his watch, and it said 6:18 AM. "I didn't realize she was such an early riser," he thought to himself.

He slowly and quietly climbed out of bed so as not to awaken Anna. He went to the closet, put on his robe and slippers and slid out the door of the bedroom, closing it quietly behind him.

When he got to the kitchen, he saw Kaitlyn sipping on a cup of coffee. "You're an early riser," Rigel said to her.

"I'm so sorry. I hope I didn't wake you," she replied. "I wanted to get a head start on the decorations."

"You don't have to go to a lot of trouble for this," Rigel started to tell her before Kaitlyn quickly interrupted.

"You just shush!", she commanded him with a smile. "I may never have this kind of opportunity to do something for the two of you again and I'm taking full advantage of it!"

Rigel just chuckled and headed for the coffee pot. Before he could even get there, Kaitlyn blocked him with her body, retrieved a mug from the cabinet and poured him a cup. "Do you take cream or sugar?", she asked.

"Just black is fine," he responded.

"So, what's your plans for today?", Rigel asked.

"My plan is to get the two of you out of the house so I can do some decorating," Kaitlyn replied.

"I don't want to wake Anna just yet," Rigel interjected, "she needs her sleep."

"No, no, let her sleep. I wasn't planning on you getting up this early and I was going to jump in the shower and do some preliminary things. I thought if the two of you could be out of the house by 10:00, that would leave me four hours to decorate everything and be ready for all your guests by 2:00," Kaitlyn offered.

"How many guests are we expecting?" Rigel asked rather surprised. "I thought it was just going to be us."

"Don't worry. It's just both of your parents and a few friends. Shouldn't be more than ten total," Kaitlyn replied.

"Then I'll leave you to it. I've got some work to catch up on while I wait for Anna to wake up. Once she does, we'll jump in the shower and be out of your hair," Rigel offered.

"Sounds like a plan," Kaitlyn said with a smile. "Thanks again for allowing me to do this. Anna is so special and it makes me feel so close to be asked to participate in the two of your lives."

"You're like a sister to her," Rigel replied, "and that means you're a sister to me as well."

With that, Rigel headed to the study where he could get started catching up on all the work he had missed lately. It wasn't long after he began that he heard Anna come out of the bedroom.

"Good morning, sleepy head!", he shouted.

"Good morning, yourself, early bird!", she replied. "Is Kaitlyn already up?"

"Up and at 'em," Kaitlyn responded quickly. "Now get showered! Rigel's taking you to breakfast!"

"I am?" Rigel asked.

"Yes, you are!", Kaitlyn responded emphatically.

"Don't I even get a vote in this?", he asked.

"No!", both Kaitlyn and Anna responded simultaneously.

With that, Anna turned around and headed toward the shower. Rigel finished the report he was working on and headed there as well.

As Anna and Rigel, both freshly showered and dressed, headed into the kitchen, they found Kaitlyn hard at work assembling decorations.

"These things are harder than they look," Kaitlyn said a bit frustrated.

"That's exactly why we didn't want you to go to so much trouble," Anna scolded.

"You just shush and get out of here. I have work to do," Kaitlyn retorted immediately.

Rigel pulled Anna away from the island countertop on which Kaitlyn was working and said, "C'mon, Momma. We have things to do." They both smiled at Kaitlyn who returned their gesture with an even bigger smile and off they went to breakfast.

Chapter Thirty

At a few minutes before 2:00 PM, Rigel and Anna pulled into their driveway. Several cars were parked along the street, so they knew the guests for the Reveal Party had already arrived. Rigel ran around the car and helped Anna out of her seat, and they walked arm in arm to the front door. As soon as they opened the door, they were met with everyone clapping. Anna's parents, Rigel's parents, the next-door neighbor, a friend of Anna's and a couple of people from Rigel's work were all in attendance.

The house was decorated everywhere with pink and blue question marks. It was so cute. After hugging her mother and father, Anna immediately ran over to hug Kaitlyn. "I love you so much," she whispered into Kaitlyn's ear. Those words drew tears from each of them. They could blame Anna's tears on hormones, but Kaitlyn's tears could only be classified as genuine.

"Well, what are we waiting for? Let's find out if this is a boy or a girl," Kaitlyn exclaimed. "Please follow me!"

Everyone got in line following Kaitlyn out onto the patio. On the table was an array of chemical lab equipment. Anna had to laugh, "Of course, the top MIT Chemistry major would set up an experiment to determine the sex!"

"How clever," Rigel thought to himself as he examined the equipment. On each end of the table was a dropping funnel filled with clear liquid. It was attached to a clamp stand support frame. At the bottom of each dropping funnel was a valve that could be turned to allow the fluid to flow into plastic tubing. The plastic tubing from each dropping funnel curled around several other support frames forming coils that wound around several times until the ends came together just above an Erlenmeyer Flask. The Erlenmeyer Flask also contained some clear liquid and at the bottom of the flask was a stirring magnet that spun around and around mixing the solution.

Kaitlyn grabbed Anna first and moved her to one end of the table. She then situated Rigel at the other end of the table. She explained, "when I count to three, I want each of you to slowly open the valve on the bottom of your dropping funnel."

"Wait, wait," Rigel interjected, "Do we open the valve as you say three or after three has already been said?" That brought a chuckle from everyone.

"Ok, smart guy," Kaitlyn scolded, "As I say three. Ready?" Both Anna and Rigel nodded.

"Is someone videotaping this with their phone? I can't supervise Rigel and tape too," Kaitlyn asked as everyone laughed again.

"I'll do the honors," Anna's father said as he retrieved his phone from the pocket of his jacket. "Ready," he said.

"One, Two, Three!" Kaitlyn yelled.

With that, Rigel and Anna both began opening the valves on their dropping funnels. The clear fluids begin flowing into the tubes from both valves. The fluid made its way around the coils of the tubing until they finally reached the top of the Erlenmeyer Flask. As the liquids splashed into the flask, the magnetic stirrer did its job to combine the fluids in the solution. For the first few seconds, nothing happened, then suddenly you could see the color of the solution begin to change and keep changing until it formed a vibrant color of blue.

"It's a boy!" they all yelled in unison!

Rigel immediately ran over and grabbed Anna in a bear hug lifting her off her feet with excitement. "Careful there, Papa. We don't want to squish this baby at his first party," Anna cautioned.

"Oh sorry," Rigel apologized as he slowly returned Anna back to her feet. "Guess I was a little excited."

"You think?" Anna said smiling.

Rigel no sooner set Anna down when the entire party ran over to congratulate them. Anna's mother reached her first and it was a hug that seemed to last forever. Rigel's mother reached him first and Rigel couldn't believe the smile on her face as she hugged him and kissed his cheeks just like she used to do when he was little. Rigel looked up to see his father looking at him. He had seen that proud look on his father's face before, but never this apparent. Rigel knew what his father was thinking and he realized he had never been so proud before either. He was going to be a dad.

After all the congratulatory hugs had died down, Rigel had to ask, "Ok, how'd you do that?"

"Oh, just a simple little chemical reaction," Kaitlyn replied, "I'd explain, but it might be a little too complicated for a physicist to understand."

Rigel loved the way Kaitlyn teased him. It was her way of showing how much she thought of him. "Try me," he challenged.

"It was just a dilute copper sulfate solution in water mixed with a solution of concentrated aqueous ammonia," she responded.

"That's exactly what I thought it was," Rigel teased.

"Yeah, right, physics boy," Kaitlyn came right back at him. "Is that why Anna still has to fix your coffee in the morning? Because you can't figure out how much cream to add?"

"For your knowledge, I drink my coffee black," Rigel retorted. "I learned how to drink it that way in college because Mom wasn't around to add the cream for me." Everyone laughed.

Rigel made his way over to Kaitlyn and gave her a big hug. "Seriously," he said, "I love you for all of this. Thank you so much."

"It was my pleasure," Kaitlyn replied. "Now what do you say we let Anna and Rigel open their gifts?" With that everyone cheered and they made their way back into the house.

As Rigel headed up the rear, his father joined him and put his arm around Rigel. No words were said between the two...no words were needed. They both understood.

Chapter Thirty-One

With the Reveal festivities over, Anna and Rigel could now focus on properly preparing the nursery for their son. As easy as "our son" was to say, it remained difficult for either of them to comprehend. They both saw the bump growing in Anna's abdomen, but neither knew how to prepare for how the birth of their son would impact their lives. They shared conversations about this, both deciding to just enjoy the process.

A few days later, Rigel received notice of another meeting he was ordered to attend. While he didn't want to leave Anna alone, he understood this meeting could carry some importance. He broke the news to Anna, and she had no qualms with him attending. She understood the importance of Rigel's job and the dedication it took.

Thankfully, it was a short trip. He would fly out on Wednesday morning and return Thursday afternoon.

When Rigel arrived at Sunport Airport on Wednesday, he entered the General Aviation Terminal. Captain Graves was already waiting for him. As they greeted each other, Captain Graves picked up Rigel's bag. "I can get that," Rigel said.

"Please, it's my pleasure," Captain Graves replied.

They walked out onto the tarmac together. "Looks like a beautiful day to fly and the weather should be perfect for landing," Captain Graves announced.

"Where are we flying to?" Rigel asked.

"I'm afraid I'm not able to say until we are actually on the plane and in the air," Captain Graves replied.

That seemed like a rather odd response, but Rigel respected it. As he walked up the steps to the plane, Jen once again greeted him. "Good morning, sir," she offered, "may I get you some coffee?"

"That would be great, Jen." Rigel made it a point to remember her name as he remembered how kind she had been to him on his previous flight. "Sit anywhere?", he asked.

"Yes, sir. Once again, you will be our only guest," Jen responded.

Rigel didn't hesitate heading directly for one of the larger chairs this time. He was still a little embarrassed at his awkwardness over chair selection on his first trip. He buckled himself in and within seconds Jen returned with a hot cup of coffee and a danish. "I thought you might enjoy one of these," she smiled and said.

"You spoil me," Rigel replied.

"That's my goal," Jen responded as she spun and headed back up to the front of the plane.

Almost immediately, he felt the plane begin moving on the tarmac heading to a runway. The plane lifted off smoothly and once they were in the air, Captain Graves came on the speaker. "I'm sorry, sir, that I wasn't able to explain where we were going while still on the ground, but that's protocol. We are headed once again to the enclave we took you to a few weeks ago," Captain Graves announced. Rigel awkwardly felt a need to respond but quickly realized his response would be to a speaker and not a person, so he just began working on the delicious danish Jen had brought him.

Rigel hadn't brought anything with him to work on, so he found himself nodding off. Before he knew it, Captain Holmberg, the copilot, came on the speaker announcing, "We've been cleared to land, Dr. Emerson, so please fasten your seatbelt and we'll be on the ground shortly."

Jen almost immediately appeared to retrieve Rigel's coffee cup and plate that held the danish. "Did you enjoy it?" she asked.

"It was delicious," Rigel responded.

Jen smiled and headed back up the aisle to the front of the plane.

They were on the ground before he knew it. Just like before, once the plane came to a full stop, Rick was there waiting for him.

"Good morning, Dr. Emerson," Rick said as Rigel walked down the steps.

"Good morning, Rick," Rigel replied.

Captain Holmberg exited the plane and retrieved Rigel's bag from the plane and handed it to Rick who placed it in the back of the SUV. It was only a short drive to the house.

Rigel was looking forward to seeing his father again, but this time no one met him at the door. "Perhaps my flight got in before my father's," he thought to himself.

Just as he was about to reach for the doorknob, Jim, opened the door. "Good morning, Dr. Emerson," Jim said.

"Good morning, Jim," Rigel responded.

"I'll place your bag upstairs in your bedroom. Please make yourself comfortable and I'll be right back," Jim told him as he started up the staircase.

Jim came back down the stairs and, as he approached Rigel, asked, "Are you hungry?"

"Thanks, Jim, but I'm fine. Jen gave me one of those danishes on the flight over," Rigel responded.

"If you don't mind, I'm going to set the security system so we can talk about a few things," Jim offered as he made his way to the security pad.

Rigel heard the locks on the door click into place and the white noise turn on in the room. When Jim returned, he started, "You will be the only guest here today. I will remain to attend to your needs, but I will stay as invisible as I can once I'm done with this briefing. Congratulations on the announcement of your son, by the way. We're all so happy for you."

"Thank you, Jim. Both Anna and I are so excited," Rigel replied.

"You may be wondering why you were called to this meeting, but appear to be the only guest," Jim went on.

"The thought had crossed my mind," Rigel offered.

"Now that things are in motion, it's time to allow you to discover additional insight as to your mission," Jim continued. "As you are now aware, there are other players in the Plan in which we participate. They have asked for you to be brought here so they can share a bit more of the mission with you. I can tell you they won't physically appear, but you will be able to communicate with them with your mind. You just need to be open to allowing that to happen. If, at any time, you feel uncomfortable, just call out my name and I will respond, but I can assure you they will not harm you in any way. They just want to properly prepare you."

"Who exactly is 'they?", Rigel asked.

"I will have to allow them to explain it to you. I hope you understand," Jim responded. Rigel just nodded his head in agreement.

"So, I will now be heading into the kitchen. I won't be participating and I won't be able to hear any of the conversations between you. I will simply be available should you need me for any reason," Jim added. "Are you okay with that?"

"Not knowing what to expect makes it difficult to respond, but I think so," Rigel replied.

"You'll be just fine. They will treat you well. Now to get started, all you need to do is sit and relax. Take a few deep cleansing breaths and then open your mind. They will take over from there. Ready?" Jim asked.

"As ready as I'll ever be," Rigel responded as Jim turned and headed towards the kitchen.

Chapter Thirty-Two

Rigel found a spot in a big over-stuffed chair. He shifted around in it until he felt comfortable and then took several cleansing breaths. He waited. Nothing happened. "Jim, nothing is happening," Rigel called out.

Jim re-entered the room and replied, "Just relax and give it time. It'll happen."

"I'll try," Rigel replied. He took a few more cleansing breaths, shifted around in the chair a few more times and then tried to open his mind. Before long he saw a very bright white light, not with his eyes, but with his mind. He didn't hear anything, but the light was inviting and he found himself being drawn to it. The more he concentrated on the light, the more open his mind became. For a moment, he thought he heard the sounds of a soft rustling, like a soft wind or breeze, but then it faded. As he tried harder to hear it, it came back, this time a little louder. It was comforting. No words, just the gentle breeze.

Suddenly a thought broke through. Was it a thought or was it a voice? Rigel couldn't tell. All he knew was he was picking up some sort of message. The message was becoming increasing clearer. He wasn't hearing any words; he was just feeling them.

"Thank you for your faith in our Plan," the message said.

What was that supposed to mean? As soon as his mind questioned the message, the message stopped, and the light began to dim. Had he offended whoever was sending the message? He wanted to hear more, so he once again cleared his mind and the light and sound of the gentle breeze returned, soon followed by that same message.

"Thank you for your faith in our Plan," the message said.

This time Rigel allowed himself to respond with a return message in his mind. "You are welcome. Tell me more."

He no sooner got this thought off when more messages began coming. The message told him to continue opening his mind further and follow. As Rigel did so, he felt himself being taken up into another realm, another dimension. He felt himself floating, but not in a way where he had to struggle to keep afloat, but rather in an effortless comforting way. He felt himself moving through a haze toward the bright light. "I wonder if this is what death feels like?", Rigel thought to himself only to immediately lose the vision and the message. He found himself once again sitting on the couch alone. Although he felt all this strange, he decided to try once again.

He took a few cleansing breaths and then cleared his mind. Almost immediately he saw the bright light and heard the sound of the breeze return. As he walked through the bright light, the breeze became increasingly louder. At some point, he felt the message. "You have returned. It's important that you refrain from extraneous thoughts during this process and allow your mind to completely focus on the message," Rigel felt the message telling him. "Do you agree to move forward?" the message asked.

Rigel immediately replied, "Yes."

"Good," the message replied, "then let us begin. I am a messenger. I will lead you to your guide. Stay with me. Focus on me. For at any time that you fail to focus, our conversation will end."

"I will try," Rigel replied.

"I understand it is difficult to focus, that your mind wants to take you to thoughts and places outside of our conversation, but you must focus on the message I have for you as it is of great importance. You will be given only a few attempts. If you fail, you will no longer be considered for this assignment. But if you are successful, I assure you it will be worthwhile for you and your family," the message continued.

"May I ask questions?", Rigel asked.

"With me, you may not. My assignment is to assess your faith and then lead you on your journey to meet your guide. Questions, at this point, indicate doubt. I need your full allegiance in order to move you through the journey to your next level. While this may appear rigid, it is necessary. As you have been tested throughout your life, our journey will be testing you on your faith and allegiance to the Plan. Do you understand?", the message stated emphatically.

"I understand and will do my best," Rigel replied.

"Initially, you doubted, even when the message was coming from your father. Why?", the message asked.

"It was all new to me. I've never experienced the thought of my father having secrets he'd kept from me or my mother, and I didn't know how to process it. It took me a while, but I trusted my father enough to continue and that should count for something," Rigel replied.

"It counts for everything, Rigel. You will need to apply the same logic here. While some things may seem strange or foreign, you must trust our Plan. It is not only essential, but worth your complete effort," the message responded. "We have proven our trustworthiness by providing you a son. This confirms our investment in you. Now we must demand your investment."

"What investment is that?", Rigel asked.

"Your total faith and allegiance," the message responded. "If you can pledge that, may we go on?"

"I pledge it," Rigel replied, "please proceed."

"How far would you go to protect the Plan?" the message asked.

This question took Rigel by surprise. He wasn't sure how to answer. He didn't even really know what the Plan was, so how could he possibly know how far he would go to protect it? "I don't know how to answer that since I don't really know what the Plan is," he said timidly.

"You are a Christian, are you not?", the message asked.

"I am," Rigel replied.

"Would you do everything within your power to do God's bidding if asked to do so?", the message continued.

"I would hope that I would," Rigel responded.

"You hope?", the message immediately demanded.

"If God asked me to do something, I would do everything I possibly could to accomplish it," Rigel replied still a little shaken. "Wait, does God have something to do with the Plan?"

"I told you no questions. You must save them for your guide," the message demanded.

"Please forgive me. I asked before even thinking," Rigel said shaken.

"Would you be willing to push all earthly things aside if God required you to do so?", the message asked.

"I would," Rigel responded.

"Including your wife and son?", the message inquired.

That was a question Rigel was unprepared to handle. He had never thought of having to make a choice between his family and his faith. As this thought raced through his mind, he saw the light becoming dimmer and the sound of the breeze becoming softer. He focused with everything he had and answered, "I would."

As soon as those words entered his mind, the light returned, the breeze returned to its previous volume, and in front of him stood a transparent entity. The form was indistinguishable. It was without form, yet it somehow remained a shape which kept shifting in appearance. It was much like a very large bubble floating in mid-air, intact, but constantly changing shape. It wasn't human, it wasn't animal, it appeared to be gaseous.

"I am the messenger," the shape said.

For the first time, Rigel actually heard the words and didn't just feel them, although he felt them just as strongly.

Chapter Thirty-Three

Rigel was in awe. Was he just dreaming? Was this just a hallucination? For a moment, he didn't know what to believe and at that moment, the shape disappeared from his vision.

"Where'd you go?", Rigel called out.

"You doubted. You had been warned that doubt would make you ineligible," he heard the messenger's voice reply.

Panic began to set in. Logic would tell him this was all just a dream, but there was something too real that was pushing logic aside. "I'm sorry I doubted. I can't control random thoughts. Please give me another chance?", Rigel said beggingly.

"It's not a matter of chances, Rigel. We can only use those that are the strongest in our Plan. We must be able to rely on them regardless of the circumstances and control of their mind and thoughts is crucial," the messenger replied.

Rigel felt defeated, more helpless than he had ever felt before. He had come this far only to allow a random thought to destroy all progress. What would happen to his son now that he had failed his first challenge? The remorse was incredible. He had ruined perhaps the greatest opportunity in his life. He had never done anything that made him feel so ashamed. "I'm so sorry, God, that I have let you down," Rigel felt himself praying silently.

Suddenly, the messenger reappeared. "Our God is a God of mercy," the messenger began. "Although we cannot offer you endless chances, we understand humans are weak. You called to God and repented. That means your faith and allegiance is strong. You have passed the test. I will lead you to your Guide."

All the pain, all the guilt, was suddenly lifted from Rigel's shoulders. He immediately thanked God for this opportunity, and he thanked his parents for bringing him up in faith.

"I am ready," Rigel announced.

"Follow me," the messenger responded.

Rigel felt himself following the messenger and moving deeper into the light. After a few moments, he and the messenger came to a wall. "This is where I leave you. Your Guide will meet you here. Stay strong, Rigel," the messenger said and with those words, the shape disappeared.

Rigel felt himself standing alone outside the wall. He didn't know whether to call out or simply remain silent. Suddenly, the entire vision was gone, and Rigel awoke from the meditative state he had been experiencing.

This sudden change surprised him, and he felt panic wondering if he had done something wrong. Just then, Jim walked into the room. "Relax, Rigel," Jim said. "You will go there again, but for right now you need a break. Follow me into the kitchen. I've made you something to eat."

Rigel nodded and started to get up from the chair finding himself a little unsteady on his feet. "Take it slow. Your body needs time to adjust," Jim said as he slowly walked into the kitchen.

"So, you know all about this?", Rigel questioned Jim.

"Let's just say I've had a similar journey. Each person's assignment is different, but all of us are led," Jim responded.

"I doubted," Rigel confessed.

"We all have doubted. We're human and let's face it, concentration and focus are not our best skills. The fact that you remain means you're doing what you need to do. You must be doing something right or you wouldn't have come this far. Don't be so hard on yourself. Use your weakness as a lesson and your resolve as a tool," Jim offered.

"I will," Rigel responded. "That looks like an incredible lunch," he said as he glanced at the salad and plate of sandwiches on the table. I'm famished. Funny how you can work up such an appetite just sitting in a chair."

"Your body may not have been active, but trust me, your mind and your soul were burning a lot of calories. Dive in. I'll eat lunch with you, but it's better if we don't talk about your experience. As I've said, each of our assignment's is different and yours will be between you and your Guide," Jim said.

"I do have one question," Rigel began, "When my father first told me about this, he referred to them as the 'inter-dimensionals". Why didn't he tell me they had anything to do with God?"

"That would be a question for your Guide," Jim responded. "C'mon, these sandwiches won't eat themselves," Jim said kiddingly.

As they enjoyed their lunch, they talked about fishing, the beautiful house, and even the Reveal Party, but the subject of the Guides didn't resurface again.

When lunch was over, Jim said, "Why don't you go out and take a quick walk before your next session? You need some fresh air and that will give you an opportunity to work off some of this lunch."

"I'll take you up on that offer," Rigel replied as he got up from the table and headed towards the door. "If I get lost and aren't back in a half hour, send out the search team," Rigel joked as he headed out the door.

Chapter Thirty-Four

Once outside, the fatigue that had built within his body began to quickly dissipate. The air was fresh and clean, the surroundings incredibly beautiful, and Rigel felt himself becoming more and more relaxed.

He followed the path, taking in all the sights. His mind wandered, but not about the visions. Instead, he found himself in awe of all that God had made. Ahead of him on the path was a doe and her fawn. As soon as they saw Rigel, they scampered off into the forest. Although he visually observed only a few, it seemed like there were hundreds of birds around him, each warbling their own particular song.

He approached a small meadow covered in prairie grasses and natural flowers. He saw bees flitting from blossom to blossom. He watched butterflies take flight and then land on the long stems of the grasses which gently swayed in the breeze. This was all so perfect, Rigel wondered to himself what the Garden of Eden must have looked like. He had heard stories about the Garden of Eden since he was a young child, but he wondered how similar it was to what he was actually viewing.

Ahead, he saw something slither across the path. It was a snake, dark in color, almost black. He didn't really get a good look at it to determine what kind of a snake it was, but it immediately send an uneasy feeling through his system. He had never liked snakes. Their movements were too erratic. No matter how docile some varieties might be, he never felt comfortable around them. He had a friend who had a pet snake, but Rigel refused to go over to that friend's house. He just didn't want to be near it. It wasn't even a venomous snake; Rigel just didn't like them.

The uneasiness was enough to turn Rigel around and head back to the house. He looked back over his shoulder several times just to assure the snake wasn't following him. He thought to himself how strange it was that he even considered the snake might be following him. Surely, it wouldn't be able to keep up. Besides, he had heard snakes don't pursue people. They are only a danger if cornered.

Ahead of him on the path, another snake appeared. This one wasn't retreating. It was coiled and looked ready to strike. Rigel stopped in his path. He watched the snake as it glared back at him. It became a staring match, and Rigel quickly realized the longer he stared at the snake, the more uneasy he was becoming. It wasn't moving towards him, but it certainly wasn't giving up any ground either.

Rigel realized he needed to get back to the house, but he wasn't going to approach this menacing snake. Walking in the tall grass to get around the snake didn't seem like a good option either. If he had already seen two snakes, how many more were hiding in the deep grass?

His uneasiness continued to grow. It wasn't yet at the point of panic, but he couldn't guarantee panic was out of the question if the snake started advancing. They were at an impasse. The snake refused to move and he refused to advance.

Rigel realized the only tool he had available was faith. "Dear Lord, please make this snake leave the path and allow me to get back to the house safely," Rigel prayed. No sooner had his prayer left his lips when the snake began slithering off the path into the tall grass.

"Thank you," Rigel whispered. He realized prayer should have been his first thought, not his last. He had spent that entire time anxious and worried. A simple prayer and God made the serpent go away.

When he got back to the house, Jim met him at the door. "How was your walk?", Jim asked.

"Interesting," Rigel replied. Perhaps the lesson he had learned should be pondered, not shared. Maybe he'd tell someone about it another time, but for now, it was between he and God.

Chapter Thirty-Five

Once he had regained composure, Rigel was ready for the next session. Jim encouraged him to take a seat in the chair and relax, opening his mind and soul to his next message. Obediently, Rigel did just that.

For some reason, this time was different. Rigel had trouble relaxing and his mind was racing with all kinds of thoughts, especially his standoff with the snake on the path. Every time he thought he was beginning to open his mind, the memory of the snake returned. Rigel didn't like snakes, but it wasn't as if he had a phobia about them. He wondered why he was having such a problem of getting past it and allowing his mind to open.

After several attempts, he called out to Jim. "Jim, are you around?", Rigel asked.

Jim came around the corner from the kitchen. "Did you need something, Dr. Emerson?", Jim asked.

"I do," Rigel replied, "and please call me Rigel. Dr. Emerson is way too formal."

"Rigel, it is," Jim replied. "Now what can I help you with?"

"I seem to be experiencing some trouble clearing my mind. Ideas keep racing through my head and there's one vision, in particular, that seems to be haunting me," Rigel went on. "Do you have any recommendations?"

"Let me fix you a cup of Ashwagandha tea. That always seems to help me," Jim responded as he turned and headed back towards the kitchen.

Within a few minutes, Jim returned with the tea. "What did you call this tea again?" Rigel asked.

"It's called Ashwagandha tea. It's a caffeine-free herbal tea that helps reduce stress, anxiety, and cortisol levels," Jim replied.

"That's exactly what I need," Rigel responded as he took his first sip. He immediately crinkled his nose. "It's a bit bitter," he offered.

"Let me add a bit of honey," Jim said as he once again headed to the kitchen. When he returned, he had a honey dispenser and proceeded to add some honey to Rigel's tea. "Stir that up with your spoon and give it a try."

Rigel stirred the concoction and gave it another sip. "Better, but still a little bitter," Rigel responded.

"Would you prefer something else?", Jim asked.

"No, no. This is fine. If this will do the trick, it's exactly what I need, so let me just push through the taste. I guess I'm not much of a tea gourmet," Rigel chuckled.

Jim laughed and stated, "I think it will definitely help, but if you would like something different, just let me know."

"This will be fine. Thanks so much, Jim," Rigel responded.

"It's my pleasure. Now let me leave you alone so you can get back to work," Jim said as he went back to the kitchen.

Rigel finished the tea, set his cup and saucer on the coffee table, and leaned back to relax. At first the thoughts were racing through his mind but began to slow down until he was finally able to focus. He took in a deep breath and let it out slowly. After repeating this a few times, he felt a sense of calm come over him.

He saw the light beginning to return, getting progressively brighter as it approached him. A soft breeze could be heard in the background and before he knew it, Rigel found himself standing at the wall. As he looked around, he discovered he was still alone. The branches of the trees swayed in the gentle breeze, and he could hear the birds chirping in the background. Their beautiful warbling songs helped calm him even more.

Off in the distance, he saw a shape moving towards him along the path. Once again, the shape was transparent and had no form, but you could definitely make out a shape, albeit constantly shifting.

When the shape neared, it said, "Rigel, it's good to meet you. I am your Guide."

Rigel wasn't sure quite what to do in the presence of his Guide. Instead, he nodded his head conveying respect.

"I'm sure you have many questions," the Guide began, "but before we get to those, we need to discuss a few things. The journey I'm about to take you on can be overwhelming for some. I need you to promise me that if you begin to feel anxious or overwhelmed, you will call out my name. Can you do that?"

"I can," Rigel replied, "but what is your name?"

"For now, my name will be Guide," the Guide responded.

"Will you be with me on whatever journey I'm about to take?", Rigel asked.

"I will be with you, but you will not see me, nor will anyone else," the Guide responded. "As you well know, this journey will involve a great deal of trust and must be clandestine at all times."

"Clandestine? Are you asking me to do something illegal?", Rigel asked nervously.

"Not illegal or immoral, Rigel," the Guide responded. "Although it may involve covert actions in which you may be asked to challenge certain policies or politics. You see, Rigel, your world involves many players and sometimes those players don't have the best of intentions. In fact, some of their intentions are quite nefarious. Part of your journey will include gathering information from some of these groups which may become useful in developing plans and strategies."

"Who sent you?", Rigel inquired.

"That will be revealed at the proper time," the Guide responded.

"Where are you from?", Rigel continued his questions.

"That also will be revealed at a later time," the Guide returned.

"Why won't you answer any of my questions?", Rigel countered impatiently.

"I will answer all of your questions, Rigel, when the time is right," the Guide replied. "It's much like your top-secret work on Project: Xaviar..."

Rigel cut the Guide off in mid-sentence, "Wait, how do you know about Project: Xaviar? That's top secret."

"Who do you think gave you the idea for that project, Rigel?", the Guide asked rather convincingly.

"I came up with the idea on my own by combining two different theories on propulsion," Rigel responded defensively.

"Did you, now?", the Guide replied.

That threw Rigel for a loop and made him suddenly doubt his own abilities. The concept he was working on was unique and it had come to him out of the blue, but he didn't remember receiving a message or anyone interfering with his thought process. On the other hand, coming up with such a different way to look at propulsion surprised even him. No one had done that before. Rigel considered himself smart, but the theory behind Project: Xaviar seemed a little too bold for anyone, even for him. Could it be true that this Guide had led him to the idea of Project, Xaviar? It wasn't as if he had developed the theory through application of principles or similar projects. Rigel supposed it could at least be feasible that someone or something more advanced had intervened. It wasn't a giant leap to consider having been guided to this idea. After all, he learned from his father he was already dealing with inter-dimensionals and if that was possible, anything was possible. Besides, how would the Guide even know about Project: Xaviar? There were only a handful of people who did.

As logic took hold, his ego began to retreat, and Rigel felt his defensiveness beginning to ease. He understood need-to-know and he surmised the Guide was only protecting what needed protection.

"What exactly is the Plan?", Rigel asked.

"I'm afraid I can't reveal that to you just yet, Rigel," the Guide replied, "But know that you are on the right side of whatever may happen. Our goal is right and we will achieve it, no matter what it takes to do so."

"It almost sounds like war," Rigel interjected.

"There will be a war, Rigel, no doubt about that. Our Plan, however, is to gather as much information as possible and develop the best strategies so that we may win this war with the least number of casualties," the Guide responded.

"A war? Casualties? I'm not sure I'm ready for this," Rigel said panickily.

"You've known about this war your entire life, Rigel. It isn't something that is unexpected. From the very beginning of mankind, this war was anticipated." the Guide said.

"Is it coming soon?", Rigel asked.

"We don't know exactly when it will come. Our goal is to be prepared so we are ready whenever it starts," the Guide shared.

"Are you going to prepare me to fight?", Rigel asked the Guide.

"I'm going to prepare you to prepare," is the way the Guide responded.

Chapter Thirty-Six

As Rigel walked, the Guide moved along the path beside him and began to paint a clearer picture for Rigel. It was hard to say how long they walked, as time seemed to have no reference or scale. It wasn't as if time was standing still; it was more because time was no longer relevant.

The Guide explained that it was important to have the proper people in the proper places when the Plan unfolded. That involved people in various categories including domestic and worldwide politics, military, finance, academia, and even science. Rigel would be a cog in that Plan. His children, and perhaps even his grandchildren or great-grandchildren may also play a role.

To provide perspective, the Guide used the category in which Rigel was currently involved, "You are currently working on a top-secret propulsion system, but you won't be on that project long."

The Guide's knowledge of Project: Xaviar still disturbed Rigel a little. Only people with top-secret clearance and need to know were supposed to know about that program. And, why wouldn't he be on the project for long? Rigel decided to let that one go, but asked, "What other top-secret programs do you know about?"

The Guide didn't respond. He just allowed Rigel time to process his own answer to that question.

"So, you know everything that's going on?", Rigel asked.

"Pretty much so. There are those who seek to do evil and keep it well hidden. Only God knows what is happening at any given moment, but sometimes He allows us to discover it for ourselves," the Guide responded.

"Let me ask you this. Do you have a God?", Rigel asked.

"I do. Your God is my God. What you know about your God is what God has made available for you to learn about Him. Your beliefs rely upon what is written in the Bible and what has been passed down through the ages. We have been allowed to learn more about Him. So, although our faith is on a different plane than yours, we still honor the same God," the Guide responded. "Just like in your Bible, there exists a battle between the forces of God and those that resist Him. We are part of God's forces, as are you. That's why we must prepare."

"When you talk about battle, you're pretty much talking about the battle between good and evil?", Rigel asked already knowing the answer but still seeking confirmation.

"Most definitely," the Guide responded. "Yesterday, as you walked along the path, what did you observe?", the Guide asked.

"I observed nature's beauty and all that God has created," Rigel replied.

"What else did you observe?", the Guide asked.

"I saw deer, birds, bees, butterflies, and two snakes on the path. One snake slithered away into the tall grass. The other coiled and stood his ground almost as if challenging me," Rigel responded.

"What were your thoughts about the snakes?" the Guide inquired.

"They made me uncomfortable. Not so much the one that slithered away, but definitely the one that seemed to challenge me from walking on the path," Rigel answered.

"I want you to close your eyes and go back to those moments in your head," the Guide instructed.

Rigel followed the Guide's urging, closed his eyes, and the vision of the walk came back to him. He was greatly enjoying the serenity and beauty of nature's beauty, when these two snakes interrupted. The first slithered away without threatening, but the second definitely wanted to challenge him.

"I think I'm picking up on what you wanted me to see," Rigel went on. "While enjoying God's beauty and how serene everything was, the first snake distracted me. My mind went from appreciating God's wonders to becoming defensive and wondering if I was going to need to act. The second snake didn't leave it up to interpretation. He was definitely challenging me, trying to frighten me, trying to take over. God's creations were good, but evil tried to redirect my thoughts, to get me to stop appreciating, and focus on dangers and threats."

"That's correct, Rigel," the Guide responded. "Evil doesn't like anyone enjoying God's blessings, so it will use fear and chaos in order to redirect our thinking. The first snake slithered away into the tall grass. That was more of a subtle warning that danger is out there and, in fact, could be anywhere. The second was definitely a challenge. Evil sent that snake to put fear in you; to show you it was in charge. It stopped you in your tracks and it knew it had command of you. When you called out to God, evil knew it could not compete and slithered away. This is what evil does in our lives. It constantly brings fear, uncertainty, chaos, and even calamity, but it knows it cannot overcome the power of God.

When someone with faith turns to God, evil must back down."

"Evil was in the form of a snake, just like in the Garden of Eden," Rigel thought to himself.

The Guide picked up on Rigel's thought and explained, "Evil appeared as a snake to you yesterday because you were already familiar with the analogy. You must be cautious, however, as evil can take many shapes and many forms, many of which can be quite deceiving."

"What does this all have to do with the Plan?", Rigel asked.

"The day will come when evil will be defeated once and for all," the Guide explained. "The Plan involves preparing for that day."

Suddenly Rigel realized how serious this all was. He had many more questions, but his mind was too busy processing all he had just heard.

"I think we've had enough for today, Rigel," the Guide told him. "Go back to the house, enjoy your dinner and get some rest. We will talk more tomorrow."

With that, the Guide vanished and the entire vision began to fade from Rigel's view. Before he knew it, he was fully aware of himself sitting alone in the chair. The sun was peeking in through the windows and inviting him outside.

Rigel got up from the chair and walked towards the door, only to be stopped by Jim. "Hold on just a moment while I turn the alarm off," Jim said as he scurried to the security system controls. "All clear," Jim announced. "Can I make you a cocktail?" he asked.

"I wouldn't mind a beer if you have one," Rigel said as he continued walking towards the door.

"Coming right up," Jim replied.

Chapter Thirty-Seven

Once outside, Rigel breathed in the fresh air. It smelled so beautiful here, like fresh pine. He watched as the trees swayed in the gentle breeze. He didn't leave the porch, he just stood and appreciated.

Jim arrived with his beverage and a tray that contained various meats, cheeses, crackers, olives and grapes. There was a small table situated between two chairs on the porch and Jim set the tray on the table. "I brought a little snack. Thought you might be hungry," Jim said.

Rigel replied, "Thanks, Jim. Do you have time to join me?"

"After all you've been through today, I didn't know if you wanted to be alone, but if you're sure, I'd be glad to join you," Jim replied.

"Yes, please do," Rigel said with a smile.

"Let me run and just get one of those cold beers for myself," Jim chuckled as he headed back into the kitchen.

When Jim returned, Rigel took a seat in one of the chairs. Jim took the other seat. "So, how'd it go?", Jim asked.

"I think it went well," Rigel responded. "We talked about..." Jim cut him off mid-sentence.

"Whoa! What you observed, what you discussed, and who you talked to are none of my business. This needs to be kept to yourself. I'm sorry my question was so vague. What I really meant to say is how are you feeling after today's session?", Jim corrected.

"I'm a bit overwhelmed, but I feel good. I have lots of questions, but I feel good," Rigel replied smiling. He appreciated how Jim always helped to keep him in line. Now he knew why his father thought so highly of Jim.

For the next hour, they sat on the porch, enjoyed their beer and snacks, and talked about the beauty surrounding the house. As Jim took his last sip, he said, "Let me get you another and you can sit out here while I prepare dinner."

"Deal," Rigel replied.

Chapter Thirty-Eight

Sleep came easily that night for Rigel. With all that was going through his mind, he thought he would be tossing and turning, but that wasn't the case. Instead, he fell asleep right away and slept like a baby. The strange part was that when he awoke, he realized he hadn't had any dreams, at least he couldn't remember any. Rigel almost always dreamed, even if they were short, so not dreaming at all was rather different for him.

In any event, he awoke refreshed and was ready for today's journey. Rigel showered, dressed and then went down to the kitchen for breakfast. He barely made it out of his room when the aroma of freshly brewed coffee and sizzling bacon hit his nostrils. There was something about this place that seemed so special. Even the aromas were unbelievable. No wonder his father had enjoyed coming here so much.

When he reached the kitchen, Jim was busy at the stove. "Fried or scrambled?", Jim asked.

"Scrambled, please," Rigel responded.

When Jim brought Rigel's plate to the table, it was loaded with scrambled eggs topped with cheese, green peppers, and sausage. The plate included strips of bacon and a cinnamon roll, which explained the other scent Rigel couldn't quit figure out.

"Please join me, Jim," Rigel said.

"Don't mind if I do," Jim replied. "Are you ready for your last day?"

"As ready as I'll ever be," Rigel responded. "It'll be good to get home, but I'm sure going to miss your friendship and your cooking."

"Well, the friendship is there whenever you want it, and the cooking is here whenever you come to the Lodge" Jim replied with a smile.

The two finished their breakfast and Jim could tell Rigel was eager to begin. "Let me just clean up the kitchen before you get started. I don't want to make a lot of noise once you get into your session," Jim offered.

"Perfect," Rigel responded.

Chapter Thirty-Nine

Rigel went over and sat in the overstuffed chair, patiently waiting for Jim to finish. Once the kitchen was clean, Jim said, "All done. I'll set the alarm, then please proceed and I'll get out of your hair."

"Thanks for all you do, Jim. I really appreciate you," Rigel said.

"It's my pleasure," Jim replied as he walked to the security panel, set the alarm, and then disappeared into another area of the house.

As Rigel relaxed in the chair, he immediately felt calm and warmth wash over him. He briefly remembered the nervous anxiety he felt just before his first session, but all of that was gone now. It was replaced with calm, but eager anticipation.

The light soon began to appear, followed by the sound of a soft breeze. Soon Rigel envisioned himself once again standing near the wall. Off in the distance, he saw the Guide approaching. Rigel felt himself smile at the thought of all his Guide would teach him.

"Good morning, Rigel," the Guide said as he approached. "Did you sleep well?"

"I slept exceptionally well, thank you," Rigel responded.

"Are you ready to continue your journey?", the Guide asked.

"As ready as I'll ever be," Rigel answered.

As they walked along the path together, the Guide began to explain. "As I mentioned yesterday, the day will come when evil needs to be defeated once and for all. Our job is to prepare for that day."

"Doesn't God have the power to just eliminate evil on his own?" Rigel asked.

"Absolutely," the Guide responded, "But God grants all of us free will. He could make everyone believe if He wanted, but He wants us to choose to believe. He could eliminate evil in the blink of an eye, but He wants to give evil a choice between submitting and repenting or being destroyed. Given Satan's ego, we all know which he will choose, so we are preparing for that battle."

"I'm not much of a fighter," Rigel interjected.

"It's not your physical abilities we need," the Guide responded, "it's the attributes you contribute to our preparedness."

"I'm not sure I understand," Rigel admitted.

"When it is time for this battle, the world must be properly positioned. We must have the proper people in place who can lead humans while forces are battling. We must have the technology that will allow life to continue regardless of the destruction being caused by the battles. We must have the systems in place to assure life is sustainable while these battles are occurring," the Guide responded.

"So, the battle must be happening soon?", Rigel asked.

"No, I didn't say that," the Guide responded. "No one knows when this is going to happen. It is our job to be ready."

"What will my role be?", Rigel inquired.

"It's quite possible you won't still be on the Earth when this happens, Rigel," the Guide replied. "This battle could take place tomorrow or it may not happen for centuries, we just don't know. What we do know is we need the help of people like you to produce the right kind of humans who will be able to govern and sustain the world when the battle begins."

"So, if I play such an important role, why isn't my son my baby?", Rigel found himself saying before he had really thought that question through.

"Let me respond to that in the best way I know how. Your father is a brilliant physicist. You are even more intelligent. You understand and are working on things far more advanced than your father could handle," the Guide responded.

"Oh, don't cut my father short," Rigel said interrupted defensively. "My father is far smarter than me and he could handle any of the things I work on if he were given the opportunity."

"With all due respect, Rigel, your IQ is higher than your father's. He has accomplished great things, but you are the next version, the next model, in a long line of progression. You are smarter than your father. Your father was smarter than your grandfather. Your grandfather was smarter than your great-grandfather. Your son will be smarter than you. There's a reason, Rigel. We need that progression to continue."

"I don't understand. If it wasn't my father's sperm, how could I inherit my father's intelligence genes, and how will my son inherit my intelligence genes if it's not my sperm," Rigel asked.

"The truth is, Rigel, your son's intelligence doesn't rely on your genes. We are developing the necessary resources we will need over time. Small incremental improvements that humans can handle. We have learned that too big of a leap at one time cannot be handled by mankind," the Guide replied.

"I don't understand," Rigel admitted.

"The only way I know how to explain this is to give you some examples," the Guide continued. "Hitler was an infectious leader. He was able to get people to follow him wherever he wanted to go. The problem was, with great power comes great responsibility. Hitler couldn't handle the responsibility. He was selfish and led his people down a path of destruction instead of leading his people to a better world. There were scientists that were given the ability to harness nuclear power. Look what you did with it. Instead of harnessing it for good, you used it for destruction. All of those things happened because we allowed too large of a leap at one time. We've learned to make smaller increments of improvement. It will take longer, but that's the only way this will work."

"So, Hitler and Oppenheimer were part of the Plan?", Rigel asked frantically.

"They were and although it didn't work out well, we learned a great deal about how the Plan had to progress," the Guide responded.

"So, I'm just a cog in a wheel?", Rigel asked.

"You are a contributor to something immensely important," the Guide replied.

"I still don't understand the gene thing," Rigel said.

"It's not about your genes, Rigel. You were created and you advance science. Your son has been created and he, too, will advance science," the Guide advised.

"Then where do my son's genes come from?", Rigel asked.

As Rigel asked this question, they approached a large rock. "Sit, Rigel. We're going in deep," the Guide began to explain. "When you first started your journey yesterday, you received some messages, thoughts that would come into your mind about commitment. Do you recall that?"

"Yes, I was asked about my allegiance to the Plan," Rigel replied.

"That's correct," the Guide replied. "Do you know why your allegiance is so important?"

"I could speculate, but I prefer you tell me," Rigel responded.

"Defeating evil in the world is not an easy task," the Guide explained. "It requires planning, training and execution of the Plan. We must assure this goes flawlessly. If it does, evil will be defeated once and for all. If it doesn't go well, the battle could continue for eons and all dimensions, including mankind, will greatly suffer."

"I still don't understand why God doesn't just eliminate evil?" Rigel asked.

"Do you have a choice as to whether or not you believe in God, Rigel?" the Guide questioned.

"I do and I choose to believe," Rigel replied.

"God gave evil a choice, as well. What benefit do you gain from believing in God," the Guide asked.

"Eternal life," Rigel answered.

"That's why I can assure you God has given His blessing to this Plan, Rigel," the Guide replied. "The Plan includes building an army of beings from many dimensions, including a human army. The human army will not be of soldiers, but of leaders who will be able to guide all human believers through this battle."

"Did God create you?", Rigel asked.

"God created ALL things," the Guide responded. "I have just as much at stake in the Plan as you do, Rigel. That's why I need to properly prepare you for your role."

"Where does God fit into the Plan?", Rigel asked.

"Isn't God a part of every plan?", the Guide replied.

The Guide allowed that to sink in for a moment before saying, "Our session is about to come to a close. Before it does, do you have any questions?"

"I have tons of questions, but my mind is so overwhelmed. Let me just ask why was it necessary to use the seed of an interdimensional to impregnate Anna? Why couldn't you use my seed? I've already committed to the Plan," Rigel asked a bit more anguished than he had intended.

"Your son will be smarter and do greater things than you, Rigel. Could you have done that on your own?", the Guide asked. "You trusted your father when this all began. All I can ask is that you give me the same level of trust going forward."

"Were you the interdimensional that impregnated Anna?", Rigel asked.

"I was not," the Guide responded. "I am merely your Guide."

"Will I ever meet the entity that impregnated Anna?" Rigel inquired shakenly.

"I don't know the answer to that question," the Guide offered, "but let me remind you that an interdimensional did not impregnate Anna, you did. It just was not your seed. Secondly, you understood going into this that it would not be your seed, but it was the only way you could have a son and offer Anna a child. Lastly, if a DNA test were ever done on your son, it would show you as the father. You will be as much of a father to your son as your father has been to you. Also remember, that you have the option at any time to withdraw from your agreement."

"If I withdraw, what will happen?" Rigel asked.

"Just like before, if you should decide to withdraw, things will revert back to before Anna got pregnant and you will have no memory of anything that has been discussed," the Guide replied.

"What if I decide to withdraw after my son is born?", Rigel asked.

"If you had not yet had the discussion with your son, then your son will never know he was different and you will not remember how he came to be. You will both live your lives as if nothing had ever happened only neither of you would be part of the Plan. If you had already had the discussion with your son and he chose to participate, then your son would know about the Plan, but you would not. You would lose all memory of it," the Guide responded.

Rigel shook his head acknowledging he understood.

"I still don't understand why I am so crucial for the Plan," Rigel confessed.

"You are an iteration, an improved version so to speak, of your lineage. We will continue making these improvements through generations, if necessary, until our army is formed and the right people are in place to implement the Plan. I know this is a lot to absorb. That's why we called you here to explain it. But I don't want you to leave here until you're completely comfortable with all we've discussed," the Guide explained.

"I don't know how that's possible," Rigel admitted. "I still don't feel I understand."

Suddenly, Rigel was overwhelmed with warmth and love. In his mind he saw visions of himself as a young boy with his father. They were taking walks, fishing, tossing a ball. He saw the love his father had for him. And then the vision changed. He saw his son being born, holding him for the very first time, teaching him how to walk, kicking a soccer ball, being so proud of having such a wonderful son.

"You sent me that vision, didn't you?" Rigel asked the Guide.

"No, Rigel. God did," the Guide replied. "He wanted you to see what lies ahead for you. He wants you to realize that once you allow your ego to let go, that you can enjoy this gift God is giving you."

"If I begin having doubts, does God just send me a pleasant vision to change my mind? Like brainwashing?", Rigel asked.

"No, Rigel. God will never force you into the Plan. He may send you a vision so you can see what life could be like, but the decision is always up to you. If you are intent on pulling away from the Plan, God will allow it," the Guide responded.

Rigel wondered why he even felt any doubt. Was it his ego that was making him question? Already his son was bringing so much joy into his and Anna's life, and the baby hadn't even been born yet. Perhaps he was being selfish. Perhaps he was being too hard on himself. Instead of fighting it, perhaps he needed to just commit to it. Deep down inside he knew this was right for him and Anna. He had to quit allowing his ego to get in the way.

"I think I'm beginning to understand," Rigel offered. "Our meeting was to teach me how important the Plan is and to help me learn how to let go of ego, wasn't it?"

"It was," the Guide replied. "The ego is a difficult thing to overcome. To do so, there must be something in your life with greater priority. I think you're starting to discover this Plan is the ultimate priority. The Plan is crucial and you play an important role. You understand that don't you, Rigel?"

"I'm beginning to," Rigel replied.

"Now go home to your beautiful wife," the Guide instructed. "We will meet again soon to help you get there."

With that, the Guide disappeared and Rigel awoke from his vision.

Chapter Forty

Upon awakening, Rigel remained seated in the chair for several minutes contemplating all he had experienced. It seemed illogical, impossible, almost a dream, yet it was happening. He realized his life had become more complicated than it previously had been and he sensed some anxiety in how he was handling it.

Almost immediately a calm came over him and the anxiety disappeared. It was replaced with an overwhelming sense of pride knowing he was a part of the Plan. Rigel realized that, up until this point, he had been viewing all of this from a personal perspective, a human perspective. This task was anything but human. He had been selected to participate, as had his father, and it appeared that his grandfather, great-grandfather, and perhaps generations of his family had been involved. He was the next iteration. He was the next generation of improvements, and his son would be an improvement over him.

Rigel realized his son would someday face the same decision he was allowed to make. Rigel also realized he would be the one that would lead his son down this path, just as his father had done for him. It was a great responsibility. He didn't fully comprehend everything yet, and he still had a lot of questions, but for once he felt totally committed to the Plan. He couldn't say that before. Although he had previously agreed to participate, it was his visions and his discussions with his Guide that made him realize the importance of what he was doing.

It was still unknown when it would all happen, but Rigel realized it was out of his control. All he needed to know is he had a job to do...to be the best father to his son that a man could be, just like Rigel's father was to him.

Sometimes it was easier for Rigel, when trying to learn a new concept, to use an example he already understood. Top secret clearance Rigel understood. It's on a "Need-to-Know" basis. A person isn't read into a Top-Secret Project unless they've already received clearance and have a need to know. There were things at work he couldn't discuss with Anna, or anyone, for that matter. Why was this any different? They would be having a child, and although it wasn't his seed, it was his love for her that made it happen. Rigel knew it was him who had made love to her. It was him who planted the seed. It just wasn't his seed. There was a reason he wasn't able to tell her everything.

There was a reason why his father told him and there would be a reason why he would tell his son when his son had a need to know. The goal of any Top-Secret project is to further the project without releasing details except to those who have clearance and have a need to know. As much as it sounded counterintuitive to Rigel, Anna wasn't cleared to learn about the Plan, therefore she didn't have a need to know. She definitely will play a role in making it happen, but it isn't in the Plan for her to understand. It was Anna's job to be a loving, nurturing, and caring mother of their child, and of that, Rigel had no concerns. Anna would be the best mother possible. She nurtured and cared for him, and Rigel knew that would grow exponentially for their son.

As he reached this conclusion, Jim walked into the room. "The plane is ready for you when you're ready to board," Jim announced.

"I'm ready. Thanks so much for all you do, Jim, and for being such a good friend. I can't imagine going through this on my own without you here," Rigel responded.

"It's my pleasure, Rigel. I hope you got some of your questions answered and feel comfortable with the mission you've been given," Jim replied.

"I have, Jim. I still have questions, but the main ones have been answered, and I am more than comfortable with this mission," Rigel remarked.

"Said like a trooper," Jim joked, "now get on that plane and head back to your lovely wife."

"I wish someday I could bring Anna here to meet you. She would enjoy that," Rigel offered.

"I would enjoy that, as well," Jim responded.

Rigel nodded as he walked to his room to get his bag. He double checked the room to make sure he hadn't left anything, and as he closed the door, he realized another chapter in this journey had just ended. He was convinced there would be many more chapters to come.

Chapter Forty-One

It felt good to be back home. Anna was off running errands when he arrived at the house. Although he couldn't wait to see her, to hold her, he realized a little time to relax after such a heavy couple of days wouldn't hurt either. He plopped down on the bed and laid there staring at the ceiling. A vision of Anna immediately appeared, so beautiful, so loving.

"Thank you for bringing her into my life," he prayed in his mind.

"You deserved someone so special," shot through his mind in response.

Whoa, that had never happened before. He often turned to prayer in his life, but never had he received such a clear response from God. Sometimes he was thanking God and showing appreciation, sometimes he was requesting something, and sometimes he was asking for guidance or forgiveness, but never had he received such an immediate and clear response.

As he pondered, he heard the garage door lifting. Anna must be home. He jumped up from the bed and raced down to the garage to meet her. She had barely gotten out of the car when he was upon her, hugging her tightly.

"Careful, Cowboy, you're squeezing the two of us," Anna joked. Rigel immediately lessened the intensity of his hug; didn't abandon it, just made it less intense.

"So, you missed us?", Anna asked.

"More than you'll ever know," Rigel responded as he finally released her.

"How'd your meeting go?", Anna inquired.

"Oh, you know. Same ole, same ole," Rigel responded. It pained him a little that he wasn't able to tell Anna everything, but deep down he understood.

"Are you here to help carry in the groceries?" Anna asked.

"It's the only reason I showed up," Rigel joked.

Anna loved how playful they were with each other. Joking and teasing brought a layer of comfort to their marriage. There were so many important things to discuss and worry about; their playfulness was a refreshing escape.

"That's a pretty big belly you have there," Rigel teased, but immediately realized he had gone too far when the smile disappeared from Anna's face.

"Am I getting too fat? Am I putting on too much weight?", Anna began panicking.

"No, no. That's my bad. I was trying to make a joke, but my teasing went too far. You're not fat. You're carrying our son. And even if you had put on a few extra pounds, even if you became as big as a house, it wouldn't matter. I'd still be madly in love with you," Rigel countered.

The look on Anna's face made it apparent he was only making matters worse. He was trying to be supportive, but he was making poor choices with his words and analogies.

Anna grabbed two bags of groceries out of the trunk, spun, and angrily stomped off into the house.

"What have I done?", Rigel thought to himself. He couldn't wait to see her, but his stupidity and his big mouth ruined it. He had just made the most important person in his life upset, no, worse than upset; he had made her furious. He somehow hurt her deeply and that's the last thing he ever wanted to do.

Rigel grabbed the remaining bags, closed the trunk lid, and sheepishly carried the groceries into the house. Anna was already emptying the contents of the bags she had brought in and was putting the groceries away. She ignored him completely.

After setting the bags down on the counter, he walked over to her, spun her until she was facing him, and said, "You married an idiot. I love you so much and I can't believe how my stupid jokes hurt you. I am so sorry. You are not fat. You are the woman I love more than anything else in the world and I can't stand the fact that I hurt you. Please forgive me."

Anna stood there for a moment just looking into his eyes. She saw the regret. Deep inside, she knew he wasn't trying to hurt her. Maybe it was the hormones. Maybe she just over-reacted. Instead of speaking, she just continued to gaze into his eyes. In them she saw a vision of him holding their newborn son. His smile was more incredible than she had ever seen on Rigel. He was proud, but more than that, he was thankful. He was going to make a wonderful father, and regardless of his lack of ability to determine when his teasing had gone too far, he was a wonderful husband. A tear spilled out of her eye and down her cheek. This wasn't a tear from being hurt; this was a tear of love, but Rigel didn't know that. To him, he had brought her to tears from his hurtful behavior and tears immediately formed in his eyes for having hurt her.

When Anna saw Rigel's tears, she realized she had now hurt Rigel, as well.

"Baby, I'm...", Rigel started, but Anna cut him off mid-sentence.

She put her finger on his lips and said, "No, Rigel. I'm sorry. I let my ego get in the way. When I was looking into your eyes, I had already gotten over it and forgiven you. The tear you saw was a tear of joy, but you had no way of knowing that. I should have told you what I was thinking. I should have explained how when I looked into your eyes, I saw a man who truly loves me. I saw a man who is a wonderful husband and is going to be a magnificent father to our son. I didn't communicate, Rigel. I left my tear up to interpretation. I'm sorry I did that and I'm sorry I hurt you."

With that, Rigel kissed her. It was a lingering kiss because they both needed it. Their lips touching was communication in another form. No words were needed. They both simply understood.

When they finally released, simultaneously they said, "I love you." As they both chuckled, Anna said, "Jinx, Coke!"

Laughing, Rigel responded, "I don't deserve you."

Rigel thought back to the first time Anna had said, "Jinx, Coke!" to him. He had never heard that expression before, so had no idea what it meant. They had been watching a hockey game together on television when their favorite team scored and they both simultaneously yelled, "Goal!" Anna immediately responded with "Jinx, Coke!" Rigel had looked at her rather strangely and Anna said, "What, you've never heard that before?" When Rigel admitted that he hadn't, Anna explained it was an old game where when two people say the same thing simultaneously, the first to yell "Jinx,

Coke!" wins and the loser has to buy them a Coke. In reality, Cokes were rarely ever exchanged, but it was kind of a fun game to play. And it just happened to be the perfect way to break the tension on such a difficult situation.

"Just remember how you think you don't deserve me the next time I ask for a foot massage," Anna teased. "In any event, I'm glad you're home. Now, fire up the grill because I bought us some steaks. Chop, chop!"

Rigel did what he was told smiling every step of the way.

Chapter Forty-Two

Later that evening, Rigel and Anna were sitting on the couch watching tv. Rigel's arm was around her and Anna's head rested comfortably on his chest. This was their favorite way to watch television.

They were watching some kind of documentary about Michael Jackson's life, and it was currently showing a concert Michael Jackson performed with Britney Spears. It was at Madison Square Garden in New York City on September 7, 2001. They were performing the song "The Way You Make Me Feel".

At first, Rigel was caught up in the choreography. Michael Jackson was known for it. He also liked the way Brittney Spears added to the story by strutting back and forth across the stage. As he began paying closer attention, he realized the words Michael and Brittney were singing closely resembled the way he felt about Anna.

The way you make me feel
You really turn me on
You knock me off of my feet
My lonely days are gone

I never felt so in love before
Just promise, baby, you'll love me forevermore
I swear I'm keepin' you satisfied
'Cause you're the one for me

He could feel Anna moving along with the music. He wondered what she was thinking, but he wasn't going to disturb the moment by asking. Instead, he pulled her a little closer and kissed the top of her head.

As Rigel continued to watch the performance, he began thinking about how talented Michael Jackson really was. From a child singer in the Jackson Five to undoubtedly one of the most popular solo artists of all times. People would die to see him and many of the dance steps he used in his performances were revolutionary. The Moonwalk, the Toe Stand, the Robot, and his precise, rapid spins were amazing and drove the crowds wild. On top of that, he was an amazing singer. His real talent, however, probably came from his ability to wow crowds. A relatively shy person in real life, this guy had the ability to command an audience like no other.

Then it struck him. Could Michael Jackson have been part of the Plan? He definitely was revolutionary in terms of his performances. He had talent that was out of this world. People went crazy for the chance to watch him perform. And, years after his passing, people were still enjoying his work today. He definitely could have been part of the Plan, for what purpose, Rigel didn't know, but being a leader in his field kind of stood out as an important clue.

That lead Rigel to thinking about other performers and the Beatles immediately popped into his head. Here was a group of four British musicians who took the world by storm and revolutionized music. Prior to the Beatles, the music industry focused mostly on single hit songs. The Beatles changed all that to an album-oriented art form. They were a self-contained band writing original music. They pioneered stadium concerts and blended several genres of music. They not only became legends, but they ushered in the rock era. The entire world moved from Elvis Presley to the Beatles as soon as they came on the scene.

Could one or more of the Beatles be part of the Plan? Could all of them? Those were good questions. Although John Lennon was killed by a lone gunman at the age of 40, and George Harrison passed away at the age of 58 from lung cancer, Paul McCartney and Ringo Starr are still going strong. After the Beatles broke up in 1970, each of them went on to solo careers and leading their own band.

"The Beatles led a revolution. They changed peoples' minds about many things. Each or all of them could definitely have been part of the Plan," Rigel thought to himself. "But why? Why did two of them die relatively young, yet two still go on?"

Rigel realized he didn't have an answer to that question. Besides, it was all speculation, and he may never know if they were part of the Plan, but it was interesting to explore how Michael Jackson and the Beatles made such an impact on humanity. Frank Sintra, Elvis Pressley, Dolly Parton, Johnny Cash, Willie Nelson, Cher, Garth Brooks, Beyonce, Celine Dion, Taylor Swift, there were so many stars that had affected humanity, and each could have been in the Plan. It was mind-boggling.

Then Rigel remembered what his Guide had told him. Sometimes people involved in the Plan were the next iteration. Maybe they were supposed to bring on the next improved generation and maybe they were just supposed to take the world to the next level. Rigel thought about that for a moment. While many of these stars had children, the next generation progeny really hadn't stepped up just yet. Maybe things were happening behind the scenes, or maybe the time was not yet right, or maybe what these stars had accomplished was enough. Maybe their assignment was to start a revolution, not necessarily start a lineage.

With Michael Jackson's concert tape finished, the documentary continued about his life. Rigel realized Anna had fallen asleep on his chest. He wasn't about to move her.

He would be there supporting her for as long as she wanted to remain in that position. He loved her that much.

I swear I'm keepin' you satisfied
'Cause you're the one for me

Chapter Forty-Three

When Rigel arrived at work the next morning, he had an important message that his boss wanted to see him. He immediately walked to his boss's office. The door was open, but Rigel knocked anyway.

"Rigel, thanks for coming in," his boss said.

"Not a problem. What's up?", Rigel asked.

Rigel's boss got up from his chair and walked over to shut the door. Rigel thought this was rather strange and was quite curious as to what was going on.

When his boss returned to his chair, he said, "Rigel, we're going to pull you off Project: Xaviar."

Immediately Rigel's mind began racing. His Guide had known about the project. He was confident he hadn't brought it up or mentioned it, yet his Guide seemed to know all about it. Was there a leak?

"We have something more important we'd like you to work on. This is even more top-secret than Project: Xaviar," his boss continued as he plopped an envelope down on the desk in front of Rigel.

Rigel looked at the envelope. He immediately noticed the designation TS//SAR-AEGIS/WAIVED at the top. He knew this meant Top Secret - Special Access Required. AEGIS must be the code name for the program and WAIVED meant the program did not require standard Congressional reporting.

As he began to open the envelope, his boss stopped him. "Not here. This may only be opened in a SCIF," his boss told him. Rigel noticed there was a seal on the edge of the envelope that would prevent someone from opening it without first breaking the seal. Although not unheard of, this was uncommon.

"I have scheduled the SCIF for you. Please go there now and read over the material. You'll find instructions and everything you'll need to get started," his boss informed him.

"What about Project: Xaviar?", Rigel asked.

"This takes priority. We will be moving Project: Xaviar to someone else," his boss replied.

"All-righty then, it's off the SCIF I go," Rigel said. As he walked out of his boss's office down to the SCIF he realized he probably should have used more professional language than "all-righty then". This seemed rather important and he didn't want his boss to think he wasn't taking it seriously. "Oh, well. What's done is done," he thought to himself.

The SCIF was on the same floor as his boss's office. In fact, it was right down the hall. Rigel was quite familiar with the protocol. Before entering, he showed his identification and signed a ledger controlled by the gatekeeper of the SCIF. He then stowed all his electronic devices in a lockbox, removed the key and took the key with him. When he was ready to enter, he moved to the biometric reader and looked into it where his retina was scanned and compared to the database. When the green light came on, the gatekeeper opened the door to the SCIF and as she did so, Rigel heard a whoosh of air. SCIF's were slightly pressurized to assure no contaminants, poisons, or harmful vapors could enter the SCIF while it was occupied. Rigel entered through the door. The gatekeeper remained outside but closed the door behind him.

Rigel walked to the table and took a seat. He was waiting for others to join him, which is what usually happens in a SCIF, but this time he saw the red light come on above the door meaning the room was being pressurized, secured, and acoustic protections were being applied to prevent anyone outside the room from hearing anything or eavesdropping. Once all systems were properly operating, the light above the door turned green.

Rigel nervously broke the seal on the envelope. He opened the flap and on the first page he once again saw the top-secret markings of TS//SAR-AEGIS/WAIVED.

"So, the project is called Aegis," Rigel thought to himself. He wasn't yet sure why this name was picked but remembered from Greek mythology that Aegis was a magical shield or breastplate. It was used to provide divine protection for Zeus and Athena, but it was also known to have spread terror among enemies.

Rigel spent the next two hours reading the contents of the envelope and then reading them again. He wasn't allowed to take notes and the instructions at the end of the package informed him he was to place the envelope and its entire contents into a burn bag and place it in the slot of the bin where documents to be destroyed were placed. They were called "burn bags" because that's exactly what would happen. They would be burned so no one else could ever read them. That meant Rigel needed to be able to remember and absorb every single word.

When he finished, he found himself wondering why he had been selected for this project. It had nothing to do with propulsion systems. In any event, he placed the envelope and all its contents into the burn bag and inserted it into the designated slot. He then walked to the door, pressed the button located near the biometric reader, looked into the scanner until he heard a beep and then waited for the gatekeeper to open the door.

Chapter Forty-Four

That night, sitting at the dinner table, Anna said to Rigel, "You look like you're deep in thought. Is something wrong?"

"No, nothing's wrong. I've just been assigned a new project at work and I'm not quite sure how to go about it," Rigel replied.

Almost immediately Rigel felt Anna's arms around his shoulders, pulling him in for a hug. She was standing behind him and kissed the top of his head as she said, "I'm sure if anyone can tackle it, you can."

Anna was always extremely supportive of Rigel, and he so appreciated that ability in her. He hoped he was being that supportive of her and that she could feel his attempts. At the same time, Rigel recognized he could probably do more. Anna was the most important thing in his life, so if he was ever to give maximum effort to someone or something, it should be her.

"You're always supporting me," Rigel began asking, "how can I better support you?"

"You support me just fine. Don't cut yourself short," was Anna's reply.

"No, I'm serious. I want to be the best husband a woman could ever have, but I don't know how to get there. I need you to guide me, to tell me what I could do to be even better," Rigel said.

"Well, I could always use more foot rubs," Anna said jokingly.

"I'd be glad to give you more foot rubs, but what else can I do?", Rigel asked.

"What I want more than anything is for you to just be you, Rigel. You're the man I fell in love with, and I love you for who you are. I hear a lot of my friends talking about how they wish they could change their husbands. I wouldn't change one thing about you," Anna replied.

"I appreciate that, pumpkin, but I want to do better. I want to be the best husband I could actually be. How do I get there?", Rigel continued.

Anna thought for a moment. "You know, there is one thing. You could share more when something is bothering you," she responded.

"You know my work dictates there is much that I cannot share with anyone, including you. And there are times when I'm thinking about some of those things when I'm around you. I know you understand I'm unable to discuss classified material, so how about this? I'm going to try harder not to bring my work home with me," Rigel offered.

"First off, I understand about your classified material completely. I may not always like it, but I understand there are things of which you're unable to discuss with me. As for the last part, you don't bring work home a lot. I rarely see you working on things from work when you're home with me," Anna replied.

"I may not bring physical things home, but trust me, sometimes there are a lot of things sloshing around in my mind. I'm going to try to do a better job of leaving those things at work. I do a good job of compartmentalizing things at work, so now I'm going to do a better job of **leaving** those compartmentalized things **at** work," Rigel responded.

"I've never considered it a problem, but if it helps you and makes you feel better, then go for it," Anna said with another hug.

"I love you," Rigel responded.

"I love you, too! Now let's get these dishes cleaned up because I'm hankering for a foot rub!" Anna said teasingly.

They both got busy cleaning up and soon the job was done.

"Can I get you a beer or a glass of wine?", she asked as they headed to the couch.

"No, thanks. I don't like drinking in front of you since you can't have one with me," Rigel replied as he grabbed the television remote and plopped onto the couch. Anna quickly joined him and assumed her cherished position under his arm with her head resting on his shoulder.

"What do you want to watch?", Rigel asked as he surfed through channels.

"You pick. I have a feeling I'm going to be sleeping in short order," she responded.

Rigel landed on a hockey game and then slid from his position on the couch.

"Where are you going?", Anna asked.

"Just getting in a better position for that foot rub," Rigel replied with a smile.

Anna so enjoyed Rigel's foot rubs. It wasn't necessarily his technique; it was more his touch. She relished his touch. It conveyed his love and there was nothing she cherished more. As he massaged, the tension began leaving her body and before she knew it, she was sound asleep.

Once he realized she had fallen asleep, Rigel slowly stopped rubbing and returned Anna's foot to the couch. He grabbed the throw from the back of the couch, draped it over her, and tucked it in around her. He slowly moved back to his original position on the couch so as not to awaken her and gently placed her feet on his legs. As he looked down at her feet, he felt a tingle move through him. Her feet were warm, delicate, and beautiful. He thought to himself how he had never really considered feet to be beautiful before. In fact, he had always considered them to be quite ugly, but Anna's were different. It was then that he realized that Anna's feet weren't just an anatomical object, they were part of Anna as a whole and in his mind everything about her was beautiful.

As he pondered that thought, he realized perhaps that's how he should look at the Plan. His part in the Plan may not be perfect and beautiful on its own, but if his participation helped make the entire Plan beautiful, maybe it was all worthwhile.

Suddenly some words, perhaps part of a quote rushed through his mind, though he had no idea of who may have said it. "Love can make things beautiful."

Chapter Forty-Five

This next morning at breakfast, Rigel said to Anna, "So, have you given any thought to names for my son?"

"You mean, OUR son?", Anna quickly responded.

"Yes, OUR son," Rigel said sheepishly.

"Well," Anna began, "I don't know what your thoughts are on this, but I think I would like to hold off until we see him for the very first time. I just have this feeling that once we see him, we'll know instantly. Are you okay with that?"

Rigel took a moment to think about it, "Well, that's a little unconventional, but there's not a whole lot conventional about either one of us. I think you might be right. I've known people who have picked out names beforehand and later wished they had named their child something else."

"My parents are going to flip out about this," Anna offered, "what do you think your parents will think?"

"I think both of our parents will expect nothing less from us," he said laughing.

While Anna was the confident bold one in the family, Rigel was the quiet analyzer. Although direct opposites, together their characteristics complimented each other's and resulted in some pretty innovative ideas. He knew both their parents wouldn't be the least bit surprised by their unconventional means of naming their son.

"I just have one request," Rigel added.

"What's that?", Anna inquired.

"That we don't name him Rigel. I've always hated that name," Rigel laughed.

"Well, I happen to love it and the man behind it, but yes, I promise you we won't name him Rigel," Anna agreed.

"And no stuffy names," Rigel interjected.

"Stuffy names?", Anna questioned.

"You know, like Sevington," Rigel offered giggling.

"Sevington? Who in the world would name their child Sevington? And what does that even mean?", Anna protested laughingly.

"Exactly," Rigel responded.

Anna, still giggling, ran over and gave Rigel a hug. "I am so crazy about you," she offered.

"Crazy ABOUT me, is fine. I have trouble with just CRAZY," Rigel said chuckling as he held her in his arms. Just as she was about to pull away, he pulled her closer and kissed her and she kissed him right back.

"Sevington," Anna chuckled as she finally pulled away.

Chapter Forty-Six

Project: Aegis was proving to be quite the challenge for Rigel. He wondered why he had even been chosen for this project since it had nothing to do with propulsion systems. It was more in the weaponization field, or anti-weaponization field.

He was introduced to some new technology that had never been used before, and he had no idea where some of it came from. All he was told was that it was revolutionary.

The project itself appeared unreachable to Rigel at first, but once introduced to this new technology, he realized that with some tweaks, it might actually be possible. The project involved neutralizing an enemy's weapon utilizing surface ablation plasma, phasing/shielding barriers, neutralized particle beams and artificial gravity wells. It all sounded like science fiction, but each component had already been proven on its own using quantum physics. Each component had its advantages, but someone had determined it would require all four components to effectively do the job. Rigel's challenge was to figure out how to use all four components together to accomplish the job.

The main gist of the project was to design a system that could be used to neutralize an enemy's weapon. This would include making the weapon incapable of firing by neutralizing the weapon or destroying the kinetic energy or projectile if it had already been fired. This was a tough enough job, but the other component was the system must do so without harming the enemy that fired it. For example, if an enemy was attempting to use an RPG, the system had to be capable of either rendering the launch system inoperable or of destroying the weapon itself without harming the person who launched it. In a larger scenario, if a nuclear weapon were launched, the system would need to be capable of neutralizing the launch system itself or in neutralizing the missile without detonating the nuclear warhead. Instead, it must prevent the warhead from ever becoming operational. Rigel could see how beneficial the Aegis system could be in the situation of a nuclear warhead as it would prevent nuclear weapons or armaments from ever being used if it somehow got into the wrong hands. It wasn't going to be a simple task, but he could quickly see how valuable it would be to the U.S.

The first element Rigel would be working with was Surface Ablation Plasma. This involved using extremely high energy to damage or vaporize the surface of a target. Although effective, he was going to have to be careful with this one as the directive of the project was to create a system that would destroy or disarm weapons but not harm the operator of the weapon. Not an impossible task, but not an easy task either.

The next element involved Phasing/Shielding Barriers. This is basically a force field created by projecting energized, magnetic, or particle fields to protect an object. They would work by absorbing, deflecting or converting energy from incoming kinetic or radioactive energy weapons. In this application, a Phasing Barrier would be used to protect the person operating the overall system so they could not be harmed while the system was in use.

Neutralized particle beams were the third component. This element involved advanced directed energy that fires neutral, high velocity subatomic particles, like neutrons, to penetrate, irradiate, or thermally destroy targets. Although not commonly used, this type of weapon was already available in the U.S. arsenal to eliminate or temporarily disarm targets. The problem Rigel would need to solve is how to utilize it without causing permanent damage. That was one of the strange parts about the objective for this project. The system he was to design was to destroy or disarm weapons but not harm the person using them.

Imagine being on a battlefield when you see an enemy pointing a gun at you. The system Rigel would be designing would be capable of eliminating or disarming the weapon without harming the operator of that weapon. That would be a pretty hefty task, but extremely valuable if he could pull it off.

The fourth and final element was Artificial Gravity Wells. This involved utilizing spinning habitats created by a constant engine accelerator or advanced "grav-plating" technology to simulate 1G of gravity, regardless of its actual G force, while also avoiding the complexities of zero-gravity.

This one would be Rigel's most difficult. Although he was very familiar with the effects of gravity in terms of propulsion systems, he wasn't used to assuring the environment remained at 1G. His propulsion systems worked in extreme conditions, such as 10, 20, 30, 40 Gs or higher, so he never had to consider how to reduce every situation to 1G and especially avoid zero-gravity. This one was going to take some work.

Rigel knew, however, that he was up for the challenge. Whatever the government gave him, he always gave his best effort to accomplish. It may take a while, but he'd see it through.

Chapter Forty-Seven

One of the things Rigel and Anna enjoyed doing was hiking. They had taken many long treks over the course of their relationship. They loved enjoying the fresh air and nature. Anna had spoken to her doctor about these hikes and asked if they were still allowed. Her doctor explained long hikes shouldn't be a problem through the 28th week of pregnancy, if she could tolerate them. Her doctor also cautioned her "not to go crazy".

Since her 28th week was approaching, that Saturday Anna recommended to Rigel that they go on a hike. He was excited about the idea and immediately knew which trail to take. They lived not too far from a national forest, and it was so beautiful this time of year. Although remote, the paths were well marked, there were very few steep inclines and the views were spectacular. He couldn't wait.

Anna packed some sandwiches and snacks while Rigel got the backpack ready. Normally they would both carry a backpack to keep the load on each of them lighter, but with Anna being pregnant, Rigel decided he would carry all the weight. He placed the rain gear into the backpack. It wasn't supposed to rain, but you never know and better safe than sorry. He also brought along a compass. It was a bit old fashioned as most hikers now used the compass on their cell phone, but it was one he had earned when he was a boy scout, and he always brought it along when hiking. They wouldn't be cooking and it wasn't supposed to get cold, so he didn't need matches or fire-starting tools, so he left them in the cabinet. There was also no reason to bring along a hatchet as that would just add extra weight. He did, however, place his pocket-knife into the backpack. His pocket-knife was loaded with all sorts of blades and tools, and you never knew how it could come in handy.

When he finished packing the backpack, he brought it into the kitchen to load up the sandwiches and snacks Anna had prepared.

"Where's my backpack?", Anna inquired.

"It's on your belly," Rigel joked. "I can carry the load today."

Anna didn't complain. Rigel filled the remaining space in the backpack with bottles of water. When everything was packed, they both grabbed their hiking boots and headed to the car.

It was only about a 30-minute drive to the trail. When they arrived, they changed into their hiking boots, Rigel grabbed the backpack and the walked to the mouth of the trail.

"I've been looking forward to this," Rigel said.

"Why? Are you stressed?", Anna asked.

"Maybe a little," Rigel confessed.

"Is it about work or because I haven't been the easiest to be around the last few weeks?", Anna inquired.

"You have been amazing through this pregnancy," Rigel explained. "I can't even begin to imagine how tough it is to have another human growing inside your body and you haven't complained one bit."

"That's because I've had the best husband in the world to help me through it," Anna said as she leaned over to kiss him on the cheek.

The hike was an easy walk, and the weather was perfect, not too hot and not too cold. The temperature was just enough to work up a sweat, but not cold enough that you became chilled when you stopped to rest.

About 30 minutes into the hike, Anna had a funny feeling. Something wasn't right. It wasn't an actual pain, but something was happening and she could feel the baby moving around more than normal. She placed both of her hands beneath her belly to try to support a little, but it didn't seem to help. Rigel seemed oblivious as he just kept hiking.

"Hold up, Cowboy," she called to him.

He had gotten about ten steps ahead of her and when he turned and looked at her, he saw a worried look on her face.

"What's wrong?", he asked.

"I'm not sure. Something just doesn't feel right," Anna responded.

Just then a large dog came out from behind the trees ahead of them. He was snarling with his mouth open, and saliva was dripping from the edges of his mouth. Rigel immediately wondered if the dog was rabid. He had never experienced a rabid dog before, but he had seen pictures on the internet. This one looked pretty close to the pictures.

The dog stopped in its tracks and continued snarling at them. Rigel moved over in front of Anna to protect her, but he didn't know how he was going to do that with nothing in his hands to fight the dog off. He knew he had a pocket-knife in the backpack, but he didn't want to make any moves to remove the backpack from his back and retrieve it. Instead, he slowly reached into his pocket for his cell phone. He kept one eye on the dog and the other on the cell phone's screen when he realized his phone said NO SERVICE. He remembered that his cell phone had the capability to switch to satellite in the event of an emergency where no cell signal was available, but just as the phone connected and started to dial, his battery suddenly went from 67% to zero. It wasn't a gradual loss of power; it was sudden and the phone went completely black. Rigel could feel his heart rate increasing. Did he tell Anna or did he keep it to himself? It took him a moment, but he decided that maybe this wasn't the time for more surprises.

He could feel Anna squirming behind him. "Are you okay?", he asked.

"I'm not sure. The baby is not liking this one bit, and neither am I," she said in a whisper.

The dog took one step closer, and Rigel and Anna took two steps backward. There was something evil in the dog's eyes and Rigel was almost sure the dog was getting ready to attack.

"Please, God, help us out of this," Rigel said softly.

As the dog moved another step closer, a hawk suddenly came out of nowhere and flew right towards the dog. It didn't touch the dog but looked like it was going to. That immediately drew the dog's attention from Rigel and Anna. The hawk swooped close to the dog's face, then quickly turned and climbed. The hawk circled and was coming in for another attempt. This time when the hawk swooped, it came in talons first. When the dog saw what was coming, it immediately retreated and ran off into the forest. The hawk, having completed its mission, simply flew away.

"Whoa," Rigel exclaimed. "That was close."

"Too close," Anna replied.

"Are you okay?", Rigel asked.

"I think the baby is starting to settle down, but I think maybe I should call my doctor," she responded.

"I agree," Rigel said. "Unfortunately, my cell phone is dead." He didn't see the need to go into any further explanation.

After he explained, Anna said, "That's strange. I thought you had it plugged in and charging as we drove up. This has all been strange and I don't like it. Let's just go home."

Anna was always one for an adventure, but he could see the panic in her eyes. He put his arm around her, and they headed down the path back to their car. It was about a 30-minute walk back, but they did not speak. They just kept walking.

When they made it back to the car, Rigel said, "It's Saturday. Is your doctor even in today?"

"She takes Saturday morning appointments to accommodate her patients that work, so I think she is," Anna replied.

Rigel got Anna safely inside the car and then plugged in his cell phone. It immediately came to life, showed it had a 5G signal and 67% of battery life remaining. Rigel had a feeling he knew what had happened, but this was no time to get Anna any more anxious than she already was. He selected Anna's doctor's number from his directory, hit the call button and then placed the phone on speaker while it remained in the charging holder.

"Dr. Anston's office, how may we help you?", the voice on the other end of the line answered.

"Is Dr. Anston in? This is Anna Emerson and I just had an episode I'd like to discuss with her."

"If this is an emergency, we suggest you go to the Emergency Room," the voice said almost coldly.

"The emergency is over; I just need to tell her what happened," Anna stated emphatically.

"I'll give the message to Dr. Anston and she will call you when she has time," the icy voice informed her. "What's a good number to reach you at?"

Anna provided Rigel's number since her cell phone was still at home and hung up.

"Huh!", was all that Anna said.

"I heard. She seemed rather blunt with you," Rigel interjected.

"That's what I thought. I've never known anyone at that office to be so cold," Anna replied.

On the drive home, Dr. Anston called. "Anna, are you okay?", she asked.

"Yes, I'm fine now but we were in a rather hairy situation and the baby started moving a lot. I just wanted to make sure this was normal," Anna answered.

"Well, it can be normal under stressful situations, but why don't you swing on by, and we'll check to make sure everything's okay," Dr. Anston responded.

"Are you sure you have time? The person who picked up the phone in your office made it seem like you were quite busy," Anna replied.

"That must have been our answering service. Sometimes my staff switches over to the answering service if they need to leave the desk for any reason. We've had complaints lately about how they are treating some of our patients when the patient calls, so when you get here, I want you to tell me exactly what happened on the call. I don't want my patients treated like that," Dr. Anston stated.

"I will. We're about 30 minutes out, so I'll see you soon," Anna replied

"Looking forward to it," Dr. Anston said and then hung up.

"Well, I guess we're headed to Dr. Anston's office," Anna said to Rigel.

"On my way," Rigel replied.

As they drove, Rigel thought about everything that had happened. It was strange to see a dog like that. They had never come across anything so scary on those trails before. It was also strange how his cell phone first showed NO SERVICE and then the battery suddenly drained. It was a fairly new phone, and he had never experienced anything like that before either. It was especially odd that as soon as he plugged the phone in when they got back to the car, that it showed it had 67% power remaining. Thank goodness that hawk came by to scare the dog away.

Then he heard it. It was a soft voice in his head that said, "Evil will threaten, but remain faithful, Rigel. I have your back." He recognized the voice immediately. It was that of his Guide's. That meant that what happened today wasn't random. He and Anna had been threatened by evil, but his Guide had intervened. Rigel wondered why evil chose them to threaten. It didn't make any sense. They weren't doing anything wrong. "Why us?", Rigel thought to himself when the Guide's voice returned, "Because your baby is extraordinary."

Whoa! Evil wasn't coming after he or Anna, it was coming after their baby? "Remember, Rigel, we will protect you and your family," his Guide said softly.

This whole day was becoming stranger by the moment.

Soon they were at Dr. Anston's office. The minute they walked through the door, a nurse scurried to greet them. "Come right on back. Dr. Anston is waiting for you," the nurse told them.

They followed the nurse into Dr. Anston's office where Dr. Anston was sitting behind the desk. When she saw Anna and Rigel arrive, she immediately stood up and asked Anna to have a seat. "First, tell me how you're feeling and then tell me what happened," Dr. Anston ordered.

Anna explained that she felt fine now but shared how she felt when they came upon the dog. She told her doctor there was no pain, just a lot of commotion going on in her belly and a lot of discomfort. She shared that she felt fine now and the baby had simmered down.

"Let me take a listen," Dr. Anston said as she took her stethoscope from around her neck, warmed up the listening bell with her hands, placed the earpieces in her ears, and then placed the listening bell on Anna's abdomen. She moved the stethoscope around and listened in several different places. "Everything sounds good," Dr. Anston told her, "but let's get an ultrasound just in case." With that, Dr. Anston exited the office and walked down the hall.

Almost within seconds, a nurse appeared and asked Anna and Rigel to follow her. She directed them to a room and asked Anna to get up on the table.

"Do I need to put a gown on?", Anna asked.

"No, I think you'll be able to just pull up your shirt a little," the nurse replied.

Dr. Anston entered the room, pulled the ultrasound machine toward the table on which Anna was positioned, applied gel to the paddle and began. It only took a few moments before Dr. Anston proclaimed, "Everything looks perfect!"

Those words were greatly welcomed by Anna and Rigel. Such a hectic day but thank goodness everyone was okay.

Chapter Forty-Eight

Rigel found himself calling to his Guide in his head. He had questions and felt he needed to meet with his Guide for some answers.

Upon arriving at work on Monday morning, he booted his computer and opened his calendar. It was going to be a busy week with meetings scattered everywhere. As he was looking at his calendar, suddenly items began disappearing, one by one. Someone was deleting his appointments and clearing his schedule. He walked out to his administrative assistant's desk and was about to inquire as to what was going on. Judy, his administrative assistant, looked up and said, "Oh, good morning, Dr. Emerson. I was just about to come in to talk to you. I just received word to clear your schedule for tomorrow. It appears an important meeting has come up that you need to attend."

"Well, that answers that," Rigel thought to himself.

"Thank you, Judy. I saw items disappearing from my calendar and wondered what was going on. Any idea what this special meeting is about?", Rigel asked.

"No, sir. I just was told to clear your schedule. I'm sure more information will be forthcoming," Judy replied.

"You're the best," Rigel smiled and went back into his office.

Later that morning, Judy came rushing into Rigel's office. "I'm so, so sorry," she exclaimed. "A clerk just delivered this envelope and without even looking, I opened it. The funny thing was the two sheets of paper inside were blank. There was nothing on them. As I relooked at the envelope to see if I could determine who sent it, I saw it had printing on it that said, 'To be opened by addressee only'. I'm sorry, I should have caught that, and I shouldn't have opened it. It's strange though that someone sent you two blank pieces of paper." Judy's face was flushed and she was obviously embarrassed for not having followed protocol.

"Well, since the pages were blank, I guess no harm done. Good thing it didn't contain anything classified. In the future, though, please check the envelope first. If this had been something top-secret or sensitive, you could have gotten yourself in trouble. You know I trust you, Judy, but the rules on handling sensitive information are rather strict," Rigel explained.

"I understand, sir," Judy replied. "I'll do a better job of watching for any markings on envelopes or packages that are delivered. It won't happen again." She was still shaken and a little teary eyed, so Rigel felt some kind words were needed.

"Judy, I trust you with my life. I have absolutely no concerns there. I just don't want to see you get in trouble. You're the best administrative assistant I've ever had, and I plan on keeping you for as long as I'm here," Rigel said trying to comfort her.

"Thank you for those kind words. They mean a lot to me," Judy said. Then she turned and left the office.

After Judy had left, Rigel decided to take a look at the contents of the envelope himself. When he pulled the two pages out of the envelope, they were indeed blank, but then something strange happened. Slowly writing began to appear on the pages. It was as if someone was typing each letter. He began to read as the words appeared, occasionally having to slow down to allow the appearance of more words. He thought to himself how strange it was that the human mind could read faster than it could type, but that appeared to be what was happening.

The message that appeared instructed him to fly to a meeting tomorrow morning. It didn't state where the meeting would be, only that he was to be at Sunport Airport at 7:30 AM on Tuesday, which was tomorrow. It didn't indicate where they would be flying to or what the meeting was about, but it did say that they would be arriving back at Sunport Airport by 5:00 PM the same day.

Rigel placed the pages back into the envelope and placed it in his briefcase.

Chapter Forty-Nine

After work that evening, when Rigel arrived home from his commute, Anna was waiting for him in the garage. The garage door was already open, as was one of the rear doors of Anna's car. She shut it when she saw him approaching so he could pull into the garage.

Rigel shut off the engine, got out of the car and walked over to where Anna was standing. He gave her a big hug and a kiss on the cheek. Then he said, "Hmmm, you appear to be deep in thought."

"I'm just trying to figure out which car seat to buy," she answered. "There's so many of them, so first I did a search on the safest, then I trimmed that list down by the most popular. Now I'm trying to figure out which color matches the interior of my car."

"So many decisions," Rigel replied. "I didn't know they even came in colors."

"Neither did I," Anna responded. "Color choices are definitely limited, but there are some choices to consider. I was originally thinking of just going with the black because that would work in both our cars, but do you think that might be too hot for the baby?"

"Hmmm, maybe," Rigel answered. "We have air conditioning, but with whatever color you choose, we'll have to remember to cool down the car first on hot days before putting the baby into the seat."

"True. Wait, what do you mean whatever color 'I' choose? I thought we were in this together," Anna teased.

"Oh, we definitely are. I just don't think you want my color coordinating abilities making decisions. Not only am I terrible with colors, but I don't have very good taste either," Rigel joked.

"Let me give it a little more thought," Anna said as she walked with Rigel into the house.

"What's for dinner?", Rigel asked.

"Absolutely nothing," Anna responded. "I had a lazy day today and I thought we could order take-out delivery."

"Sounds like a plan to me," Rigel said.

After Rigel changed into more comfortable clothes, he walked back out into the kitchen and saw Anna was on the phone. "Pizza okay, or would you prefer Chinese?", she whispered as she covered the mouthpiece of the phone with her hand."

"Pizza is fine," Rigel answered.

While Anna was finishing the call, Rigel went to the refrigerator and pulled out a pitcher of iced tea. He held it up, lifting his eyebrows in attempt to ask Anna if she wanted one without interrupting her. She shook her head affirmatively, so he got out two glasses from the cabinet, filled them both with ice and then added the iced tea.

With the call ended, Anna walked over to grab her glass and then sat on one of the stools at the kitchen island. "So, how was your day?", Anna said kind of sing-songy.

"It was good, but I have to fly to a meeting tomorrow," he replied.

"Oh, no. Gone again?", Anna protested.

"Don't get your underwear in a wad, it's only a day trip. I should be back here by six or six-thirty," he teased.

"That's not so bad. I think I can handle that. What's your meeting about?", Anna asked.

"Not sure. Must be some of that secret stuff because they didn't include anything in the invite. Works for me because that means I don't have to prepare anything," he replied.

"You boys......and girls....with all your top-secret stuff. You can have it. I don't like to have to keep secrets. I'm always afraid of slipping up," she quipped.

"Ahhh, so you have secrets?", Rigel asked.

"Only about my hot boyfriend," Anna teased. "He's this big brave scientist who goes to secret meetings all the time."

Rigel loved the way Anna teased him. She always got this little twinkle in her eye and a smirk of a smile on her lips. He was so in love with this woman.

Anna grabbed her iPad and began showing Rigel the different child car seats she was considering. He wasn't really interested, but he knew this was important to her, so he feigned it. He could tell she was leaning towards this one model, so he pointed that one out and said, "This one looks good."

"That's exactly what I was thinking," Anna said gleefully. Rigel just smiled.

It wasn't long before the doorbell rang. The pizza delivery person was at the door. "I'll get it," Rigel said as he made his way to the door.

When he opened the door, he saw a young girl holding a large pizza box. "Emerson?", she asked.

"That's us," Rigel replied.

"The total was $22.05," the young girl said.

Rigel reached into his wallet and grabbed two twenties. "Here's $40. You can keep the change."

"Wow! Thank you. I don't usually get such good tips," the girl said with a smile as she took the money.

"You're very welcome and thanks," Rigel said.

"No, thank YOU!", the girl replied as she spun and walked away.

"Pretty generous of a man who has to support a family," Anna teased.

"I liked her eyes. I'm thinking of keeping her around in case you run off with that boyfriend of yours," he teased right back.

Chapter Fifty

The next morning, Rigel arrived at the airport about fifteen minutes early. Already waiting for him was Captain Graves.

"Good morning, Dr. Emerson," Captain Graves greeted him as he walked through the door.

"Good morning," Rigel replied. "Are we going to the Lodge? That's a long flight for just a day."

"No, sir. We have a different destination for you this morning. I can't say much more than that until we get into the air. Hope you understand," Captain Graves offered.

"Not a problem," Rigel replied as he followed Captain Graves out onto the tarmac.

As Rigel boarded the plane, he saw Captain Holmberg in the pilot's seat going over some weather charts. "Good morning, Captain Holmberg," he offered.

"Good morning, Dr. Emerson. Looks like it will be smooth flying all the way to our destination," Captain Holmberg replied.

Rigel turned to walk down the aisle of the airplane and saw Jen waiting for him near the seat he had most recently been using. "Good morning, Dr. Emerson," Jen smiled and said.

"Good morning, Jen. So good to see you again. Same routine?", Rigel asked.

"Yes, sir. Sit anywhere you'd like. You are our only passenger again today," Jen responded.

Rigel sat in his usual spot and buckled up. Jen immediately returned with coffee and a fresh danish. "You spoil me," Rigel said to her.

"That's what I enjoy doing," Jen said with a smile.

It wasn't long before they were in the air. Once they had climbed above 10,000 feet, Captain Graves came over the loudspeaker. "Thanks for flying with us this morning, Dr. Emerson. It's a rather short flight this morning. We will be headed to Groom Lake. It should be smooth sailing the entire way and we will be there in about an hour and a half, so sit back and enjoy your flight."

"Groom Lake? That's Area 51," Rigel thought to himself. He had not been there before, but he'd heard lots of strange stories. He couldn't help but wonder if he would be seeing aliens. He'd heard stories about how some may be there. Perhaps this was going to be an exciting trip after all.

It wasn't long after Rigel finished his danish that Captain Graves once again came on the loudspeaker and reported, "We are beginning our initial descent into Groom Lake. We should touch down in about 20 minutes."

Rigel glanced out the window but saw nothing but desert below. Perhaps they were still too far away to see anything.

As the minutes ticked by, Rigel continued glancing out the window. "Nope, don't see anything yet," he thought to himself.

He then felt the plane make a steep left turn and descend quickly. It was only a matter of minutes before he felt the tires hit the surface of the runway. As the plane slowed, he could barely eek out seeing some buildings in the distance. Some of them looked like airplane hangars and others looked more squarish. At one point, the plane exited from the runway down a ramp towards the buildings.

When the plane came to a complete stop, he unbuckled and started to get up from his chair. Jen quickly ran towards him. "Please stay seated, Dr. Emerson. It's standard procedure for them to board the plane and check credentials prior to allowing you to deplane."

Rigel wasn't surprised about the additional security procedures. They were uncommon, but he supposed the utmost precautions were needed at this facility.

Jen scurried up the aisle to open the cabin door. Very quickly, two rather large men dressed in what almost appeared to be SWAT uniforms boarded the plane and headed right for him.

"Dr. Emerson?", one of the men asked.

"That's me," Rigel replied wishing he had chosen words that were a little more professional.

The man pulled out a small device. "Please place the tip of your right index finger on the glass." Rigel did as he was instructed knowing this was a fingerprint scanner. The light on the device immediately turned green. Using the same device the man instructed him to look into the eyepieces attached to the end of the box. This was obviously a retinal scanner and the light on the box turned green as soon as he looked into it.

"Thank you, Dr. Emerson. That's all we need. Now please follow my colleague to one of the waiting cars," the man said.

Rigel, following directions, rose from his seat and followed the other gentleman down the aisle of the plane, through the door and down the steps. Waiting on the tarmac were two black SUVs with blackened windows. He was directed to the second vehicle where the man opened the door for Rigel. Rigel climbed inside, took a seat and the man closed the door behind him.

Once the door was shut, Rigel found the inside of the vehicle to be pitch black saving for a strip of lights under the counsel in front of him. The windows were completely blacked out. There was soft music playing, but Rigel detected some white noise mixed in as well. He couldn't see into the driver or front seats of the vehicle due to a partition between them. Nothing was said, but he could feel the vehicle slowly start to move. He couldn't see where they were going due to the blackouts. He felt a few turns, but not knowing the layout of Area 51, he had no idea where he was. At one point, Rigel felt the vehicle may have gone in a circle or at least retraced a path, but it was hard to tell. Soon the vehicle came to a stop.

When the door was opened, Rigel discovered the SUV was inside a hangar. The man opening the door greeted him, "Good morning, Dr. Emerson. Welcome to Groom Lake."

"Thank you. Interesting place," was all Rigel could get out.

As he gazed around, he discovered there was nothing else in this huge hangar, not a plane, not a helicopter, not a truck, not an alien spaceship. He chuckled to himself as he thought of the last one. He wondered if they were real and if he'd have a chance to see one.

"Please follow me," the man said as he led Rigel to a door. When they arrived, the man used the retinal scanner to unlock the door for them to enter. They walked down a long hallway with nothing but cinder blocks on each side. No windows, no doorways. When they reached the end of the hall, there was another door. The man again used a retinal scanner to open the door and allow them through.

They had entered what Rigel recognized as a gowning room. This was a room where people put on gowns in preparation for entering a clean room. The man escorted Rigel over to a bin where the gowns were wrapped and sealed in plastic.

"Do you know how to put one of these on?", the man asked.

"Yes, sir. I've spent some time in clean rooms, so I am familiar," Rigel replied as he opened the package and began putting on his gown. These gowns had boots built right into them, which was a little different than the ones he was used to wearing, but he could see why these would be more effective. Rigel zipped up the gown, and the man handed him some nitrile gloves. Once the nitrile gloves were on, the man directed him over to a door with a window glass. Inside the room, Rigel could see a lab with lots of equipment. The man opened the door for Rigel and motioned him to enter.

Once inside the door, the man, remaining in the gowning room, quickly shut the door behind Rigel. Finding himself alone inside the lab, Rigel looked around and saw someone in a similar clean room gown walking towards him.

"Dr. Emerson, I presume," the man said. The voice was a bit muffled in the suit, but clear enough that Rigel could understand.

"Yes, and with whom do I have the pleasure?", Rigel asked.

"I'm Dr. Sharma and this is my lab," Dr. Sharma informed him. "We've asked you here today because we achieved a breakthrough with our gravity well and we were told this may be of interest to you."

Rigel was a little confused as he was thinking he would be meeting his Guide, but this sounded pretty interesting. "I'd love to see it," Rigel replied.

"Great, let's get started," Dr. Sharma said as he walked to the control panel. "Instead of explaining what we've discovered, I think it would be better if I just showed you first, then we can discuss and answer questions."

"Sounds good," Rigel replied eagerly.

Dr. Sharma pressed several buttons, and Rigel heard the machine starting up. There was a loud whirring sound that continued to get higher in pitch.

"I'm going to place this metal ball into the holder," Dr. Sharma explained as he placed a one-inch steel ball into a tripod type of holder. Once the ball was in place, Dr. Sharma returned to the panel.

Dr. Sharma pointed to a second tripod holder located about three feet away from the first. That holder was empty. "Now watch what happens," Dr. Sharma said as he hit a button.

The one-inch metal ball that was in the holder disappeared and suddenly reappeared in the previously empty holder three feet away.

"Wow! You transported it!" Rigel said.

"Not exactly, "Dr. Sharma began. "A transporter converts matter into energy or information, transmits it, and reconstructs the subject at a new location. What you just saw was the result of a Gravity Well. It's a bit deceiving because it looked like the ball disappeared and then reappeared on the second tripod, but in actuality, the ball was accelerated by negative gravity to the second location. It happened so quickly, your eye couldn't catch it. If we were to watch this at extreme slow-motion speeds, you would see the ball moving from one place to the other."

"That's pretty interesting. Is this the first application for which this has been used?", Rigel asked.

"To our knowledge, no one has ever done this before. We've used several different types of objects to verify the material used didn't impact the results, but the results have all been the same."

"Have you tested to see if any physical changes happened to the ball as a result of this test?", Rigel asked.

"We have. So far, we've detected no changes in the host material whatsoever," Dr. Sharma replied.

"Has it been tried on anything living?", Rigel questioned.

"No. We've only used inanimate objects. We would need to do a lot more testing before we would try it on anything living," Dr. Sharma responded.

"This experiment moved the object what looks to be about three feet. Have you tried other distances?", Rigel inquired.

"Not yet," Dr. Sharma replied. "We plan to conduct additional experimentation varying the distances and materials, but we were told to contact you right away as it may have some kind of impact on a project you may be working on."

Rigel had not been informed that Dr. Sharma or anyone at Area 51 had been read into Project:Aegis, so he refrained from talking about his project. Instead, he said, "Yes, thank you. This helps me a great deal. May I see it a few more times and may I review the slow-motion video to see the ball actually moving?"

"Absolutely," Dr. Sharma replied. "Let me just reset the system."

Dr. Sharma and Rigel spent the remainder of their time rerunning the experiment. They didn't vary any parameters as the discovery was so new, the math had not yet been worked out completely.

Rigel could see how this new discovery could assist his project. He had been thinking of gravity wells in a completely different way, but the way the gravity well was used in this experiment could be very beneficial.

The hours went on, but soon there was a knock on the glass of the door to the gowning room. Both Dr. Sharma and Rigel turned to see what it was. The man who had led Rigel from the plane was motioning for him to come over. As Rigel neared the door, the man pressed the button on the intercom and announced, "I'm sorry to interrupt you, but Dr. Emerson, you have another appointment."

With that, Rigel thanked Dr. Sharma and returned to the gowning room where he removed his gown and freshened up for his next appointment.

When he was ready, the man led him back down the long hallway and back to the hangar where the black SUV was parked. He opened the door for Rigel, and Rigel climbed back inside.

The next drive only took a couple of minutes. This time they stopped outside one of the block buildings. The man opened the door for Rigel and led him to the front door of the building. The man pressed a button, and a voice came across the intercom saying, "May I help you?"

"Dr. Emerson has an appointment with Colonel Wages," the man spoke into the intercom.

"Please ask him to come in," the voice said as the door buzzed and unlocked. The man opened the door for Rigel and directed Rigel inside.

Rigel found himself standing in a lobby. No one was around, but a man in uniform soon came down the hallway. Extending his hand to Rigel, he said, "Dr. Emerson, so good to have you. I'm Colonel Wages. I'd like to spend a few minutes debriefing you on your visit."

Debriefing him? Did that mean his visit was over? Rigel totally anticipated seeing his Guide. Not that the trip hadn't been worthwhile. After all, he learned a new use for gravity wells, but he was hoping to spend some time with his Guide and ask a few more questions.

Colonel Wages led Rigel back to his office where they spent the next 20 minutes in a security debriefing. In the debriefing, Rigel learned what he could and could not say about the project he just saw. Basically, it was what he could not say. The only thing he could tell anyone was that the trip was worthwhile. He wasn't allowed to mention gravity wells, or anything else he may have seen on the base. In fact, he couldn't even tell anyone he had been to Groom Lake. He could only say the trip was worthwhile.

Rigel was asked to sign an NDA. Kind of jokingly he said, "And what if I refuse to sign?" As soon as the words came out of his mouth, he regretted saying them. The look on Colonel Wages' face was a little startling and Rigel realized he may have just gotten himself in trouble.

"You may choose not to sign, Dr. Emerson, but then you will not be allowed to leave the base," he said sternly.

"Understood," Rigel said as he signed the NDA.

Chapter Fifty-One

Immediately after signing the NDA, Rigel was ushered to the SUV, which drove him out to the plane. Captains Graves and Holmberg were waiting for him and had already completed their safety check of the plane.

Rigel boarded the plane and Jen welcomed him aboard. "Can I get you anything?", Jen asked as Rigel settled into his seat.

"No thanks, Jen. I'm fine," Rigel replied. Jen nodded and went to buckle into her jump seat in preparation for takeoff.

The plane took off and quickly rose to cruising altitude. Rigel felt himself nodding off, so decided to tip the seat back and take a quick nap.

Once asleep, Rigel immediately began to dream. He envisioned himself driving his car on the highway. He suddenly had the urge to urinate. This was kind of strange because he rarely experienced such urges and never so suddenly. In any event, he pulled into a truck stop along the highway.

In his dream, after relieving himself, he picked up a pack of gum to purchase. It never felt right using a restroom at a truck stop without purchasing something. After making the purchase, he was exiting the building when he happened to notice a man sitting under a tree just off the edge of the concrete of the truck stop. It was a distance from the building, but the man still caught his eye.

For some reason, in his dream Rigel saw himself walking towards the man. He had long hair, a beard, and was dressed rather raggedly. He saw the man watch him as he walked over.

When Rigel reached the man, he could sense there was nothing to be concerned about, so he said, "Mind if I sit here?"

"Help yourself," the man replied.

Rigel set on the ground, not right next to the man, but close enough where they could carry on a conversation if the man was so inclined. He sensed the man was unaccustomed to people approaching him, so Rigel said nothing for a couple of minutes to give the man some time to adjust.

After a couple of minutes, Rigel asked, "You live around here?"

"Bout a mile down the road," the man replied. That would explain the bicycle leaning against the tree, Rigel thought to himself.

"My name's Rigel. What's yours?", Rigel asked.

"Troy," the man replied reaching out to offer a handshake. Rigel immediately extended his hand and the two of them shook.

"You look like a man with a story," Rigel said.

"We all have a story," Troy responded.

"I won't pry if you don't want me to, but I'd enjoy hearing yours," Rigel continued.

"Not much to tell," the man began. "Graduated from high school and began working on a ranch in Texas. The Gulf War started, so I decided to enlist. Served two tours of duty in the Middle East. Got injured. Got out, got married, had a son." The man suddenly stopped there.

"Where are your wife and son?", Rigel asked.

"Heaven," Troy replied.

"I'm sorry," Rigel offered.

"I'm sorry, too. Lost them both in a car accident. Not sure why I survived. I wish it had been me and not them. A semi came across the median. I swerved to miss him, but he caught the left corner of the car. Rolled and spun us. I was knocked unconscious. Woke up in the hospital only to hear the news that I had lost them both," Troy explained.

"I'm so sorry, Troy," Rigel said.

"They're with our Lord now. I'm just bidding my time until I can be with them," Troy responded.

"Are you hungry?", Rigel asked as he realized how thin the man was.

"I could eat," was Troy's response.

"Any preferences?" Rigel asked.

"Just about anything will do," Troy replied.

With that, in his dream Rigel saw himself get up and walk back into the convenience store side of the truck stop. He picked up a cheeseburger, some fries, an apple, and a Coke, brought them to the counter, paid for them, and then delivered them to the man.

When he handed the food to him, Troy just looked up with amazement. No one had ever done anything like this for him before. Times had been rough since losing his family. Between the grief and the PTSD, he had as a result of being injured in Afghanistan, he hadn't been able to hold a job. He lived in a run-down trailer about a mile away. He'd ride his bike here to shower in the truck stop showers and then he would often just sit under the tree and watch people.

Troy opened the sack and pulled out the cheeseburger. "Want half?", Troy offered.

"No, I've already eaten. That's for you," Rigel replied.

Troy didn't wolf the food down, but it disappeared quickly. Who knows how long it had been since he had eaten.

"What sort of wisdom do you have for me, Troy?", Rigel asked.

Troy thought for a moment and then replied, "Trust God in all things, even when you think it's hard."

Those were profound words and words he would put to good use. Rigel reached into his pocket and pulled out his wallet. He thumbed through the money he had in there, quickly counting it as he thumbed. It was $212. He pulled it all out and offered it to Troy.

Troy just looked at him and said, "I can't accept that."

"Sure, you can, and you will," Rigel told him. "You befriended me as a stranger and now, I'm helping my new friend. Our paths may never cross again but I have the strength of your advice and the satisfaction of knowing I tried to help."

With that, Troy took the money and said, "God bless you."

"God bless you, too, Troy," Rigel said. Then he turned, walked to his car and drove out of the parking lot.

Rigel awoke from his dream, but he remembered everything. He appreciated the advice the man had given him, and he wouldn't soon forget it. He wasn't sure why, but he knew this dream was going to stick with him for a while.

Just then, Captain Graves came on the intercom and advised Rigel to buckle up as they were nearing their final approach.

Chapter Fifty-Two

As soon as the wheels of the plane touched down, Rigel took his phone off "Airplane Mode" and it immediately began lighting up with missed phone calls and messages. He checked the messages first.

There was one from his father. His father rarely ever texted him. It said, "Rigel, call me as soon as you get this." He also saw a message from Anna that simply said, "Call your father."

Rigel wasted no time and dialed his father immediately. When his father picked up, Rigel said, "What's going on?"

"It's your mother," his father started. "She's had a heart attack. She's in surgery now."

"How bad is it?", Rigel asked.

"We don't know completely yet, but they needed to insert a stent right away. I'll call you as soon as the doctor updates me," his father advised.

"I'll catch the next flight out," Rigel said in a panic.

"No, let's wait until she's out of surgery and know more," his father responded.

"I want to be there for her, and you," Rigel interjected.

"I understand, but let's just let this play out. There's no reason to rush into anything. Besides, it's so close to Anna's due date that she shouldn't be flying and you need to be with her," his father replied.

Thinking about the emergency, Rigel had momentarily forgot about Anna being so close to delivering their son. He didn't know what to do.

"The doctor is coming down the hall now. I'll call you back after I talk to him," Rigel's father said and hung up.

He wasn't even off the plane yet and he was in full panic mode. As Jen came walking down the aisle, she recognized how pale Rigel had become. "Is everything okay?" she asked.

"My mother just had a heart attack," Rigel answered.

"Is she alright?", Jen questioned?

"Don't know yet. My father is talking with the surgeon now," Rigel replied.

"Let's get you off this plane so you can do what you need to do," Jen responded as she helped Rigel out of his seat.

Rigel exited the plane and didn't even recognize Captain Holmberg had said something to him on his way out. He just kept walking. A strange look appeared on Captain Holmberg's face as Rigel had never acted like this before. "I'll explain later," Jen said to Captain Holmberg.

Once Rigel got to the car, he called Anna. "My mother has had a heart attack," Rigel told her.

"I know. Your father told me. He called me when he was unable to reach you. He said he wanted to be the one who told you, so I didn't say anything," Anna told him.

"I'm not sure what to do. Should we fly there? Should I fly there? Should I wait to hear more?" Rigel said throwing out options and hoping Anna would help him pick one.

"Rigel, pray. What your mother and father both need right now is God's help," Anna replied.

That was good advice. He hung up from Anna and started to pray when he remembered his dream. Rigel remembered the words Troy had told him, "Trust God in all things, even when you think it's hard,"

"Dear Lord, please be with my mother and help her to pull through this. Be with my father because I know how hard this is on him. Protect Anna and our baby. Last of all, help me make the right decisions. Guide me. Tell me what to do."

Before he could even get "Amen" out, his cell phone rang. It was his father.

"The surgeon said your mother came through surgery well. They caught it before too much damage was caused. She'll be in ICU for a while and she'll probably need to make some lifestyle changes, but the doctor is expecting her to recover well," his father said.

"Oh, that's a relief. I'll talk to Anna as soon as I get home and then I'll make arrangements to fly out," Rigel said.

"No, Rigel," his father said emphatically. "You need to be there for Anna. Your place is there with her right now. I can handle this. There's no reason for you to fly out here and just sit in a hospital room."

"But I want Mom to know I'm there for her," Rigel pleaded.

"Think about it, Rigel. What would your mother be telling you right now?", his father asked.

"She'd be telling me to stay with Anna," Rigel answered.

"Absolutely," his father replied.

"But if anything changes, I'm hopping the first flight out," Rigel demanded.

"We'll cross that bridge if we come to it," his father responded. "They told me it would be about an hour before your mother was in a room and I could see her, so I think I'm going to get something to eat."

"That's a great idea. Keep me posted?", Rigel asked.

"I promise. Love you, son," his father replied.

"Love you too, dad," Rigel responded and then heard the call disconnect.

Rigel sat there in the parking lot for a few minutes thinking. He received devastating news, but by applying the words Troy had told him in his dream, everything worked out alright. Rigel had always been a strong believer, but he had also been the kind of person that felt he needed to do things on his own. He wasn't used to relying on anyone. Maybe the lesson he learned today was to stop being so stubborn and to let God handle the things that he was unable to handle on his own.

Just then, he heard his Guide's voice. "Remember all those questions you had for me, Rigel? Do you still have them?"

"No," Rigel replied, "I think relying more on God provided the answers I needed. I know you will tell me more when the time is right. I will just trust in God and in you knowing you both are working in my best interest."

For the first time since the plane had landed, Rigel felt himself at ease. His mother was still in the hospital, and Anna would be delivering soon. Both of those would be reason to worry for Rigel, but he was no longer panicking. He was in good hands. He had learned where to turn and who to trust.

Chapter Fifty-Three

When Rigel arrived home, Anna met him in the garage.

"Any word on your mom?", she asked.

"My father had called me. She's in a room now, awake and resting. It was quite a scare for both my mom and my dad," Rigel explained.

"I'm sure it was," Anna replied. "Are you going to fly out there?"

"No. My father seems to think he has it all under control. Besides, I need to stay here with you," Rigel responded.

"I'm fine. You could go out there for a few days if you wanted. My due date isn't until next week," Anna protested.

"No, she's in good hands. My father promised to keep me updated and if something happens, I can decide then whether or not to fly back then," Rigel replied.

Anna was a bit relieved, although she would never let Rigel know that. She knew she could go into labor at just about any time and not having Rigel around for the birth of their son would be difficult. At the same time, she would understand if he changed his mind.

"I have dinner waiting. When we're done, if you're not too tired, could you help me put the finishing touches on the nursery?", she asked.

"Never too tired for you. Let's eat! I'm starving," Rigel said giving her a hug. He snuck in a little kiss on her head in the process.

They walked arm in arm into the kitchen. Anna pulled a roasted chicken out of the oven. It smelled so good. She had made roasted carrots and potatoes to go along with the chicken. As she prepared to move the chicken onto a platter, Rigel said, "Let me do that." He bumped into her playfully which caused her to stumble and knocked the spatula she was using out of her hand. The spatula hit the floor with a splat from having been covered with the juices of the chicken from the bottom of the pan. Anna didn't say anything. She just gave Rigel one of her looks.

"Perhaps I'll go change my clothes before dinner," he said sheepishly as he walked into the bedroom.

"I think that's a fine idea," Anna chuckled.

At dinner, they talked a little more about Rigel's mother and Rigel shared everything he knew at that point. His mother had been treated for high cholesterol for years, so he had hoped that was enough to prevent a blockage. Apparently not.

When dinner was finished, Rigel was quick to remove the dishes to the sink. He rinsed them off and placed them in the dishwasher. Anna worked on the roasting pan to remove a stubborn remnant of chicken stuck to the bottom. It finally released, so she rinsed the pan and handed it to Rigel to be dried. Rigel dutifully complied and then handed it back to her to put away. Her hands immediately came up in protest.

"It goes on the top shelf, Cowboy," she instructed him.

"Wait. Then how did you get it down?", he questioned.

Anna just nodded to the pantry where they kept the stepstool.

"You're not supposed to be climbing ladders," Rigel quickly interjected.

"That's not a ladder, Einstein," she teased.

"Close enough," Rigel blurted out realizing what happens when he's not home to do things for her. Anna was strong-willed enough that she would just do things herself, even if cautioned against it.

With the kitchen chores done, Anna brought Rigel into the nursery. Rigel had painted it a sky-blue color the previous weekend. He realized he hadn't been back into the room since, because Anna had almost finished the room. She had the furniture back in place, the crib assembled and located near the wall, and several sports decorations hung.

"How did you get the furniture moved?", he asked.

"Don't go there, Rigel," she responded. He was smart enough to back off when he needed. He didn't like the idea of her moving furniture around, but he hadn't been there to do it for her. He also dreaded the thought of battling with hormones. It was a battle he knew he could not win.

"It looks nice," was all he said.

"I have one more decoration to hang and I thought it would be nice to do it together," Anna said as she picked up a cross from the table. It was made entirely of ceramic and had a little boy kneeling in the center. "I thought it could go above the door. Kind of like protection for our son."

Rigel thought that was a strange place to put it as you really couldn't see it unless you happened to look up when exiting the room, but he wasn't about to go there. If that's where she wanted it; that's where he would hang it. Besides, he liked the idea of the extra protection for his son.

As Rigel went to get the stepstool, Anna retrieved a hammer and a nail from the garage. Rigel got on the stool and placed the cross about where he thought it should be.

"A little lower and to your right," Anna instructed. Rigel moved the cross following her instructions. "A little more. A little more. Now back. No, too far."

Rigel could feel his impatience starting to build. He swallowed, took a deep breath and continued moving the cross until he heard the word, "Perfect!"

Rigel wasted no time marking the spot and driving the nail. He hung the cross on the nail and stepped down from the stepstool.

"There, now everything's perfect," Anna proclaimed.

"You're going to be such a great mom," Rigel said as he pulled her close. They both stood there looking at it.

It was a few seconds before she said it, but finally, "You're going to make a mediocre dad," she said giggling.

That's the Anna that Rigel had fallen in love with, the one who would tease him to no end. Every tease was a term of endearment to Rigel. He knew she only teased the people she truly loved.

Chapter Fifty-Four

It was only 9:15 PM when Rigel announced he was tired and going to bed. Perhaps today had taken more out of him than he realized.

He wanted so much to tell Anna about his trip to Groom Lake, but the NDA he was forced to sign prevented it.

Anna started turning off the lights around the house. "You don't need to come to bed so early if you don't want to," Rigel told her.

"No, I think I'll just come to bed and read for a while. For some reason that chicken didn't sit right with me," she said.

Rigel changed into his pajamas and hopped in bed. He was always amazed at the extensive ritual Anna needed to follow before retiring. She changed into her pajamas first. Then she scrubbed her face with this foamy stuff like you'd scrub the white walls on a car. She dried her face and then applied some cream. Then she applied some other cream. Then she checked her eyebrows for any strays. Then she brushed her teeth. Finally, she was ready for bed.

Rigel was already asleep by the time Anna got to bed. She shut off the light, opened her iPad and began reading.

Rigel felt a nudge. He looked at his watch. It was 1:15 AM. "I can't get comfortable," Anna said. "Would you mind getting a pillow out of the closet and putting it under my knees?"

Rigel rolled out of bed and retrieved the pillow. He gently placed it under her knees and said, "How's that?"

Anna jostled around a little and said, "Push it a little closer to my thighs." Rigel did as he was told. "I'll try that," she responded.

Rigel jumped back into bed and immediately fell back asleep.

Rigel hadn't slept long when Anna jostled him again. "I've got terrible indigestion," she said. "Do you think you could get me a Pepsid?"

"Absolutely," Rigel said as he jumped out of bed to retrieve the medicine. The Pepsid was chewable, but he brought a glass of water to help wash it down.

Rigel jumped back in bed, but this time he had trouble falling asleep. Anna kept moving around and he was concerned about her indigestion. After about fifteen minutes he heard, "There it is again."

"Is your indigestion coming and going?" Rigel asked.

"Yeah, it's strange," Anna replied.

"Do you think you might be in labor?", Rigel inquired.

"No. If I were in labor, I'm sure I'd know it. Just go back to sleep. I'll be fine," Anna told him.

It wasn't long before she started jostling again. "I can't get comfortable and the indigestion's back."

"Do you think maybe we should call the doctor?", Rigel asked.

"No, I'm sure it's nothing. It'll be fine," Anna retorted.

In thirteen minutes, it happened again. Anna was now getting concerned. "Maybe it is contractions. I've read about them but never experienced them before so I don't know what they should feel like."

"Let's call your doctor," Rigel said.

"Ok, get me my phone," Anna replied. Rigel knew this was serious if she was going to call the doctor, but he was relieved just the same. He didn't like seeing her so uncomfortable.

"I'm not due for another week," she said under her breath as she dialed.

Rigel listened as Anna spoke with the answering service who told her they would relay the message to Dr. Anston. Within minutes, Dr. Anston called. Rigel was only hearing one side of the conversation, so as soon as Anna hung up, he said, "What did she say?"

"She said it sounds like contractions and to head to the hospital," Anna said still in discomfort.

Rigel went into full panic. He ran to the closet to change his clothes, then he ran back to the bed realizing he hadn't even checked to see if Anna needed help getting up. Once he had helped her get up and going, he ran back to the closet to change. He grabbed the bag they had prepared for the hospital, carried it out to the car, backed the car out of the garage and left it running so it would cool the inside down, and then ran back to get Anna.

Anna was taking her time, and this was driving Rigel crazy. "C'mon, we have to get going," he exclaimed.

"Settle yourself, Cowboy. This may be my first rodeo, but at least I know enough not to just jump in with the bulls," she said teasingly.

He helped her to the car, got her inside, backed out of the driveway and sped down the street towards the hospital. He was wishing his car was equipped with red lights and sirens.

"Slow down, Rigel. We have plenty of time and we don't need to be getting into an accident," Anna proclaimed.

"I'm not going to get into...." Rigel barely got the words out of his mouth when he heard the siren and saw the red flashing lights coming up behind him. "There's always a cop when you don't need them," Rigel thought to himself.

The policeman pulled him over and got out of his police vehicle. He walked to Rigel's door. Rigel had already rolled down his window. Before the policeman said anything, Rigel blurted out, "My wife is in labor. I have to get her to the hospital!"

"Is this your first?", the policeman asked.

"Yes," Rigel replied.

"I figured," the policeman said chuckling. "How far apart are your labor pains, ma'am?"

Anna replied, "About thirteen minutes."

In a very calming voice, the policeman said to Rigel, "You have plenty of time. The important thing is that you get to the hospital safely. I can assure you that your baby won't be here for hours. I want you to take your time, drive within the speed limit, and get your wife to the hospital safely."

"Don't you think you should lead the way with lights and sirens?", Rigel asked. Both Anna and the policeman laughed at that one.

"There's no need for that, sir. Just take your time and get her there safely. There's not a lot of traffic on the streets this hour of the night, but I want you to still observe the speed limits. Is that clear?", the policeman asked.

"Yes, sir," Rigel said sheepishly.

"Then good luck and congratulations," the officer said before turning and walking back to his vehicle.

Rigel stared straight ahead. He didn't dare look over at Anna. He simply put the car in gear and slowly pulled away from the curb. He followed speed limits the rest of the way to the hospital.

He did well, but as soon as he pulled into the emergency room entrance, he began to get wired again. He pulled up right in front of the doors, jumped out of the car, ran to Anna's door, and helped her out. "Wheelchair!", he called out, "Woman in labor!"

An orderly came through the doors with a wheelchair. Both Rigel and the orderly helped Anna into the chair and the orderly wheeled her inside. Rigel followed, but as he reached the door, a security officer stopped him. "You can't leave your car there, sir," the security officer told him.

"My wife's in labor," Rigel said as he tossed the security officer the keys.

"No, no, no," the security officer interjected. "I am not your valet. You will need to move your own car to the parking area."

"What about my wife?" Rigel said in panic.

"It will only take you a minute and she will be right inside waiting for you," the security officer said.

Rigel turned around, ran to the car, moved it to the designated parking area and then sprinted back to the emergency room. Once inside, Anna asked him, "Did you bring the bag?"

Rigel turned immediately red, spun around, ran out the door, retrieved the bag from the car and then sprinted back. By the time he got back in the emergency room, he looked like someone who had just run a marathon.

Anna couldn't help it. She put her hand over her mouth trying to hide her laugh.

"What?", Rigel asked. Anna looked down at his shoes. He was still wearing his slippers.

"The guy's literally a rocket scientist," she said to the clerk at the window laughing.

Anna had pre-registered, so they had all her information. The orderly wheeled her through a pair of automatic doors into the emergency room. Rigel quickly followed.

Once in the room, the orderly helped her out of the wheelchair and then left the room with the wheelchair in tow. A nurse walked in, instructed Anna to get into a gown and get on the exam table. Once on the table, the nurse took her blood pressure and temperature. An ER doctor entered the room.

"So, you think you may be in labor?", the doctor asked.

"Well, I think so," Anna began to explain, "but with all this commotion, I'm not so sure. I haven't had any pains in a while." Anna was a little embarrassed about this, but the doctor was reassuring.

"Sometimes a woman can have Braxton-Hicks contractions, which often come and go like you're describing. Let's just take a look and see what's going on," the doctor told her.

When he completed his exam, he removed his gloves and said, "Yes, I think they were definitely Braxton-Hicks. You're not dilated and this baby is telling us it's just not ready yet."

"So, this was all for nothing?", Anna asked.

"I wouldn't say that," the doctor replied with a smile, " it was good practice for the real thing."

Anna looked over in the corner where Rigel was sitting in a chair. Just the sight of him made her giggle. His hair was uncombed and wild. He was still breathing like someone who had just ran a marathon. He was pale. And he was in his slippers.

"Round 'em up, Cowboy, we're headed home," was all she said.

Chapter Fifty-Five

They didn't arrive home until almost 5:30 AM. Rigel was tired, but he felt like he had gotten his second wind, so he decided to shower and go into the office. Anna was exhausted and went right to bed.

After showering and dressing, Rigel went over to give Anna a kiss before leaving for work. She was sound asleep. She was so beautiful and looked so peaceful, he decided not to wake her. Instead, he just bent down and kissed her on the head.

As he exited the room, he heard, "Did you change out of your slippers, Cowboy?"

Rigel ran back to the bed and jumped in on the other side. The bounce almost bounced Anna right out of the bed.

"I'm so sorry. Another bad decision on my part. Love you. See you tonight," he said sheepishly as he climbed out of the bed and left the room.

On his drive to work, he thought of how he could apply what he had learned about gravity wells to Project: Aegis. He had only just gotten started on the project, so he wasn't quite sure. Perhaps he would just document what he gained from the trip so he could recall it later.

When he arrived at the office, no one was there yet and all the lights were off. There was enough light in the main hallway for him to find his way to the office, so he didn't bother turning any lights on. He just headed towards his office. The break room was just off the main hallway, so he stopped to get a cup of coffee, not realizing that since no one was yet in the office, no coffee had been made. He didn't know how to operate the coffee contraption, so he moved over to the soda machine and purchased a Coke. "The caffeine will help and the sugar won't hurt either," he thought to himself.

When he made it to his office, the door was shut. He unlocked it, opened the door and almost stumbled over an envelope that had been shoved under the door. He picked it up, looked at the address and return address label and deemed it important enough to open. It was from the War Department informing him he had been cleared to work on his old project. He chuckled to himself as he had been working on that project for the last six months and had gotten verbal approval right away, but it took this long to receive written confirmation. He shoved the letter into his desk drawer.

Rigel sat in his chair and turned on his computer. Several meeting requests popped up once his computer had booted. One was from his boss wanting to set up a meeting with the new person that would be working on his old project. It was scheduled for 9:00 AM today and was expected to last two hours. That must mean his boss wanted him to bring the new guy up to speed. He didn't really have two hours to spend with this guy and, having no sleep, he was sure he wasn't going to be a very good host, but he accepted the invite anyway. For the next couple of hours, Rigel jotted down notes from his trip and went through emails. When he looked up, it was already 8:55 AM.

He had been so lost in thought that he hadn't realized that the office was now buzzing. There were people everywhere. Coffee. That was his first thought, and he wasted no time making his way to the break room.

As he was coming back with his coffee, his boss and the new guy were standing in the door.

"Rigel, this is Rick Labenz. He will be taking over your old project," his boss said.

Rigel reached out his hand to shake Rick's. There was a slight hesitation, but then Rick reached out and the two shook hands.

"Nice to meet you, Rick," Rigel said. "I don't recognize you. Are you new to the division?"

"Yes. I come from private industry. Just started today," Rick replied.

"Oh, what company did you come from?", Rigel asked.

"It was rather small. I'm sure you haven't heard of it," Rick responded.

Rigel sensed avoidance, so he pursued. "Why don't you try me? What was the name of the company?", Rigel continued.

"AD," Rick replied.

"What does AD stand for?" Rigel asked.

"The actual name of the company is AD," Rick responded coyly.

"I'm sure AD stands for something. What do the initials represent?", Rigel dug a little deeper.

"Aetherion Dynamics," Rick responded obviously agitated.

"You're right. Never heard of it," Rigel said as he walked Rick into his office and motioned for him to sit.

"I'll leave you two alone so you can chat. I've scheduled a couple of hours for both of you, so take your time," Rigel's boss said.

Before Rigel's boss could walk away, Rigel said, "May I have a moment?", and ran after him. He caught his boss in the hall and said quietly, "How much information am I to provide him. Does he have security clearance and has he been read into the project?"

"They're working on his clearance now, but I'm sure there won't be any problems. You can tell him as much as you feel comfortable telling him. I'm sure that will be alright," his boss replied.

"Sir," Rigel said stoutly, "I asked for guidance. Without clearance, I don't feel comfortable telling him anything."

Rigel's boss leaned in and whispered, "Look, I'm not so sure about this guy either. I got the word from further up to brief him in on Project: Xaviar. Like you, I'm skeptical about him not yet having clearance, but I've been told to brief him anyway. Give him what you can without releasing anything important. Got it?"

"Got it," Rigel replied. With that, he walked back to his office, stepped inside and closed the door behind him.

"Let's start out with you telling me what you already know about Project: Xaviar," Rigel began.

"I'd rather hear it from you," Rick said smugly.

"Look, I'm going to be honest with you, Rick. You don't yet have security clearance," Rigel started.

Rick stopped him mid-sentence. "I will have security clearance within days. That shouldn't stop you from doing what your boss asked you to do."

Rigel didn't speak; he just looked at Rick. There was something in his eyes Rigel didn't like. It went beyond his attitude. He was definitely dealing with an A-Type personality, perhaps even a narcissist, so he would need to proceed cautiously to prevent being manipulated.

"Why don't we start with you telling me about yourself," Rigel countered.

"I'm a Princeton graduate with a doctorate in Physics. My specialty is advanced propulsion systems. I've joined this project because I intend to take Project: Xaviar to the next level," Rick responded rather smugly.

"What level would that be?", Rigel asked. "I'm curious since you've not yet been read into the project."

"Whatever level it's currently at, I know I can improve on it," Rick responded.

Rigel knew this was going to be a long two hours. "Tell me about some of the propulsion systems you worked on at AD," Rigel requested.

"I'm afraid that's proprietary information that I'm not allowed to divulge," Rick said arrogantly.

"Ok, then, tell me how you intend to use your current knowledge to advance Project: Xaviar," Rick asked.

"I'm not here for an interview, Dr. Emerson. I'm here to be read into Project: Xaviar," Rick responded.

"I have no intention of interviewing you, Dr. Labenz. I'm simply trying to establish a baseline so I can determine the best way to bring you up to speed on the project," Rigel replied.

Rick was obviously agitated. He shifted uncomfortably in his seat. "Perhaps you'd prefer that I tell your boss that you were uncooperative," Rick barked.

"Our meeting is over. I suggest you find my boss and tell him just that," Rigel said firmly as he got up and opened the door for Rick to leave.

Rick got up from the chair and walked out of the office without saying a word. Rigel just shook his head and walked down the hall to get another cup of coffee. He replayed in his mind how arrogant Rick was. As he walked, he sensed a message coming from his Guide.

"You used your senses well, Rigel. There are many who will try to deceive," his Guide told him.

Rigel thought about that for a minute. He wasn't quite sure what his Guide meant. Was Rick trying to deceive him or was he just being arrogant? Guess it didn't matter now. He would live with the consequences of possibly upsetting his boss or further ups. At least his Guide knew he was on the right track.

The rest of the day went without any more confrontations, although Rigel was definitely feeling the effects of a lack of sleep. By late afternoon, he wasn't even thinking straight. There was a fogginess hanging over him. He finally gave in and decided to call it a day. It was almost 5:00 anyhow, so no harm done.

Chapter Fifty-Six

When Rigel arrived home, Anna was all refreshed.

"Hey, Cowboy," she called out as he walked into the house.

"Why this 'Cowboy' thing all of a sudden?" he asked.

"Well, for one thing, you look like a cowboy whose been out on the trail all day. Looks like you might be dragging a little," she replied.

"Yeah, pretty tired, but you've been calling me 'Cowboy' for the last few days," Rigel said.

"I'm not sure," Anna responded. "It just seems to fit you." Then she giggled like a little schoolgirl. Rigel loved when she giggled like that. If calling him Cowboy made her that happy, then Cowboy it was.

"I guess I could call you Slippers Boy, if you prefer," Anna teased.

"Nah, that's alright. I'll stick with Cowboy," Rigel said as he walked over to hug her.

"Any more contractions," Rigel asked.

"No, but the baby is moving around a lot more," she replied.

"I hope that's a good sign," Rigel offered.

"I think it probably is," she returned.

They enjoyed a nice quiet dinner and then retired to the couch to watch some television. It was only a few minutes before Rigel fell fast asleep.

Anna woke him and said, "C'mon Cowboy. Let's get you to bed. You had a busy night."

Rigel didn't complain; he simply let her lead him into the bedroom. He quickly changed into pajamas, brushed his teeth, and then jumped into bed. He was asleep before his head barely hit the pillow.

Chapter Fifty-Seven

The next morning was Saturday. When Rigel awoke, he realized Anna wasn't in bed. He heard some stirring in the kitchen, so he got out of bed and walked to the kitchen.

"How'd you sleep?" Anna asked.

"Like a baby," Rigel responded.

"Well, this baby didn't sleep. He had me up all night moving around. They warned me about this, but I'm uncomfortable. I'm ready to get this baby out," she said.

"What can I do to help?" Rigel asked.

"I thought maybe this morning we'd go to the store. There are a few things we need and walking may make me feel better," Anna offered.

"I'm up for that. Should we just get ready and pick up breakfast on the way?" he asked.

"You can, if you want," she replied. "I'm not very hungry. I'm just too uncomfortable to eat."

With that, Rigel went in to shower and change his clothes. Anna had showered the night before, so she was ready when Rigel got out. They made their way to the car and headed for the store.

They went up and down the aisles while Anna placed items into the cart Rigel was pushing. In one aisle, he had gotten slightly ahead of her when he heard a crash and the sound of glass breaking. He turned around and saw Anna had dropped a jar of pickles on the floor and the glass had shattered. There were pickles and brine everywhere.

"C'mon, let's go," Anna said as she grabbed him by the arm and pulled him towards the exit.

"What are you doing? Let me get someone to clean that up," Rigel protested.

Anna looked him sternly in the eye and said, "Let's go" in no uncertain terms.

"It's not a big deal, Anna. I'll just pay for the pickles," Rigel said.

She didn't even have to say anything this time. He could just tell by the look on her face that she meant business.

"Let me just pay for these groceries," he said referring to all the items they had in the cart.

"Leave them," Anna barked, pushed the cart aside, and literally drug Rigel out of the store.

As they were exiting, they heard an announcement over the store's intercom. "Clean up on aisle 5." Anna and Rigel just ran faster.

Once outside, Rigel said, "What's the big deal? It was only a jar of pickles. It was an accident."

"It wasn't an accident, Rigel," Anna said sternly. "I dropped them on purpose."

"On purpose? Why?", Rigel inquired.

"Let's just get in the car and I'll tell you," she said a little louder and harsher than she had meant.

Once inside the car, Anna said, "My water broke."

"What do you mean, your water broke?", Rigel asked.

"I mean my water broke. The baby is coming," she said feeling like she was going to have to spell it out for him.

"Ohhh," Rigel said when he finally caught on. "And that's what made you drop the jar of pickles?"

"No, Einstein. I dropped the pickles because I was embarrassed that my water was all over the floor," Anna kind of yelled.

Rigel looked at her and began chuckling. At first, he was trying to hold it back. His silent chuckles became louder and soon his smile had spread across his entire face. She didn't think it was funny.

"Only you would think to cover up your water breaking by dropping a jar of pickles," he said still laughing.

"Can we just get to the hospital?" she asked, finally starting to giggle herself.

"Oh, oh, yeah. Man, I was so busy laughing, I almost forgot," he said as he put the car in gear and headed out of the parking lot.

"Now remember, speed limit," Anna reminded him.

"I know. I learned my lesson. Besides, this time I'm a lot calmer," Rigel offered.

"Why are you so calm this time?" Anna asked.

"Maybe it's because I didn't get woken up in the middle of my sleep," he said laughing.

Chapter Fifty-Eight

When Rigel pulled into the Emergency Room entrance, he got out of the car and waved for an attendant. A man with a wheelchair exited through the automatic glass doors and headed toward their car. Once they had Anna safely in the wheelchair, the man started wheeling her inside.

"I'll move the car and meet you inside," Rigel called out to her. Anna just gave him a thumbs up.

Rigel moved the car to the designated parking area and then headed inside. He found Anna near the receptionist's desk.

"Had you been having contractions all morning?" Rigel asked her when he got there.

"Yes, and most of the night," Anna replied.

"Why didn't you say anything?" he asked

"Because I was afraid they were Braxton-Hicks. I didn't want to go through that again. Once my water broke, I knew for sure," she responded.

A nurse came through the sliding glass doors and said, "Anna, I'll be taking you back." She grabbed the handles of the wheelchair and off they went through the doors and down the hall with Rigel in tow.

The nurse turned into a room and pulled the curtains shut around them. She then helped Anna remove her still damp clothes, put on a gown and get on the table. She took Anna's blood pressure, respirations and temperature, noting them in a tablet. "The doctor will be in shortly," she said as she exited the room.

It wasn't long before the doctor came in. It was same doctor from a few nights before. "Hi, Anna. How are we doing?", the doctor asked.

"My water broke," she answered.

"Funny story. We were in the grocery...," Rigel interrupted.

"Not now, Rigel," Anna said to him with one of her looks.

"Well, let's see what we have going on," the doctor said as he helped Anna place her legs into the stirrups and began to examine her.

"We're about 4 centimeters dilated and about 30% effaced, so we still have a ways to go, but today will be the day," the doctor said.

Anna took a deep breath. Was she ready for this? She knew she was. She couldn't wait to see her baby, and she was getting pretty fed up with being pregnant. She looked over at Rigel. She was proud of how well he had kept his composure this time. She still had to guide him on appropriateness and timing, but he was doing fairly well.

"Oh, no," she heard him suddenly exclaim.

"What's wrong?" she asked.

"We forgot your bag," he said a little bewildered.

"There's nothing in there I absolutely need. You can run home and get it after the baby is born and everything settles down. I'll just need his outfit to bring him home," she said as she saw him relax a little.

"I need to call my parents," he said.

"And my parents, too, please," she asked.

"Will do," Rigel concurred.

Rigel stepped out of the room to make the calls. His mother was still in the hospital but was expected to be released today. He hoped this news wouldn't interfere with that in any way. He dialed his father's phone first. When his father answered, Rigel asked, "Are you with mom?"

"I am," Rigel's dad replied.

"Let me talk to her," Rigel requested.

Rigel proceeded to fill his mother in on all the details, including the pickle episode at the store. Since Anna wasn't within hearing distance, he knew he wouldn't get in trouble. He had been dying wanting to tell someone. He then called Anna's mother to whom he also told the pickle story. Anna's mother just laughed and said, "That's our Anna."

With all the calls made, he went back into Anna's room. By this time, they had her hooked up to monitors and she seemed to be resting comfortably. Suddenly he saw her hands grip the rails of the bed and she started gritting her teeth. A contraction was coming. Rigel ran over and grabbed her hand. He immediately went into Lamaze coach mode, helping her guide her breathing and blowing away the pain.

The contractions were coming about every six minutes. Rigel hated seeing Anna in so much pain, but he understood it was all part of childbirth. Soon their son would be here, and it would all be worth it.

Chapter Fifty-Nine

It had been a few hours, and the contractions were now coming every few minutes. The doctor came in to check on her, performed his exam and said, "It's showtime. You're ready to go. Let's get her into the birthing room."

With that, two nurses immediately unlatched the locks on the bed and wheeled Anna into another room. Rigel wasn't sure what to do with himself. Did he wait here? Did he follow? Just then another nurse came in and said, "Follow me, Dad. Let's go get your baby."

The nurse led Rigel into a room just off the birthing room where he was instructed to put on a gown, cap, mask, gloves, and some footies. He was then led into the room where they had Anna already propped up into position.

He could hear the doctors giving orders and working underneath the draped sheet. The nurse led Rigel to the head of Anna's bed. Anna reached up and grabbed Rigel's hand.

"Here comes another one. Now with this one, I want you to push, Anna," Rigel heard Dr. Anston say. Rigel was surprised to see Dr. Anston there. He expected her for the delivery, but since the other doctor was working with Anna, he didn't realize she had come in.

"Push, Anna, push, push, push," Dr. Anston commanded. As Anna pushed, her grip tightened around Rigel's hand. It was a strong grip, but it was becoming stronger. Way stronger.

"We have a crown," Rigel heard Dr. Anston say. "Now with the next contraction, I want you to push with all your might."

The contraction came quickly. As Anna pushed, the grip on Rigel's hand tightened down like vise. He could no longer feel his fingers. He had no idea his wife had such strength. He was just about to complain when he heard the doctor say, "He's here." Just then Anna and Rigel both heard the most wonderful sound a parent could hear, the cry of their newborn baby.

He was crying at the top of his lungs, covered with blood, and squirming like a banshee. The nurse held him over Anna's abdomen as Dr. Anston waved Rigel over to help cut the umbilical cord. Rigel loosened the death grip on his hand, went over, took the scissors from the doctor's hand and cut the cord exactly where the doctor had indicated.

Their new baby was whisked over to a table, and nurses scurried to clean him up. He cried the entire time. Once he was clean and swaddled in a blanket, they returned him to Anna who held him for the very first time. He immediately quit crying and opened his eyes. Anna looked into them and said, "His name is Michael. Michael James Emerson."

Chapter Sixty

Rigel noticed the tears streaming down Anna's face as she held Michael for the very first time. He pulled out his cell phone and snapped some quick pictures. He would send them to his family once everything quieted down.

As Dr. Anston finished up, the nurse took Michael from Anna and handed him to Rigel. Rigel was a little timid at first. He had never really held a baby before, but he followed the nurse's instructions on how to properly support Michael's head and body. The nurse said, "Give me your phone and I'll take a picture for you." He handed the nurse his phone and she snapped some quick shots. The nurse then took Michael from Rigel's arms and returned him to the table so the pediatrician could examine Micheal more thoroughly.

"Everything looks good. You have a healthy baby boy. Congratulations," the pediatrician said as they wheeled Michael off to the nursery. Rigel looked at Anna and they both had tears in their eyes. This was the greatest moment in both of their lives.

The nurse told Rigel that if he needed to make any calls, he could step out of the birthing room, remove his gear and go to the birthing waiting room. Phone reception was better there, she advised. Rigel walked over, kissed Anna on her forehead and said, "I better go call your Mom and Dad or I'll be in big trouble."

"BIG trouble," she said giggling.

Rigel left the birthing room, found the waiting room and immediately sent the photos he had taken to both Anna's parents and his. He inserted the caption, "Will call soon."

As soon as the message sent, he dialed Anna's mother. "He's here!", Anna's mom yelled into the phone.

"He is indeed," Rigel responded.

"Tell me everything," Anna's mom insisted.

Rigel gave Anna's mom all the details including Michael's weight, length and exact time he was born. It was 3:00 PM on the dot. Anna's mom said she would be hopping the first flight and would stay with them for a week or two to help them out. Rigel appreciated this. He planned on taking a couple of days off from work, but that's about all he could afford with this new project and having to pass off the old one. There were a lot of things he had to complete as deadlines were rapidly approaching.

When he hung up, he dialed his parents. His mother answered and quickly called Rigel's father over to the phone so they could hear everything together. Rigel repeated just about everything that he had previously told Anna's mom. He also informed them that Anna's mom would be coming to help out for a week or two.

Rigel's mother was glad to hear Anna's mom would be coming. Having just gotten out of the hospital, she wasn't quite up to traveling just yet and she needed to make sure she could take care of Anna and not have to have Anna take care of her. They agreed that his parents would travel once his mom had gotten clearance from her doctor to do so. With that, Rigel ended the call.

He realized he was hungry and since they said Anna wouldn't be taken to her room for another half hour or so, he decided to go to the cafeteria to grab something to eat. The doctors had told him, unless there were complications,

Anna and the baby would be released from the hospital tomorrow, so he had some time to retrieve the bag they had forgotten and do some things around the house in preparation.

Once he had eaten, he headed up to Anna's room. They had just wheeled Michael in for his first feeding. A member of the nursing support team came along to help Anna with breastfeeding and to show her a few tips. Michael seemed to latch on right away and was doing just fine.

After feeding, they wheeled Michael back to the nursery. With them now alone, Rigel approached the bed. "Hello, momma," he teased.

"Hello yourself, pappa," she teased him right back.

Rigel leaned down and kissed her. "Can I get you anything?", he asked.

"No, I'm good. Just tired. I think I might want to take a nap. Why don't you go home and get some rest. You can come back up later and bring the bag," she told him.

"Are you sure?" he asked. "I could just sit quietly in this chair."

Anna chuckled. "You absolutely would not be able to sit quietly in that chair. Best scenario, you would fall asleep and wake me up with your snoring. Worse scenario, you would be clicking on your phone the entire time."

"I don't snore," he objected.

"You snore, Cowboy, trust me," she countered.

"Okay, Pickles. It's home I go. By the way, that's my new nickname for you. Pickles. I think it fits." They both started laughing.

Rigel kissed her on the way out and then headed for home.

Chapter Sixty-One

On the ride home, Rigel called his boss with the news using the hands-free feature of his car. His boss congratulated him but then gave him a heads up.

"Take whatever time you need, but when you get back, I'm going to need you to meet with Rick Labenz again," his boss told him.

Rigel groaned into the phone. He hadn't even got out any words when his boss said, "I know. I'm getting pressure from higher ups. His security clearance has come through and they're eager to get him started on this project."

Rigel told his boss his mother-in-law was coming to help out, and he thought he'd be able to make it into the office by Wednesday. He asked his boss to set up a meeting, and he'd do whatever he needed to do to get Rick up to speed.

They ended the call just as Rigel pulled into his driveway. He pulled into the garage and shut the car off. As he walked into the house, he hit the garage door button on the wall, and the garage door began to close. As the door closed, out of the corner of his eye, Rigel saw a black snake slither into the garage on the other side. He knew immediately what to do. He prayed, "Father, please remove this snake from my garage and keep it far from me." He no sooner got the words out of his mouth when the snake slithered back out of the garage just before the door came completely down.

"What is it with snakes?" Rigel thought to himself.

With all the commotion, Rigel thought he'd lay down and take a little nap. It was apparent Anna wanted him out of her hair, so he might as well take advantage of some free time.

He got to sleep almost immediately and quickly he began to dream, only this time it felt real. Instead of a true vision, he saw the transparent shape of his Guide.

"Congratulations, Rigel, on the birth of your son," the Guide said.

"Thank you," Rigel replied.

"I have some things to discuss with you, so I will schedule for us to visit next week," the Guide informed him.

"What's going on?" Rigel asked.

"Now that your son is born, I can fill you in on a few more details," the Guide answered. "I also bring you a warning. Rick Labenz is not who he says he is. He's been assigned to work on Project: Xaviar, but he's more interested in getting information out of you on Project: Aegis. Be careful with him."

"I sensed something was off with him," Rigel replied.

"He can be very manipulative, so be on your guard. If you find yourself in a position where you need help, just call out my name and I will be there," the Guide told him.

"I will," Rigel responded.

The vision was over just as quickly as it had come. Rigel slept soundly for another hour. When he awoke, it was already nearing 6:00 PM. He decided to shower and grab something to eat before heading back up to the hospital.

When he got out of the shower and had dried his hair, he dressed, then went into the kitchen and opened the refrigerator. He was looking through the leftovers trying to decide which one to pick when he saw it. It was a small coconut cake in a plastic display container. It was setting at the back of the fridge, and he had to move some leftovers to get to it. Coconut cake was his favorite. When he finally pulled it out, there was a note attached. It said, "For the Best Dad Ever".

Chapter Sixty-Two

Rigel returned to the hospital at around 7:00 PM. Michael was in the room, sound asleep in a bassinette. Rigel kissed Anna first saying, "Love you, momma", and then went over to look at Michael. He was so peaceful lying there. He couldn't believe that was his son. For a brief second, a thought flashed through his head, but he was able to ignore it. He realized it wouldn't have been a good thought and there was no reason to go there. He had to focus on how blessed he and Anna had become.

Around 8:15 PM, the nurse came in to help Anna get Michael ready for nursing before bedtime. That would mean they would be returning him to the nursery. Rigel didn't really like that idea, but he wasn't going to cause any problems.

Michael finished nursing around 8:45 PM. It was more like he had fallen asleep and wasn't able to pay attention to the job at hand. Anna had tried to wake him up several times, like the nurse had taught her, but he kept going back to sleep. Michael had quite a day, too, so it wasn't surprising he was so tired.

The nurse asked Anna if she'd like to leave Michael in the room with her or take him to the nursery so she could get some sleep. She chose to leave him with her. The nurse reminded Anna that if was too fussy and she wasn't able to sleep, she shouldn't hesitate to hit the buzzer for the nurse, and they would take him to the nursery.

"I might as well get used to it because I won't have any nurses to help me at home," Anna chuckled.

"Yes, you're correct, but that's exactly why some mothers choose to get a good night's sleep now when there are still people to help. Your choice. I'm fine with whichever you choose," the nurse replied. She then left the room.

"I found the cake," Rigel said.

"What cake?" Anna asked.

"The one in the refrigerator that said 'For the Best Dad Ever'" Rigel replied curiously.

"Oh, that wasn't for you. That was for my dad when he comes," Anna teased.

"Well, too bad for him because I ate it all," Rigel laughed.

"You ate the whole cake?" Anna asked.

"Almost. Saving a piece for bedtime," he said smugly, with a little grin.

He so loved how they could tease each other. It was something special they shared between them. It was never vicious or hurtful, just playful and fun. He had to admit that sometimes he took the teasing a bit too far, but Anna was never shy about putting him in his place and reigning him in.

Before long, Anna fell asleep. Rigel found himself watching a Hallmark movie with no sound. He was trying his best to read the lips of the actors when Michael let out a cry. Rigel jumped to his feet, ran over to the bassinette and said, "What do I do? What do I do?"

Anna awoke and just laughed at Rigel. For an MIT graduate with a doctorate in physics, he sure was shaken by the littlest of things.

"Just gently rock the bassinette," Anna said.

Rigel began to gently rock it, and Michael went right back to sleep.

"See? I've got this!", Rigel quipped.

"Yeah, you got it alright, Cowboy," Anna said smirking.

"Pickles!" It was the only comeback he could think of at the time.

Anna returned to sleeping and Rigel returned to the soundless movie. Before long, he fell asleep and began snoring. His snoring woke Michael up, who woke Anna up. The funny thing was, Rigel didn't wake up. He just kept snoring.

Anna couldn't get out of bed yet because of all the tubes she was hooked up to, so she reached out and pulled Michael's crib over to her bed. She gently lifted him out and placed him on her chest. He fell right back to sleep.

They stayed like that for a half hour or so when Rigel suddenly woke up. He saw Michael's bassinette pulled over to Anna's bed and saw Michael asleep on Anna's chest.

"What did I miss?" he whispered.

"Go home, Cowboy. I've got this. Get some sleep and come see us in the morning," Anna said.

"Are you sure?" Rigel asked.

"Absolutely, 100% sure. I've never been so sure of anything in my entire life," she giggled.

Rigel went over to bed, kissed Anna on the forehead and kissed Michael on the back of the head.

"We're not supposed to kiss the baby for a while," Anna whispered.

You could tell by the look on his face, Rigel was trying to keep from laughing as he said, "Oh, sorry. Note to self: No kissing Pickle's baby!" Holding back the laughter made him snort and his snort woke Michael again. Michael moved his head back and forth until he found a comfortable spot and then went back to sleep.

As Rigel was gathering things to leave, the nurse came in, saw Michael asleep on Anna's chest and said "We don't recommend you hold the baby while he's sleeping and you're so tired. It would be too easy for you to fall asleep and lose your grip. Not trying to be mean. Hope you understand."

"That makes sense and I understand completely," Anna said as she gave Michael to the nurse.

"Are you sure you don't want me to take him back to the nursery?" the nurse asked.

Anna thought for a moment and then said, "Maybe that's not such a bad idea after all. I've been trying to sleep but someone keeps snoring."

"I'm leaving. I'm leaving," Rigel said as he blew her a kiss and walked out the door.

Chapter Sixty-Three

The next morning, Rigel was awakened by his phone chirping indicating a message had come in. He rolled over in bed and grabbed his phone off the charger on the nightstand. It was 6:32 AM.

"Are you awake?" the message said. It was from Anna.

"Sure am," he replied even though it was a bit of a lie.

"My mother's plane gets in at 10:03. Can you pick her up at the airport and then come get Michael and I? We're supposed to be discharged sometime between 11 and noon," she messaged.

"Sounds like a plan," Rigel wrote back.

"Don't forget the car seat," she texted.

"I put it in the car before I went to bed, so we're all set," he texted back.

"Do you want me up there before I go get your mom?" he asked.

"No, no need," she texted back.

"Okay, see you soon. Love you," he wrote.

"Love you, too," she added and then the messages stopped.

Since he was up, Rigel thought he might as well get in the shower. It was about an hour's drive to the airport and if he hurried, he could stop for breakfast along the way.

When he was finished showering, he dressed and then ran around tidying up the house before Anna's mother came. The house wasn't messy. In fact, Anna kept an impeccable house, but he wanted to make sure things were perfect before she came.

When he finished, he headed to the airport with a quick stop at IHOP for breakfast.

He arrived at the airport at about 9:45 AM. "Good timing," he thought to himself. As he waited, he thought about what he should call Anna's mother. He's always had a little difficulty calling her "Mom", because that was his own mother's special name. He would never call her by her first name; he felt that was disrespectful. In the past, he had always gotten around it by not getting himself in the situation where he actually had to call her by any specific name. When he introduced her to anyone, he always reverted to introducing her as "Anna's mother". He decided now that Michael was born, he could call Anna's mother "Grandma". Of course, his mother would be "Grandma" as well to Michael, but she would always be "Mom" to him.

He was so deep in thought, he didn't see Anna's mother come down the escalator at the airport. She was almost to him before he happened to look up and saw her. He jumped to his feet and greeted her with a big hug. "I'm so proud of you and Anna," she said, "and I can't wait to see my grandson."

Rigel retrieved her luggage from the baggage claim, and they headed for the hospital. It was only about 40 minutes from the airport. They arrived at 11:15 AM, just as the nurse was having Anna sign discharge papers. Michael was in the bassinet near the bed and Grandma ran directly over to him almost knocking Rigel out of the way. She whisked him out of the bassinette and was dancing around with him when Anna said, "Good to see you, too, Mom."

"Oh my," she said as she dashed over to give Anna a hug and a kiss on the cheek while still holding Michael. Anna understood. Her mother had always wanted a grandchild and her being an only child, she was their only hope.

With all the paperwork signed, the nurse helped Anna into a wheelchair. "I can walk," she protested, but was quickly shut down by the nurse saying, "Hospital policy."

Once she was comfortably in the chair, the nurse retrieved Micheal from Grandma, turned to Rigel and said, "Did you bring the car seat?"

Rigel proudly replied, "It's in the car."

The nurse informed him he was supposed to bring the baby carrier portion into the hospital so she could strap Michael into the seat before leaving the room. Another hospital policy. Michael started running out the door when the nurse stopped him. "Also," she said, "pull the car up to the door so we can load your wife and your baby."

"Yes, ma'am," Rigel yelled as he ran out to the parking lot.

Rigel returned shortly with the baby carrier. The nurse took it from him, set it on the bed, made a few adjustments to the straps and then laid Michael into the seat. You could tell she had done this before because she buckled and pulled all kinds of straps before she was ready to release them.

With Michael firmly buckled into the baby carrier, an orderly came to push Anna while the nurse carried Michael in the seat.

"Grab the flowers and gifts," Anna said to Michael.

There were two flower bouquets, one balloon, one stuffed animal and three boxes. He stacked the boxes, placed the smaller flower bouquet on top, tucked the stuffed animal under his arm and grabbed the larger flower bouquet with his remaining free hand.

Anna kind of tipped her head toward the table, "The balloon?", she said.

Rigel stood there for a moment trying to figure out how he was going to grab it. He walked over and tried to catch the ribbon tied to the balloon with his teeth. Anna, her mom, the nurse, and the orderly all chuckled in unison. Anna's mom went over and grabbed the balloon.

Down the hall, down the elevator, into the lobby, until they found themselves at the entrance. The car was waiting just outside the door. Rigel went out first to unload what he was carrying, but when he got to the back of their SUV, he realized he didn't have any hands left to push the button. "Little help," he called out. Grandma ran over and hit the button, the hatchback lifted and Rigel put everything in the back of the vehicle, carefully supporting the vases of the bouquets so the water would not spill.

He then ran back to open the rear door where the base of Michael's car seat was installed. The nurse set Michael down on the sidewalk and then checked the installation of the seat base. "Looks good. Nice job," she said. Dad had a proud moment.

The nurse inserted the baby carrier into the car seat base, and a loud click confirmed it locked in place. The orderly rolled Anna up to the front passenger door which Rigel had opened. She got out of the chair and stepped into the vehicle. "Ugh," she uttered.

"Are you okay?", Rigel asked in a bit more panic than he wanted to admit.

"I'm fine, just a little bit sore," she said as she plopped into her seat and began to buckle up.

Rigel closed Anna's door and then ran over to open the rear driver's side door for Grandma. She was still holding the balloon and as she got into the vehicle, the ribbon holding the balloon suddenly went limp. The balloon had become detached from the ribbon and was slowly drifting away.

"I'll get you another one, Michael," he said as he stuck his head inside the vehicle. Everyone laughed.

Rigel closed Grandma's door, thanked the nurse and the orderly, then got into the driver's seat to drive them all home.

There wasn't much traffic on a Sunday, so it was smooth sailing. Rigel found himself driving a little more cautiously than normal. "Baby on Board", he thought to himself.

Once home, he pulled into the garage, got out and opened Grandma's door first. Once she was safely out, he ran around to Anna's door and helped her out. Then he unlatched the baby carrier from the car seat base and carried Michael into the house.

"Welcome to your new home, buddy," he said as they entered.

Rigel set Michael, still in the baby carrier, on the kitchen counter. Anna immediately went over, unbuckled him and pulled him out. He began crying and Anna knew immediately that he was hungry. He hadn't eaten in several hours. While Anna and Grandma went into the nursery to feed him, Rigel retrieved all the gifts from the back of the SUV. One of the vases had tipped over and the carpet was soaked. Once he had all the gifts out, he left the hatchback open so the carpet could dry out.

Rigel carried the gifts inside and set them on the counter. He had no clue where Anna would want them, so he thought that was as good as place as ever. He realized it was almost 1:00 PM, so he yelled into Michael's room, "Anyone hungry?"

He heard a tiny little voice respond, "Pizza, please." He had never heard that voice before. Who said that? He poked his head inside the nursery and Anna and Grandma were laughing. "That was me pretending to be Michael," Anna confessed.

"Well, I hope when he says it, it's more like 'PIZZA'", Rigel said in a low deep voice. They all laughed again.

Rigel ordered the pizza and it arrived within the hour. They were all quite hungry, so it went quickly.

"If you don't mind, I think I may lay down for a bit," Anna said after finishing lunch.

"I think that's a wonderful idea, honey," Anna's mother replied as she cleaned up the kitchen.

"Here, let me do that," Rigel said to her.

"No, Rigel, let me feel like I'm needed. You go relax and let me do this. Please. I insist," she countered.

Having Grandma around was going to be nice.

The rest of the day went well. Rigel recognized how much Anna enjoyed having her mother there to help and her mother enjoyed the fact that she could be there and be useful.

Rigel grilled some hamburgers for dinner and while eating, Anna asked Rigel if he was going to go into work tomorrow. "No, I'm going to take a couple of days off to help around here," Rigel responded.

"Nonsense!" Anna's mother replied. "We have everything under control here, so if you need to go into work, you go right ahead."

"I agree," Anna said. "With mom here, what are you going to do besides sit around and be bored?"

"Are you two sure?", he asked.

"Absolutely," they said in unison.

That settled that. Rigel was going into work on Monday.

Chapter Sixty-Four

The alarm went off at 6:00 AM on Monday. Rigel shut it off and rolled over to see that Anna was also awake.

"I can't believe Michael slept the whole night," he said. Anna smiled.

"He didn't sleep much at all, for your information," Anna began. "You just didn't hear him."

"Oh," Rigel replied sheepishly as he slithered out of bed and into the bathroom.

After showering and dressing, he went out to the kitchen and started the Keurig. He preferred fresh brewed coffee, but when he was in a hurry, the Keurig would do. He poured the coffee into a travel mug with a tight lid and then headed out the door.

He was half-way to work when he realized he hadn't kissed Anna or Michael goodbye. He didn't dare call in case she was sleeping. He'd have to apologize later.

When he walked into work and pulled up his calendar, the first thing on his schedule was the meeting with Rick Labenz. "I thought that was supposed to be scheduled for Wednesday," Rigel thought to himself.

He barely got started ready emails when Rick showed up at his office door. He knocked twice and waltzed on in. "Hey, Buddy. I hear congratulations are in order," he said.

"Yes, thanks. Mother and baby are home and doing well," Rigel offered trying to be cordial.

"I understand your security clearance has been approved, so I can share everything with you now," Rigel started.

Rick got up and shut the door. When he came back to his seat, he said, "There'll be plenty of time for that, but first tell me about this new project you're working on. I hear it's amazing."

"Well, I don't know what you've heard, but I hope you understand that I'm not allowed to discuss it with you," Rigel informed him.

"I have security clearance now. You don't have to go into details, just tell me about the concept," Rick continued to dig.

"You haven't been read into that project, so I'm unable to discuss anything with you," Rigel said firmly.

"Well, if you want to be a jerk about it," Rick dared, giving him that challenge look.

Rigel immediately saw right through it and realized this was an attempt to intimidate him.

"I guess I'll have to be a jerk, because I'm not allowed to share anything with you. Now if you'd like to talk about Project: Xaviar, I am prepared to do that," Rigel said.

That shut Rick down, for the moment, and they spent the next hour and a half going over details of Project: Xaviar.

"Is your new project an off shoot of Project: Xaviar?" Rick probed.

"I will not discuss my new project with you," Rigel responded.

"What's the code name for the project? I've heard a lot of rumors, and I'd just like to know which one is real," Rick continued to dig.

"I'm not going there, Rick. Not now. Not ever. If you have no more questions about Project: Xaviar, I suggest we wrap it up for today," Rigel told him.

"We're on the same team here, Rigel. I don't know why you always have to be such a jerk," Rick said as he slowly gathered up his folder trying to goad Rigel into a response.

Rigel knew how to play the game. He said nothing. He let Rick take all the time he needed to gather his things and leave the office.

A huge feeling of relief came once Rick had gone. He was so glad his Guide had warned him ahead of time. He would have hated to have fallen for one of Rick's tricks, not only because he would have gotten in trouble, but because he hated to lose to guys like that.

"Nice job," he heard in his mind and recognized the voice as that of his Guide's.

Chapter Sixty-Five

At home that evening, Rigel seemed to be in a rather good mood. Anna sensed it immediately. Anna's mother had cooked dinner and as they sat around the table, Rigel was especially helpful and cordial. She liked this in him. The stresses he had been under at work lately was apparent; it had been showing on his face lately. But tonight, a smile replaced that tension in his face worry often caused.

"Did something good happen at work today, Rigel?", she asked.

"Why do you ask?", he asked.

"You just seem less tense," she replied.

"Life is good. Michael is here and healthy. You went through the delivery without any problems. Your mother is here to help us. Life is good," he remarked.

"No, there's something more," she said intuitively.

"Well, if you have to know, I slayed a dragon at work today," he said with a satisfied smile.

"I'm not sure what that all means, but I know better than to ask. I'm just glad to see you so happy," she said.

"I'm the happiest man in the world," Rigel said as he got up from his chair to give Anna a hug and then repeated the hug on his mother-in-law.

"I have more good news," Anna advised. "Your mother has been released to travel, and they will be here on Saturday."

"That's great news," Rigel replied. "Can't wait to see the look on my father's face when he sees Michael."

"Oh, and I forgot to tell you, Anna. Your father is flying in on Friday. He wrapped up the project he'd been working on a day early," Anna's mother told them.

"Even better news," Rigel replied. "The whole family will be together."

Anna smiled, but inside she was a little uneasy. It wasn't that she had a bad relationship with her father, but he had always seemed to be a bit distant. She still never forgave him when he disapproved of Rigel the first time she introduced Rigel to him. Her father had told her she could do better. He called Rigel a "strange duck". What was probably an off-hand remark to him, stun like a whip to Anna. She was crushed that he would even say that and their relationship had been a bit cold ever since. She decided not to dwell on it. Despite her reluctance, she was glad he was coming so he could meet Michael.

As they were finishing dinner, they all heard Michael cry out in the other room. Anna got up to get him, but Rigel beat her to it.

"You sit," he instructed. "I'll go get him and bring him out."

"You'll probably have to change him," Anna quipped.

"On it," Rigel replied as he walked into the nursery.

"Hey, little man," Rigel said as he gently lifted Michael from the bassinette. He brought Michael over to the changing table, unzipped his sleeper, and went to undo the pins fastening his diaper. He searched for them, but he found sticky tape holding the diaper on instead. He pulled the tabs and the diaper released. Rigel pulled the diaper out from underneath Michael and reached for a new one. Just then, Michael started going again. Pee was everywhere and Rigel had to stop the stream with his hand so it wouldn't hit him in the face.

"Little help here," Rigel called out.

Both Anna and Grandma came running. They both began laughing as they entered the room.

"Looks to me like you've been christened," Anna said.

Anna gently shoved Rigel out of the way and took over. "Mom, can you get the baby basin and fill it with warm water. I think we're going to need to rinse him off?"

Grandma retrieved the baby basin from the closet and scurried off to the kitchen to fill it.

"Ready," Grandma called out from the kitchen.

Anna picked Michael up and carried him to the kitchen. She placed him in the warm tub of water. He seemed to like it. He didn't know quite what to do, but his eyes were blinking and he wasn't crying.

Anna washed him off and then rinsed him with clean water as Grandma went to fetch a baby towel. They had special towels for Michael that included a make-shift hood that could be put over his head while you dried him off. Grandma laid the towel out on the counter and Anna lifted

Michael from the water. She sat him on the towel and Grandma pulled the hood over his head. Anna then began drying him off.

As Anna dried, Grandma hurried back to the nursery to clean and sanitize the pad on the changing table that Michael had wet. She used the wipes Anna had on the table and then let the pad air dry as she headed back to the kitchen.

Michael gave a little shiver from the cold. "He's freezing," Rigel said.

"He'll warm up as soon as I get him dry," Anna said calmly.

"Anna already has this mother thing down," Rigel thought to himself. "Looks like I still have a long way to go."

Once Michael was completely dry, they took him back into the nursery, put him on the changing table, applied lotion to his skin, put on a new diaper and then selected a new sleeper for him to wear. Once he was completely dressed, Anna looked at her watch.

"I think I'll just feed him," she said. "That will help him warm up as well."

Rigel exited the nursery. Grandma stayed to help Anna get settled in the rocking chair and then came back out to the kitchen.

"I guess I didn't handle that so well," Rigel confessed.

"That was your first time. Don't be so hard on yourself, dear. Next time you'll know with little boys, you have to be prepared at all times," she said chuckling.

Rigel laughed with her and thought how good it was to have her here helping out.

Chapter Sixty-Six

The next day at work, his administrative assistant came in with an envelope. Rigel opened it and saw orders for him to fly to a meeting tomorrow. It would be another one-day trip, so he wouldn't be gone long, but he still thought about asking if the meeting could be postponed since they had a newborn to take care of. As he began to type the email requesting the postponement, he realized Anna's mother was still there, so it might be a good time to go after all. At least he wouldn't have to worry about Anna and Michael being alone and not having any help. He deleted his response to the message.

Since it was only going to be a day trip, he wondered if he was going back to Groom Lake. They definitely wouldn't fly him to DC for just a day. That was too long of a trip. He'd find out tomorrow.

The next morning, he arrived at the airport on schedule. As he walked into the General Aviation Terminal, Captain Holmberg was waiting for him.

"Good morning, Dr. Emerson," Captain Holmberg greeted him.

"Good morning, Captain Holmberg. Where are we headed today?", Rigel asked.

"We'll let you know once we're in the air," Captain Holmberg responded as he turned and led Rigel out onto the tarmac and to the already opened door of the plane.

Rigel climbed on board and, just like always, Jen was there to greet him. He saw Captain Graves in the co-pilot seat completing checklists.

"Good morning, Captain Graves," Rigel said as he turned and walked down the aisle of the plane.

"Good morning, Dr. Emerson," Captain Graves replied back.

It dawned on him that the pilots switched off every once in a while. One would serve as the pilot on one trip and serve as the co-pilot the next trip. That was probably a good idea so each of them could record flying time and stay familiar with the plane.

"Good morning, Dr. Emerson," Jen said standing by his seat. She was holding a tray which had a fresh cup of coffee and a muffin. "They were out of danishes this morning, so I hope a muffin will do."

"Good morning, Jen, and a muffin will do just fine," he told her.

He barely got buckled in his seat and settled when he saw Jen close the door to the plane. He then heard the engines coming to life. Within seconds, they were rolling down the ramp to reach their designated runway.

Once in the air, Captain Holmberg came over the intercom advising they would be flying to a private airport near Tucson. The flight would only take about 45 minutes.

Rigel barely had time to eat his muffin and finish his coffee when Captain Holmberg came over the intercom to announce they were making their final descent and would be landing in about 10 minutes.

Jen immediately appeared and retrieved the tray with the coffee cup and saucer. She took them to the galley, then climbed into her jump seat and buckled in.

The landing was smooth. Rigel could tell it was a short runway by the way the pilot had braked so quickly after touching down. They taxied for a few minutes, and Rigel saw a small shack come into view. Rigel wondered what this was all about, but he had learned not to ask questions and just trust.

Once the plane came to a complete stop, Captain Graves came back to talk to Rigel.

"Dr. Emerson, you are to remain on the plane. We will be exiting and will be in that shack right over there. We will remain there for the duration while you remain on the plane," he said pointing out the window to the shack. He continued, "A generator is being hooked up to the plane as we speak so you will have air conditioning. Should something come up or you need anything, please press this." Captain Graves handed him a fob, similar to the fob of a car, but it had only one button.

"Do I talk through this?", Rigel asked.

"No, it isn't a two-way communication device," Captain Graves responded. "It will just ring a buzzer inside the shack, and we will come and help you. Just so you are aware, your cell phone will not work."

Rigel interjected, "Where the heck are we?"

"We're on a private airstrip just outside of Tucson and that's all I'm able to tell you. Once we leave the plane and secure the door, you will need to relax like you've done before and you will receive instructions," Captain Graves said.

"Roger that," Rigel replied.

With that, Jen rushed down the aisle with a bottle of water. "Just in case you get thirsty," she said as she set it in the cup holder near his seat and then headed towards the door of the plane and promptly followed Captains Graves and Holmberg out.

Once the door was secure, Rigel sat back in his chair, closed his eyes and tried to clear his mind. Almost instantly he visioned himself near the gate he had seen in previous visions. Down the path came his Guide, still a transparent blob, so to speak.

As his Guide approached, he said, "Rigel, I'm going to offer you something we rarely ever offer. It only happens in specific circumstances. If you choose to participate, I will lead the way. If you don't, that's your choice."

"What are my choices?", Rigel asked.

"It has become necessary to provide you with more information about the Plan." Rigel's Guide began, "It's not that you will need to do anything differently once you've received this information, rather what I'm about to tell you will provide clarity. You must be able to trust the Plan completely, and we recognize this will be extremely difficult if you aren't provided additional details and clear on the Plan's purpose. Our discussion today will provide you with that clarity, Rigel. We will share additional information about the Plan, but you won't remember our discussion or any of the details we discuss."

"Then's what's the purpose?", Rigel asked.

"It's important you feel comfortable with the purpose of the Plan. Here's how we will achieve that. We will share additional information with you which will provide clarity, but you won't remember that information. Your inner conscience will, however, and it will understand. It will allow you to make better decisions, even if some concepts seem foreign. The easiest way to explain it is with an analogy. Have you ever had a gut feeling about something, Rigel?"

"I have," Rigel responded.

"That gut feeling came from somewhere. Your inner conscience was able to keep you away from danger because it knew more than you realized. Sometimes our minds can't handle everything, so your inner conscience has been given the ability to understand more than your mind. You may have experienced a time when you knew something but were unsure how you knew it. That was your inner conscience sharing with your mind. The inner conscience is so much more complex than your mind, Rigel. And it has the ability to anticipate just how much your mind can handle."

"I can see that," Rigel replied. "Maybe that's why an idea pops into my head out of nowhere while I'm working on a project?"

"Exactly," the Guide said. "Your inner conscience already knew and understood the idea, and determined it was allowable to share with your mind."

"You mentioned that I had a choice. Why would I choose not to participate?", Rigel asked.

"Even your inner conscience has limits, Rigel. When you push those limits too far, it can cause confusion and distrust. We will attempt to provide you with only the amount of information you can handle, but if your inner conscience becomes unable to handle it and cries out, we will have to remove you from the program."

"Removed from the program? What about my son?" Rigel questioned.

"In that situation, your son would still have an opportunity at some point in his life to participate in the Plan, but he will not be guided by you. We will provide a surrogate. As for you, you will finish out your life having no knowledge whatsoever of the Plan, the seed that produced your son, or that we have ever talked. You will be taken care of, but you will no longer actively participate in the Plan."

"And if I choose to participate?" Rigel asked.

"Then you will be exposed to things you have never imagined. You will not remember those things, but your inner conscience will. Your inner conscience will help guide you the rest of the way through your journey."

"Why have I been chosen to gain this extra knowledge?" Rigel questioned.

"That will be revealed if you choose to participate. I'm afraid I'm unable to explain that now," the Guide informed him.

Rigel thought for a moment. "What are the pros and cons?"

"The pros would be that you will be better prepared for what is ahead and you will experience a higher level of inner peace when conflicts arise. The cons would be a chance your inner conscience could become overloaded. If that happens, it could be determined you should no longer participate in the program. You would forget all that has happened so far and just go on with your human life," the Guide explained. "We would like your help and cooperation, Rigel, and we will try our hardest not to overload your inner conscience."

Rigel thought for a moment. Everything that has happened so far was beyond his understanding, yet he participated and things have gone well up to this point. He now had a son that he otherwise wouldn't have had, his career was taking off, and he had a loving and supporting wife. He had everything that really mattered. "I'm in," he said.

"Good," his Guide said. "Now please take your mind deeper. Draw everything on the outside in until you feel it rush toward you in your mind. Tell me what you are seeing, Rigel."

"I see things rushing towards me. They're beginning to move faster. They're now moving very fast. They're spinning like a whirlpool around a drain. Like a black hole. Things are getting sucked in. They're moving extremely fast now. Wait! Suddenly, everything went black. I see nothing," Rigel said.

"Rigel," his Guide said as the form of a man came into view. It was initially like looking at a blurry picture, but as the seconds passed, the form became clearer until the man became completely clear in Rigel's eyes.

"Is that you?" Rigel asked.

"It is I. My name is Raphael," his Guide told him.

Raphael had a shape and outward appearance of a man, but there was something different about him that didn't exactly look human. His body was muscular and perfect, almost like the action figure of a superhero, or someone on steroids. He was wearing strange clothing, and his skin had a bit of a luminescence to it. His hair was dark and flowed down to his shoulders. He had a beard which matched the color of his hair. The clothing he was wearing was unlike anything Rigel had ever seen. The entire outfit had a black base with what appeared to be magenta overtones, which gave it a dimensional effect. Raphael's pants were tight on his legs, which accented the muscles in his thighs and calves. Over his torso was a coat or jacket of some sort with many pockets. In fact, the entire jacket appeared to be covered in pockets. The jacket was bound tight around his waist. The top of the jacket was loose and allowed for movement. As he looked closer, he realized it wasn't a jacket at all, but more of a vest as it didn't continue down his arms. On his arms was material, similar to the pants, that extended down to his wrists.

Rigel just stood there for a moment gazing. He didn't quite know what to make of what he was seeing. Was this someone from another planet? He couldn't tell for sure, but he had a feeling Raphael wasn't human.

"Before we get in too deep, I want to remind you to keep an open mind. Try to discard all your pre-conceived ideas and focus on absorbing what you will be learning," Raphael told him.

"Are you from another planet?", Rigel asked.

"I'm from another realm, another dimension," Raphael responded.

"How many dimensions are there," Rigel interjected.

"There are many dimensions," Raphael responded.

"Like beings on other planets?", Rigel inquired.

"Some are beings on other planets, and some are only consciousness requiring no planet, no space," Raphael replied.

"So, there are aliens?", Rigel asked.

"'Aliens' is a human term, Rigel. You call anything not living on your Earth, alien. You are the human race, Rigel. There are many other races, and yes, many other planets are inhabited," Raphael explained, "but we're getting off topic. I want to focus on the Plan. I know it's difficult to comprehend. To make it easier for you to understand, let me ask you a few questions. What do you know about the biblical Millennium?"

"In Revelations, the Bible describes the Millennium as a 1,000-year period in which Jesus will rule the Earth and Satan will be bound," Rigel answered.

"Humans describe things using their own perception, and that was how the Millennium was described in the Bible, but you are mostly right. After Satan is bound, there will be a period of peace on the Earth, correct?" Raphael asked.

"Yes, at least that's what I think the Bible says," Rigel responded.

"How will Satan be bound?", Raphael asked.

"I'm not sure. The Bible doesn't tell us. I suppose God will bind him," Rigel replied.

"God will use his Radians to do so," Raphael responded.

"What is a Radian?", Rigel asked.

"A Radian is what you would call an angel. They are creatures of God who radiate God's glory and mercy," Raphel answered.

"Are you a Radian?", Rigel asked.

"I am," Raphael replied. "You see, Rigel, both you and I are creatures of God. God made us. We exist in different dimensions, but we all serve one purpose and that is to the glory of God."

"What about Satan?", Rigel questioned.

"Satan was once a Radian, but fell away from God," Raphael said.

"How did that happen? Why did God allow that to happen? I've always wondered that," Rigel inquired.

"Just like humans, God allows Radians free will to choose. He had endowed free will in all of us. Satan's name was once Morningstar, but when he chose to go a different path and challenge God, God cast him out. God said, 'Begone, Morningstar, your light is no longer Mine.' When that happened, God changed Morningstar's name to Lucifer, but he is often referred to as Satan."

"How many angels are there, or should I say Radians?", Rigel asked.

"There are more than your ability to count," Raphael said. "Each is different. Each has a purpose or a job to complete. Some provide protection, some, like me, are guides, and some are warriors that will fight the last fight against Satan."

"When will this fight take place?", Rigel questioned.

"Only God knows the answer to that. Our job is to be ready when the time comes. The battle will precede the Millennium, when Satan will be locked away," Raphael answered.

"So, the Plan has to do with the final battle?", Rigel asked.

"It does. We must be ready when God gives us the call," Raphael responded.

"What's my part in the Plan?", Rigel inquired.

"Your job is to produce the next level of human. You see, Rigel, it is important that we have the right people in the right places when the battle begins. Chosen human people must take command of the human world to assure peace while the Radians fight the battle with Lucifer and his legions. That's why chosen humans need to be part of the Plan; to make sure the vision of the Plan is followed."

"So, we won't actually be fighting in the battle?", Rigel continued.

"No, only the Radians and the Legion will be fighting that battle. Lucifer's angels are called Legion," Raphael answered.

"You make it sound like the Plan only involves our world, Earth. Does it not include all planets? The Universe?", Rigel asked.

"The Plan is specific to your planet. God banished Lucifer to live under the Earth. That's why the Plan focuses there. The Millennium will only take place on Earth," Raphael explained.

"You said it was rare that you ever shared such detail with someone. Why are you sharing it with me?" Rigel asked.

"There is evidence that Lucifer has gotten wind of the Plan. Just like I am guiding you, Lucifer has guides that he has assigned to tempt and guide other humans, all of which are unbelievers or have turned away from God," Raphael explained. "Humans who have been contacted by Lucifer's guides have been trying to infiltrate our network. We have reason to believe Rick Labenz may be one of these people. It's important that we share no information with him or anyone else."

"That makes sense. I felt there was something strange about him. I just get a creepy feeling being around him," Rigel said.

"That's why we have decided to share more information about the Plan with your inner conscience. It will help you as Rick's probing gets more intense. Your inner conscience will not only help guard you and prevent you from saying anything you shouldn't be saying, but it will also help you become more assertive in dealing with Rick. Once you have the upper hand, Rick will become weaker and will fail."

"Who will lead the Radians into battle?", Rigel asked.

"Michael," Raphael responded.

The mention of that name threw Rigel for a loop. It took him a couple of seconds before he could even think.

"My son's name is Michael," Rigel said quietly.

"I know that," Raphael responded. "His seed came from Michael."

Rigel could feel himself getting faint. He was becoming overwhelmed.

"Breathe, Rigel," Raphael instructed.

After Rigel took a couple of deep breaths, he calmed a bit, not much, but enough that focus was starting to return.

"Babies are normally not named after their seed provider, Rigel. That wasn't something we anticipated. Your wife came up with that name," Raphael explained.

"She said she would know the baby's name when she saw him. The minute she looked into his eyes, she said 'His name is Michael'," Rigel said still trembling.

"Is that such a bad thing, Rigel? That means that Anna can see deeply into your son's soul. I would take that as a blessing. It means she will be able to connect more deeply with your son than most mothers can connect with their children. It means Anna will always know there is something special about your son," Raphael explained.

"Does she know about the Plan?", Rigel said now in a panic. "I don't want her knowing I'm not Michael's father."

"I'm specifically talking to your inner conscience now, Rigel. Anna does not know about the Plan, nor will she ever know. In her mind, Michael is a product of your seed and hers. Any DNA tests ever done on your son will confirm you are the father. There will be no doubt. What you must grasp is that YOU are Michael's father. You conceived him, you were there when he was born, you will raise him, you will take care of him, you will protect him, and one day you will have the conversation with him like your father had with you," Raphael said slowly, but emphatically.

"I'm Michael's father," Rigel emitted.

"Yes, you are Michael's father and always will be," Raphael confirmed.

"Why did we need Michael's seed? Why not just use mine?", Rigel questioned.

"We are advancing civilization. We are making marked improvements in human intelligence and abilities. We can't do that with only your genes, Rigel. We needed something extra. We needed powers greater than you could provide," Raphael responded.

"Let me explain this another way," Raphael continued. "After Morningstar had fallen from grace, he took many angels with him. He made them promises, none of which he kept, but promises that were attractive enough to entice some angels away from God. Many of these fallen angels bred with human females and produced Nephilim."

"Those were giants. I read about them in the Bible," Rigil interrupted.

"Yes, you are correct. God saw the evil and damage these Nephilim were causing and sent a flood. All Nephilim died in the flood. Satan and his angels were trying to build a race of part human/part Legion to take over the world," Raphael explained.

"Why wouldn't they just take over the world themselves? Why did they need to be part human?", Rigel asked.

"Because humans would not follow Legion. They will only follow another human. By interbreeding with humans, they looked like humans to other humans, but they had extra powers," Raphael said.

"So, the Plan includes interbreeding angels and humans to produce beings that look like humans, but have special powers?", Rigel inquired.

"Not exactly," Raphael explained. "We are not trying to produce special powers like the Legion did. We're trying to improve the human race. We want to evolve them to the point where they are capable of accomplishing the Plan. All humans must come together under one leader if we are to assure peace in the world for the entire Millennium. You see, Rigel, peace cannot be assured if there are different factions governing. There must be one vision that drives the entire Earth and one governing body."

"How does physics, and especially my work, fit into this?", Rigel inquired.

"Physics is the heart of all things, therefore it must always have a role. Specifically, you will be working on a device that disarms all weapons, everywhere, but doesn't harm people. Do you see how that fits in?", Raphael asked.

"I see that now," Rigel admitted. "Why didn't my son's seed come from you?"

"God determines all matters when it comes to interbreeding. He doesn't want to take the chance of another angel falling and misusing the interbreeding process. I will be the seed for many babies, just as Michael will be the seed for many babies. One important point that you need to understand, Rigel, is when Legion interbred with human females, they physically took part in the impregnation. Through God's method, Radians don't take part; we place the seed in the husband."

"It's cleaner and purer, isn't it?", Rigel asked.

"All part of the Plan," Raphael said.

"So, I won't remember any of this?", Rigel questioned.

"Your inner conscience will, but your mind will not. Your inner conscience will help guide you when you begin to doubt or have questions. You'll be in a better place, and your consternations will all disappear," Raphael explained.

"If it brings peace of mind, why don't you do this with everyone?", Rigel asked.

"Because not everyone has your level of integrity, Rigel. And not everyone can compartmentalize information. One of the reasons you have been given such high security clearance in your job was because the U.S. Military could trust you not to reveal secrets. Your inner conscience is strong and guides you when a top-secret topic comes up. You know how to deflect or avoid questions. You know how to prevent secrets from inadvertently slipping. That's your inner conscience, Rigel. Not everyone has an inner conscience that is so strong. We can trust you. Someday, we may even share more, but today you've been provided the information for which you had a need to know. Now you can tuck that information away and allow your inner conscience to help you deal with stressful situations. We're going to end our meeting today, Rigel. Before I go, do you have any questions?"

Rigel thought for moment and said, "More of a statement than a question. Thank you for trusting me and thank you for Michael.

Raphael smiled and said, "You're going to make an amazing father, Rigel. Until next time."

Raphael's form disappeared and the vision began to fade. Rigel awoke in his seat, shook his head to clear the cobwebs, and looked down at his watch. A little over three hours had passed. He knew he had met with his Guide, but he couldn't remember what they had discussed. He thought harder. It still wasn't coming to him. "Oh, well," he thought to himself, "Maybe I'll remember later."

Once fully awake, Rigel clicked the button on the fob he had been given. Within minutes, Captain Graves, Jen, and Captain Holmberg came out of the shack and headed towards the plane.

Chapter Sixty-Seven

The flight home was smooth, as was the drive home from the airport.

When he arrived home, Anna was on the floor playing with Michael. He couldn't get over how cute that scene was. Michael couldn't really do anything yet. He just laid there and kicked every once in a while, but Anna was having the best time. She was trying to make him laugh, but he hadn't quite mastered that trick just yet. Grandma was sitting on the couch taking it all in.

"Hey, Cowboy," Anna called from the floor.

"Hey, Pickles," Rigel called right back.

"Cowboy? Pickles? Since when did you start this?", Grandma said as she giggled.

"Just recently. Inside joke," Anna said.

"I know at least part of the inside joke, Pickles," Grandma said.

"You didn't," Anna looked at Rigel half mad and half hurt.

"It was a funny story and besides, I think it was ingenious!", Rigel exclaimed. "I was so proud of you thinking so quickly; I had to tell someone." That seemed to ease the angst in Anna.

Rigel went over to where Anna and Michael were on the floor. "Hey, buddy," he said to Michael, "ready to go throw around the football?"

Grandma said, "That may take a couple more years, but it'll be here before you know it."

"What smells so good?", Rigel asked.

"Mom made her famous stew for us," Anna yelled out.

"Smells delicious, I'm famished," Rigel replied.

"I hope you're not too famished. It still has another 30 minutes in the oven," Grandma told him.

" I can wait," he replied.

"How'd your meeting go?", Anna asked.

Rigel just stood there for a minute without asking. It was like he was searching his memory banks. "Okay, I guess," was all he was able to mutter. "How did my meeting go?" he thought to himself as he headed to the bedroom to change his clothes. He realized he couldn't remember anything about the meeting. He knew he flew to a private airport outside of Tucson, but he doesn't remember much after that except flying home. He wasn't going to dwell on it, but he sure hoped he hadn't been so forgetful during the meeting.

The rest of the evening went fine. Dinner was delicious. He had no trouble sleeping that night and to his knowledge Michael didn't wake up even once. He later learned Michael had been up several times during the night, but he just didn't hear it. He slept right through it.

The rest of the week went along as normal with Rigel at work and Anna and Grandma hovering over Michael.

After work on Friday, Rigel would swing by the airport and pick up his father-in-law. His flight was supposed to arrive around 5:30 PM. Rigel was at the airport on time, but the flight was delayed at least an hour due to weather, so Rigel went into one of the restaurants and ordered himself some wings and a beer.

He hadn't ordered wings and a beer in a restaurant for a very long time. Ever since meeting Anna, when they ate in an airport, it was at more upscale places than the ones Rigel had previously frequented. Their menu at this restaurant was rather sparse. That's why he decided on the wings. He didn't want to eat heavy because he knew they would be having dinner when they got home, but he felt he needed a little something to tie him over.

The plane landed at 6:15. Rigel saw his father-in-law coming down the escalator and ran over to greet him.

"Congratulations," Anna's dad said as he hugged Rigel.

"Thanks, Grandpa," Rigel responded.

"Grandpa. Has a nice ring to it," Grandpa kidded.

They retrieved his bag, got in the car, and headed towards the house. It was about an hour drive, so they had plenty of time to talk. Grandpa asked how work was going and what projects Rigel was working on. Rigel informed him work was going well and made up some projects that sounded important but didn't reveal any top-secret information. The rest of the trip, Grandpa discussed how well things were going at his work. Rigel learned all about the new expansion their company was undertaking.

When they arrived home, Anna heard the garage door go up, grabbed Michael and headed for the garage with

Grandma close behind. Rigel no sooner got the car turned off when Grandpa bolted out the door and headed for Michael. As he grabbed Michael from Anna's hands, he gave her a peck on the cheek, but then all his attention went to Michael.

"Be careful with him. He's only a baby!", Grandma commanded.

"I can handle a baby, Mother. I handled that one," he said as he nodded towards Anna.

"You didn't handle her a lot. You were always traveling," Grandma retorted.

"Okay, Okay," Anna jumped in. "Let's get inside. Dinner is ready."

Once inside, Anna put Michael in his infant seat and then set him on the counter.

"If you don't mind, I thought we would eat at the counter instead of the table so we can put Michael up here with us," Anna exclaimed.

"Perfect," Grandpa said.

"I think that's a lovely idea," Grandma chimed in.

Rigel just watched it all happen. There was a certain dynamic in Anna's family that he never quite understood. Sometimes it was easier for him to keep his mouth shut and his eyes and ears open.

Chapter Sixty-Eight

Saturday morning, Rigel awoke to Michael crying. He realized this was the first time Michael had awaken him. That meant that Anna had been carrying the entire burden. He made a note to himself to work on that. He needed to do more around the house to help Anna, especially since her mother would be leaving on Tuesday.

Rigel's parents were expected to fly in at 2:42 PM. He'd head to the airport around 1:30 to pick them up. That would give him time to park and get inside the terminal.

"Do you want me to ride with you, Rigel?", Grandpa asked.

"No, you stay here and spend quality time with Anna and Michael," Rigel responded. He caught himself thinking "Whew!" He didn't want to be like that around Anna's dad, but he had run out of things to say halfway home from the airport when Rigel picked him up.

Once in the car, Rigel turned up the music and just enjoyed the ride. He arrived at the airport on schedule and was inside the terminal when he saw his parents coming down the escalator. The closer he got, the clearer he could see them, and he realized the toll the heart attack had taken on his mother. She looked frail. She was only in her early sixties, but she appeared much older and walked like an old lady. She was a little hunched over and his father was supporting her as she walked.

When they got off the escalator, he was right there. His mother reached out for a hug, but Rigel said, "Let's move over here first so as not to cause a traffic jam coming off the escalator."

They moved to one side, and his mom pulled Rigel down to him. "Doesn't appear you've lost any strength," he teased her.

"Almost as good as new," she replied as she kissed his cheek. Rigel looked up to see the look on his father's face. He knew instantly that his father was also concerned about how frail the heart attack had made her.

When Mom finally released him from her hug, his Dad stepped in and hugged him. "Love you, son," he whispered in Rigel's ear. "Love you, too, Dad," Rigel whispered back.

Rigel retrieved their bags from baggage claim, and they headed to the car. On the drive home, they talked about how excited they were to have Michael in their lives.

"Just out of curiosity," Rigel's mother asked, "how did you decide on the name 'Michael'?"

"I don't know," Rigel replied, "maybe it was divine intervention. When Anna looked into his eyes for the very first time, that's what she saw. I must admit, I saw it, too. I don't know why, but that's what we saw."

Rigel's mother was comfortable with that response and moved on to asking questions about Anna, the nursery, Rigel's work, and the likes.

When they finally arrived home, Anna came out of the house to greet them. She was carrying Michael. Rigel's mother took one look at him and exclaimed, "He looks just like you, Rigel!" Rigel immediately looked over at his father who just smiled.

Rigel's mom raced into the house with Anna. She couldn't wait to hold this little bundle of joy. Anna's mother and father met them as they came through the door. The greetings were cordial with the obligatory hugs, but you could tell Rigel's mother was focused on only one thing. She placed her purse on the couch and sat in one of the overstuffed chairs. She looked at Anna, held out her arms and said, "Come to Grandma, Michael." Anna smiled and graciously handed him over.

Meanwhile, Rigel and his father were retrieving the bags from the car.

"I'm glad everything has gone so well, Rigel," his father said.

"It's gone exceptionally well," Rigel responded. "I was skeptical at first, but this was the right move."

"We were all skeptical at first, Rigel. The concept is pretty far out there, but I'm glad you got to the point where you found it acceptable. You and Anna will enjoy many wonderful years with Michael," his father replied.

When they made it into the house, Rigel took the bags to the guest room where his parents would be staying. Rigel's father went over to see Michael. He pulled back the blanket and saw his grandson sound asleep. He was as beautiful as an angel. He held out his hands to hold him, but Rigel's mother turned away, "I'm not done yet!" she uttered.

"Now, now, children," Rigel said as he walked back into the room. "We have to share. Besides, you'll be with us for a couple more days and they'll be plenty of holding time."

Rigel's mom's face turned a little red and she held Michael out for Rigel's father. He gently took him and just studied his face knowing what a precious bundle he was holding.

The next few days went well. There was no feuding and both sets of parents were getting along fine. They were sharing time with Michael. The best part was, Anna and Rigel were both a little pampered having both sets of parents spoiling them.

Chapter Sixty-Nine

With both sets of parents there, Rigel had intended to take the next few days off, but he received a text message from his boss asking if they could meet first thing on Monday morning. So, on Monday, Rigel went into work. His boss was waiting for him outside the door to his office.

"Do I have time to grab a cup of coffee?", Rigel asked as he made his way down the hall.

"Sure. Grab me one, too, while you're at it," his boss replied.

"Cream and sugar?", Rigel asked.

"Just black," his boss responded.

Having poured the coffee and placing lids on the cups, Rigel headed for his office. He walked in and closed the door behind him.

"What's up?", Rigel asked.

"I'm concerned about Rick Labenz," his boss started. "I'm getting feedback that you're not being cooperative. He's told his boss that you are withholding information."

"I've given him everything, but he began asking a lot of questions about Project: Aegis and I refused to answer him," Rigel responded a little agitated.

"Good. Don't give him anything about Project: Aegis. He doesn't have a need to know. Why would he even be asking?", his boss asked.

"I have no idea. He's quite manipulative and I don't trust his intentions," Rigel responded.

"I don't know either, but I'm going to find out why he's poking around. Someone high up is behind this guy and I intend to find out who it is and why they're sticking their noses where they don't belong. How much do you think he knows?", Rigel's boss asked.

"I don't think he knows a whole lot. He didn't even know the name of the project. He just became agitated when I refused to give him any information," Rigel responded.

"Well, keep it up and make sure you let me know if he tries anything. I don't trust this guy," Rigel's boss said as he got up and made his way to the door.

"Is that it? Couldn't we have had this discussion over the phone?", Rigel asked.

"No, there's one other thing. Rick has scheduled another meeting with you this morning. He's saying it's urgent, so be ready for him," his boss advised.

"I will," Rigel said as his boss opened the door and Rigel left his office.

When Rigel booted his computer, the first thing that popped up was an urgent request for a meeting from Rick Labenz. Rigel clicked on it and the proposed time was 8:30 AM. It was now 8:15. "This guy wastes no time," he thought to himself.

At 8:30 AM prompt, Rick appeared at his door. "Hey, buddy. Thanks for fitting me in," Rick said.

"Not a problem. Have a seat," Rigel replied. "What's up?"

"I went over the material you shared with me on Project: Xaviar. I had a few questions," Rick started.

"Okay, shoot," Rigel replied.

Rick asked a few technical questions which could easily have been answered by looking at the drawings Rigel had provided him. Then came the real reason for Rick's visit.

"I'd like you to request I help you on your new project," Rick said.

"I'm not able to do that," Rigel responded.

"Sure, you can. They listen to you and you can have all the resources you want, including additional people," Rick said.

"I don't need additional people at this point," Rigel responded.

"We work together well and think how much more we'd accomplish if we were working together on this project. Besides, I could learn so much from you," Rick replied.

Rigel saw right through this as another attempt at manipulation.

"At this point, my project is proceeding well and on schedule. I have no need to add any additional resources," Rigel said firmly.

"Maybe your project won't be progressing so well if the higher ups know that you have failed to provide me with all the information you had on Project: Xaviar," Rick threatened.

"What do you mean? I provided you access to everything," Rigel said angrily.

"I suspect there are some files I didn't receive. If an internal review was ordered for some reason, they would go through everything, and it might take months. In the meantime, you would be prevented from working on your new project," Rick said with a smirk on his face.

"I have provided you everything and you know that," Rigel responded getting quite agitated.

"You know that and I know that, but maybe that's not what my boss will hear. All it takes is a little doubt and an internal review will be ordered," Rick threatened.

"I think our meeting is over. Please leave," Rigel instructed Rick.

Rick just smiled, got up and headed for the door. Before exiting, he turned and said, "You make things so hard on yourself, Rigel." Then he walked through the door.

As soon as Rigel heard his footsteps disappearing down the hall, Rigel reached over and hit the "STOP RECORD" button on his phone.

Chapter Seventy

As he began going through emails on his computer, there was a knock on the door. When Rigel looked up, someone he didn't recognize was standing in the doorway.

"Envelope for you, Dr. Emerson," the person said as he walked forward and handed it to Rigel.

"Thank you," Rigel replied as he saw the person walk back out through the door.

"That was strange," he thought to himself. "Usually, letters and packages are delivered to Judy and she brings them in." When Rigel opened the envelope, he pulled out a single sheet of paper. It said: "URGENT: Your flight leaves at 10:00 AM today. Day Trip."

That also was strange. He'd had day trips before, but never without some kind of notice. Rigel quickly emailed his boss to let him know he'd be out of the office for the remainder of the day. His boss responded immediately, "I'm aware. Safe travels."

It was already 9:10 AM. The airport was about 45 minutes away, but that was without any traffic. He dashed to his car and got on the road.

He made it to the airport just in time. Captain Holmberg hurried him out to the plane. Jen had his coffee and danish waiting. They were in the air in no time. This time neither of the pilots announced over the intercom where they were going, but within about 35 minutes, Captain Graves announced they would be landing shortly. When the wheels touched down, Rigel looked out and recognized the private airstrip they had previously been to near Tucson.

The plane pulled to a stop near the shack and all three crew members promptly exited the plane without saying a word. Rigel could feel the air conditioning kick on, so he knew the plane had been connected to the generator. When he heard the door of the plane shut, he sat back, closed his eyes, and focused.

Almost immediately, he was at the gate. He recognized the translucent form of his Guide approaching. Rigel didn't remember that he had actually seen his Guide on their last visit. In fact, he didn't remember anything at all about the visit, but his Guide knew.

As he approached, Rigel's Guide said, "Something of great importance has come up, Rigel. We need your help."

"I'll do whatever I can," Rigel replied.

"During our last visit, I shared with you information about the Plan. More information than we normally share, but we felt it was necessary. You were told you would not remember any of it, but that it would remain with your inner conscience," his Guide told him.

None of this rang a bell with Rigel, so he just tried to focus and listen intently.

"When we visited, you asked if aliens were real. Only humans refer to other beings as aliens. I informed you that there were other inhabited planets along with other interdimensional beings. There are beings from another planet from a distant solar system headed towards Earth. They are God's creatures and God created them just like he created humans, but they are not within the control of the Radians."

"What are Radians?", Rigel asked. This confirmed he remembered nothing about their previous conversation.

"Just like I am your guide, there are other guides and messengers. We are called Radians," his Guide explained.

"Why is this an emergency and why am I involved?", Rigel asked.

"Humans are not yet ready for this. Earth has been visited for many years, but the visitors have been too advanced and too creative to get detected. Yes, there has been some detection efforts going on and strange things have been sighted, but up until now, there has been no definitive proof alien forms exist. This visit will confirm their existence once and for all, and I'm afraid it's going to throw all humans into a panic," his Guide went on.

"Are they dangerous?", Rigel asked.

"Their technology is far more advanced than yours, Rigel. They could destroy your entire planet within seconds, but that's not why they're coming," his Guide explained.

"Then why are they coming," Rigel stammered.

"Their planet is in danger, and they are searching for a place to colonize. If they find your planet suitable, they may attempt to claim your planet for themselves," his Guide responded. "It is vitally important that your world stands as one, that your strength comes from one common vision. All nations must band together and establish a centralized government from which to negotiate. Their weapons are far more advanced than yours. If you attempt to fight them, you will lose. And if one nation, or even one person, goes rogue and fires on them, it could result in the destruction of the perpetrator and perhaps even all mankind. Your people must come together as one. Leaders will need to step up. Egos will need to be put aside. Strategy and cohesiveness must be used to prevent violence, not create it. Where humans have fought each other for centuries, you must now come together to fight as one, using your minds, not your weapons."

"How do I fit into this?", Rigel asked.

"To avoid panic and riots, Project: Aegis must be implemented at once. It must be capable of disarming all weapons, everywhere, simultaneously, without harming the people operating them," his Guide explained.

"But I'm years away from making Project: Aegis work," Regis interjected.

"That's why you are here, Rigel. We will give you the knowledge to advance the technology you will need," his Guide said.

"So, we will use this against the alien invaders?", Rigel asked.

"It will be useless against them," his Guide said emphatically. "It is to be used only on humans, to prevent them from firing any weapons, including atomic weapons, at the aliens or anyone else. That's why this is so important, Rigel. If humans fire upon the aliens, they will return fire with weapons humans have not yet even imagined. You will be saving humanity by implementing Project: Aegis. This is vitally important."

"I'll do whatever I can to help," Rigel said rather shakenly.

"Do you have any questions?", his Guide asked.

"How will I gain the knowledge to advance the technology? What will happen if I fail? How do I get started?", Rigel had a host of questions, but he could tell he was in panic mode and wasn't thinking clearly.

"Breathe, Rigel. I need you clear-headed. Now is not the time to panic. You will be flown back home. As you are flying, you will sleep. A vision will come to you in the form of a dream. It will provide you with everything you need to know," Rigel's Guide told him. "You have to trust us, Rigel."

"I do. I trust you. What do I do if I have questions?", Rigel asked.

"Just think deeply and call my name. My name is Raphael," Raphael advised.

Suddenly Raphael disappeared and Rigel felt himself wake up. He sat for a moment and then hit the button on the fob as he had been instructed to do on the last flight. He immediately saw the crew come out of the shack and head towards the plane. They prepared the plane for takeoff, but Rigel didn't pay any attention. He was lost in thought.

Once in the air, Rigel felt himself fall asleep. A dream appeared. He was standing in a public square. There were people everywhere. In the sky, high above their heads, was what looked like some sort of enormous craft. It wasn't moving. It was just floating. He saw a man with a shoulder mounted surface-to-air launcher run through the crowd. The man moved to an open area, knelt down on one knee, adjusted the sights, and was about to fire the missile at the craft.

Rigel heard himself call out, STOP! Don't do it....."

If you enjoyed:

Book 1: *Millennium: Preparations Begin*

The Plan is in motion.
Generational improvements have been made.
Key participants have received their assignment.

Get ready for the next book in the series

Book 2: Millennium: Unexpected Visitors

Timeline for Project: Aegis is modified due to unexpected visitors.
Technology advances exponentially from inter-dimensional assists.
Survival of mankind hangs in the threads.

www.ingramcontent.com/pod-product-compliance
Lightning Source LLC
LaVergne TN
LVHW010603100826
845148LV00014B/2825
9798986370729